THE GOOD PATIENT

ALEX STONE

Boldwood

First published in Great Britain in 2023 by Boldwood Books Ltd.

Copyright © Alex Stone, 2023

Cover Design by Head Design

Cover Photography: Shutterstock

A CIP catalogue record for this book is available from the British Library.

Paperback ISBN 978-1-80280-332-7

Large Print ISBN 978-1-80280-331-0

Hardback ISBN 978-1-80280-330-3

Ebook ISBN 978-1-80280-333-4

Kindle ISBN 978-1-80280-334-1

Audio CD ISBN 978-1-80280-325-9

MP3 CD ISBN 978-1-80280-326-6

Digital audio download ISBN 978-1-80280-329-7

Boldwood Books Ltd
23 Bowerdean Street
London SW6 3TN
www.boldwoodbooks.com

For Abhi.

1

NOW (SEPTEMBER)

Not again.

The foggy drowsiness that weighed against me was disturbingly familiar. As was the throbbing in my head that penetrated through the darkness. It was persistent. Nauseating.

I knew pain. I was used to it. Numbed to it. It had been a part of my life for so long. But it was a part that I had promised myself was over now. Enough was enough.

At least that was the plan.

And yet...

My eyelids fluttered as I tried to summon the strength to open them. Shards of bright sunlight instantly blinded me and I scrunched my eyes closed again.

I lay still, sheltered in the darkness. My brain felt lethargic and hazy. It was tempting to allow myself to drift back to sleep.

Not again.

That one thought was enough to cling to. Enough to keep me going. Enough to survive.

I fought to focus my thoughts, internally checking in with every part of my body, assessing the damage. Nothing felt broken.

Nothing else hurt. Cautiously I wiggled my toes. I could still move them.

A rhythmic beep caught my attention. There was something familiar and calming about it. I inhaled deeply. The overpowering bitter clinical scent filled my nostrils. I smiled slightly. I knew that smell.

Most people hated it and what it represented. *Where* it represented. But to me it was safety. It was kindness.

'Ms Taylor,' a deep voice disrupted my thoughts, and I cautiously opened my eyes again.

I squinted at the figure beside my bed, dark haired with a light-brown skin tone. He was wearing blue scrubs and the stethoscope around his neck gleamed as the sunlight reflected off it.

He poked his black framed glasses with his forefinger, pushing them higher on his nose. 'I'm Dr Menon,' he said, with a soft, lilting accent. 'I treated you about six months ago.'

Abhilash.

'I remember.' My voice was groggy and faint. Despite the drowsiness, I remembered him. How could I forget?

'That was quite a blow you took to your head,' he continued as he studied the notes in his hands. He looked up and his eyes met mine. 'You had us worried.'

I could see the concern etched into his features. He was telling the truth. His concern was genuine. He had been worried.

About me.

I swallowed. 'I'm sorry,' I mumbled softly. Guilt pressed against my chest. Another sensation I was too acquainted with.

'I'm just glad you're okay. That's all that matters.'

I started to nod, but the pounding in my head made me instantly regret that action. But he was right; despite the pounding in my head, I was okay. In fact, I was better than okay. I was back in hospital, but this time was different. Everything was different.

'Keep your head still and follow my finger with your eyes, please,' he said as he leaned towards me and raised his index finger. Disappointment washed over me as he moved his finger slowly in an H pattern about thirty centimetres in front of my face.

What had I expected? He was just doing his job.

'There are a couple of police officers here,' he said, straightening his back.

'Police?' I shifted awkwardly.

'They want to ask you some questions if you feel up to it?'

There was a protective tone to his words. He would send them away if I asked him to. He'd do it for me.

'It's fine,' I told him. There wasn't much point in delaying it. He would only be able to hold them off for so long. I might as well deal with their questions now.

He nodded and backed out of the cubicle. 'Okay,' I heard him say. 'You can go in now, but only for a couple of minutes. She needs to rest.'

I swallowed as two uniformed officers walked towards the foot of the bed.

'Ms Taylor, I'm PC Smith and this is PC Jennings.' The other officer nodded as PC Smith said her name.

'Can you tell us what happened?' PC Jennings asked.

I tried not to flinch at the question. It was one I'd been asked so many times before. People always wanted to know. Wanted to help.

At least that's what they claimed.

But the reality was no-one was that selfless. There was always a reason. A motive. Something to gain.

I glanced at the open doorway. Well, maybe not everyone.

'Ms Taylor...' PC Jennings prompted, stepping into my line of sight.

I drew in a deep breath and tried to recall. How had I got here this time?

'I was in the water,' I said slowly, the vague memory of my body rhythmically bobbing, swept up in the current, as darkness descended upon me like morning fog creeping in.

'Yes, you were found unconscious in the water. The coast-guard said your life vest saved you from drowning.'

'My head.' I lifted my hand and tentatively touched my fore-head. It was bandaged, but even so, my gentle touch made me wince. 'I hit it.'

The police officers watched me. Silently waiting for me to continue.

I squinted, trying to summon the memories from the murky depths of my mind. Why was I in the sea?

Your life vest saved you.

PC Jenning's statement circled in my brain. If I'd been swim-ming, I wouldn't have been wearing a life vest. I only wore that when I took the jet-ski out.

'The jet-ski.' That was it. 'I was out on the jet-ski.'

The officers glanced at one another, and I knew from their expressions that this revelation wasn't news to them. 'But how did you end up in the water?' PC Smith asked as he shifted position, attempting to block the low September sun from his eyes.

I frowned. There was something about the sunlight that felt off. As though it didn't fit. 'Wasn't there a storm brewing?'

PC Smith nodded. 'This morning. It got pretty bad for a few hours. The rain has stopped now, but the wind is still strong. Not really ideal weather for jet-skiing. Why did you go out in that?'

'It wasn't that bad when I set out. I thought I'd beat it.'

PC Smith's expression showed how reckless he thought that

decision had been. He was right. It had been foolish. And yet... I closed my eyes. I could almost feel the spray in my face.

The jet-ski lifted as I flew over the crest of another wave. I was going so fast. Too fast for the choppy conditions. But I didn't care. I felt powerful. Strong. Free.

There was another wave already heading towards me. It was even bigger this time. Common sense told me I should slow down. Head back to shore. I'd never ridden when the sea was so rough before. I wasn't experienced enough.

My heart pounded. I felt alive for the first time in so long.

I tightened my grip and accelerated more.

I was tired of being sensible. Contained. I wasn't ready to go back.

A surge of power rippled through my body as the jet-ski sped up and then suddenly the engine spluttered.

I glanced down at it, taking my gaze off the horizon as the steering became heavy and sluggish. I was no longer flying over the top of the water but trudging through treacle.

Something was wrong.

Panic welled in the pit of my stomach, my body instantly recognising that everything had changed in one split second. Without power I would be stranded out here.

I looked up and gasped. I wasn't just stranded; I was defenceless. Without the power of acceleration, the wave no longer looked like a tempting challenge, but a terrifying monster. I lurched forward, hunkering down against the jet-ski, praying it would offer some protection just as the wave hit.

* * *

My eyes flew open. 'The engine cut out and I got knocked off the jet-ski.' My fingers instinctively gripped the bedsheet that covered me, as though it could offer any protection from the force of the impact. I could feel the blow as the wave threw me forwards, banging my head against the jet-ski. It was like being thrown headfirst against concrete. Hard. Disorientating. Painful.

And yet, alongside the pain, there was something else too. Disappointment. A void I felt inside from the absence of power.

Immersed in the icy water, I felt my grip slip before everything faded to nothingness.

'And Josh Carter?'

I blinked. 'What about him?'

'What happened to him?'

I frowned. 'I don't understand?'

'He's missing.'

'Missing?' I repeated the word slowly, as my brain struggled to make sense of it. 'What do you mean, he's missing?' A sense of dread weighed heavily against me.

'You were the only one pulled from the water. The coastguard hasn't been able to find Josh yet.'

My eyes widened as I stared at them. 'He had an accident too?'

The officers exchanged an uncertain look. 'He was with you on the jet-ski,' PC Jennings said, hesitantly.

I shook my head. 'No. I was alone.'

'Are you certain?' I heard the doubt in her voice.

I lifted my hand back to my forehead, but it did nothing to help ease the pounding that reverberated through my skull. 'I was alone,' I repeated. I knew I was. I wouldn't have gone out with Josh. Not today. Not ever again.

'Josh sent a text to his brother, Paul, saying that the two of you were going out on the water together. Just like usual.'

'Why would he tell him that?' I shook my head.

'We found your car in the Harbourside car park in Poole.'

I nodded. 'I use the Baiter slipway there.'

'We found Josh's car at the other end of the car park.'

I blinked. 'You did?'

'Sunday morning is when you and Josh usually take the jet-ski out?'

'Well, yes, but...'

'The two of you? Together?'

'Normally, yes.'

'So why not today?'

'I...' The pounding in my head grew stronger. More persistent. This wasn't how it was supposed to be. 'I...' I ran my fingers through my blonde curls, wincing slightly as they caught on a knot from the dried salt water that had matted my hair.

'Sorry, officers,' Dr Menon's voice from the doorway cut through the silence. I stared at him, stunned. I hadn't even realised he was there. 'You're going to need to leave now so my patient can get some rest.' He was protecting me again.

'Just a few more questions—'

'My patient sustained a severe head injury.'

PC Jennings nodded. 'We'll come back when she's less confused.'

I frowned. Was I confused?

PC Smith nodded as he followed his colleague out of the cubicle. I stared after them, relieved they were leaving. But unease still churned in the pit of my stomach. They were police officers. They were good. They helped people. Except they had the power to turn my world, my life, upside down.

Just like before.

'Thanks,' I said as the officers left.

Dr Menon nodded and turned to the monitor. 'Your vitals

look okay,' he said, before turning back to me. He placed his hand beside mine. 'Can you squeeze my fingers?'

I wrapped my fingers around his and squeezed as instructed.

'Pull my hand towards you, and then push me away, so I can check the strength of your upper limbs.'

I obeyed again.

'Good. And the other hand?'

We repeated the process.

He nodded again as he started to pull his hand away, but he paused. He glanced over his shoulder, before turning back to me. The corner of his mouth twisted upwards in a hopeful smile. 'So, Lauren,' he whispered, 'did you do it?'

2

FOUR MONTHS EARLIER (MAY)

I hugged my right wrist to my chest as I sat in the waiting room. It was broken. Even with my non-existent medical training I could tell that.

The two paracetamol I'd already taken weren't really doing anything to numb the pain, but it wasn't anything I couldn't handle. After all, I'd handled worse.

I glanced down at it, studying the deformed shape. I didn't want to see it and yet, something kept making me look. Some sense of morbid curiosity perhaps; like covering my eyes when watching a scary movie, but still peeking through my fingers. Because even though I told myself I didn't want to know, didn't want to see, the truth was, some part of me did.

I was fascinated. Repulsed, but fascinated.

My gaze drifted around the busy waiting room. Everyone looked harassed and worried. I watched as new patients entered, wide eyed as they studied the signs, desperately checking they were in the right place. They looked overwhelmed by it all.

They didn't want to be here. I couldn't blame them. It was unfamiliar and scary.

At least to them.

Hospital staff zig-zagged through the crowd, their pace hurried and decisive. There was an order to it all. The atmosphere felt charged with a buzz of energy. It was structured. Purposeful.

Safe.

'Lauren Taylor.' I turned at the sound of my name being called. A male doctor stood in the corridor, his eyes scanning the room. I stood up and walked towards him, protecting my wrist against my body as I moved.

'Ms Taylor?' he asked, and I nodded. 'I'm Dr Menon.' His subtle Indian accent added extra warmth to his tone. 'This way please.' He led me through to a small cubicle and signalled to a chair. 'Have a seat and let's have a look at that wrist.'

I sat on the edge of the chair and slowly held my wrist out for him to examine. I inhaled sharply as he touched my fingers.

'Sorry,' he said, instantly. 'I'm afraid it's broken.'

I nodded.

'It looks like a possible fracture dislocation and may need manipulation, but I'll need an x-ray to confirm.'

I nodded again.

'How did you do it?' he asked.

'I fell off a ladder.'

He arched his eyebrow.

'I'm such a clutz,' I added, pre-empting his next question.

His gaze flitted to my face for a second before returning his attention to my wrist. But that split second was long enough.

'It's not the first time you've been treated here.'

There was an unspoken question suspended in his words.

I shook my head and laughed. 'Like I said, total clutz.'

His expression didn't change. He didn't even crack a smile at my feeble attempt at a joke. He just looked up and studied me intently.

'There were some questions raised by the doctor who treated you last time.'

I felt cold.

I remembered those questions. I remembered the way the doctor had looked at me. Pitying and fearful.

He was just trying to help of course. Just like the doctors before him. I understood that. But I didn't need it. I was fine.

'The frequency of your injuries had raised some concerns.'

I should have known it would be in the file. I should have known they would document it. Their doubts. Their theories.

I was taking up their time again. Time that they needed for other patients. I was either careless or I was...

I swallowed. 'They're not that frequent.'

Dr Menon tipped his head to the side. 'Well, it's not as though you're here every month, no. But you are here more than normal.'

Normal.

That was a word that had long ceased applying to me.

'And given your history—'

'That was years ago,' I cut through his words, my voice hard and cold. I didn't need him bringing up the past. It was *my* past. My burden.

Mine alone.

'In situations like yours it's not unusual for...' He paused. He was searching for the right words. The ones that would enable him to say just the right thing. The right way.

But there was no right way.

There never had been. Not about this.

I could hear my own breathing. Fast. Laboured. Loud. The sound of it seemed to echo in the small cubicle. Could he hear it too? Could he sense the panic rising in my chest?

'When children experience what you did...' He started again. Hesitant. Unsure.

'I know the risks,' I interrupted, saving him from his own internal battle. And saving me from hearing those risks laid out.

Again.

'The therapist explained at the time.'

He nodded. 'And?'

It was such a simple word. But it held such weight. Such implication.

'I'm not my mother.'

3

NOW

'W-what?' The word came out so broken and distorted that I wasn't even sure it had been my voice. Only the bewilderment on Abhilash's face as he stared at me, told me it had been me who had spoken.

'Did you leave him?'

'Oh,' my breath escaped my lungs in a gush. 'That.'

Abhilash chuckled. 'Of course, that. What did you think I meant?' A frown creased his forehead. 'Unless...' his head turned as he glanced back over his shoulder to where the police officers had departed.

'We ended it on Saturday,' I blurted out without emotion.

Abhilash's eyes widened. 'We?'

I nodded, conscious that 'we' sounded mutual, as though we'd both agreed. Yet, in reality, it had been a long time since Josh and I had agreed on anything.

'So, Josh was okay with it?' Abhilash covered my hand with his. 'He was okay with you?'

I nodded again. I knew what he meant. What he feared.

What I had made him fear.

'I would have come with you, you know. We could have handled him together.' Abhilash squeezed my hand, as though trying to telepathically transmit his sincerity.

I smiled. 'I know.' He'd offered before. Repeatedly. It was one of the things that had drawn me to him: that determination to protect me, to keep me safe.

I relaxed back against the pillows. His sincerity was what made him so different to Josh. With Abhilash they weren't just words and empty promises. I had no doubt that he really would do anything for me.

I inhaled sharply. Well, anything except perhaps one thing.

The one thing that I wanted most of all.

'How come you didn't call me afterwards?' He tried to pass it of as a casual question, but I could hear the undercurrent of hurt in his voice.

I shrugged, pretending that it wasn't a big deal. Even though we both knew it was. 'It was late when Josh left and I didn't want to disturb you. I knew you had an early shift this morning. You needed your sleep.'

Abhilash rolled his eyes. 'I still would have found a few minutes to talk to you.' He shifted awkwardly, his expression suddenly apprehensive. 'Unless you didn't want to talk to me?'

'Of course, I did,' but my voice lacked conviction.

Abhilash's frown deepened, and I knew he'd heard it too.

My words sounded like a lie. But they weren't. I had wanted to call him. To talk to him. But he would have wanted to know the details.

And right then, in that moment, I probably would have told him.

I shook my head. 'I think I just needed a little time alone to process it all.' I paused. 'Josh was everything at one point. I'd imagined us spending our lives together, growing old together. I know it was my choice to end things and I know it was the right decision. But I think I still needed a moment to accept that it was really over.'

It was the truth.

At least partially.

Abhilash nodded. 'I understand. You needed time to grieve.'

Grieve.

I stared at him as the word churned my stomach.

'For your relationship,' Abhilash added hesitantly.

'Right,' I nodded a little too forcefully. Grieving was exactly what I'd done. In my own way.

'So, you haven't seen him since yesterday?'

Josh is missing.

The police officer's voice repeated in my brain.

'No,' I replied firmly. There could be no doubt. No question. The alternative was unthinkable.

And yet, it was what I'd wanted. Josh gone from my life. Totally. Completely.

The how was irrelevant.

Wasn't it?

What had happened to him beyond Saturday night wasn't my concern. *He* wasn't my concern. Not any longer.

We'd ceased to matter to each other the moment we broke up. If not before.

We had limped along in denial for so long, it was hard to know the exact moment that we had stopped caring. It hadn't been instantaneous. I was sure of that. It had been slow. Like a gradual death. One that neither of us had predicted. And neither of us could prevent.

But then again, perhaps only one of us had really been trying.

4

THEN

An uncomfortable silence hung between us. Perhaps I'd been too abrupt. Dr Menon was only expressing concern for me. I sucked in a deep breath. Doctors were *always* concerned for me.

It came from a good place, I knew that. It was part of their training. Or perhaps their nature. They wanted to help. To heal. I liked that part of it. The care. The attention. But I knew, beneath it all there was an undercurrent of fear. Almost expectation. They thought they knew me based on what was in my file. My past.

And *that* part did not feel good.

'The doctor you saw before wondered if you'd hurt yourself intentionally.' Dr Menon persisted. He wasn't giving up.

My skin bristled. 'I didn't.'

'And this time?'

And there it was. The inevitable question that I'd known would come eventually.

The doctors always came back to the same theory. They thought Mum's instability had become my own. Her need for attention had been so desperate, so excessive, that it had come with a price. One I had paid. Repeatedly. Things like that damaged you. The doctors knew it.

And so did I.

'How could I break my wrist intentionally?'

'FOOSH,' Dr Menon said. 'It stands for fall on outstretched hand,' he clarified as I frowned. 'It could be the result of an accident or potentially the fall could be intentional.'

I sat straighter and met Dr Menon's eyes. 'I told you, I fell off a ladder.' My voice was firm. I didn't show any sign of weakness. No hesitation. No indication, even for one split second, that I might be lying.

Perhaps I was wrong.

I was like my mother after all.

'Right, because you're just clumsy.'

I knew from the tone of his voice that he didn't believe me. He didn't even try to disguise it.

I said nothing. I was good at keeping quiet. Biting my tongue and keeping my head down. It was the best way to stay under the radar.

Not that it was always successful.

'I read the notes about your mother in your file.'

I nodded. That wasn't surprising. Cases like hers, like ours, were rare. But they were also dangerous. Everyone involved took great care to document even the tiniest detail. They tried to protect me.

Tried, but failed.

'I'm sorry.'

I blinked. Dr Menon's apology startled me. I was used to concern. I was used to questions and assumptions. But an apology...? 'What for?'

'That you went through that. That no one helped you sooner.'

I nodded slowly.

'Both of you,' he added softly.

I swallowed.

He wasn't just sorry for me. He was sorry for her too. He pitied us. Pitied the life that we'd led. The life we'd lost.

My breath caught in my throat. I felt something shift. A tiny crack in the wall that I had spent years building up around me.

I tried not to think about the past. About her. It was better to stay angry. To hate her. If I allowed myself to feel compassion, to feel sad for her, then it opened the door to many more emotions that I didn't want to feel.

Emotions that I had fought to block out.

And yet, they tormented me still.

They were relentless. Unwavering. The doubt. The guilt.

I should have done more.

I should have *been* more.

'Can you tell me what's really happening?' Dr Menon's voice cut through my self-loathing.

I swallowed. He knew. Somehow, despite my adamance. Despite my well-rehearsed performance. He knew.

My jaw clenched as I gritted my teeth and tried to keep my emotions in check. He didn't say anything, but I saw the flicker of recognition cross his face and I knew he'd noticed my reaction.

It made me look guilty.

I couldn't let him think that. The other doctors had had doubts. Questions. But they didn't have anything concrete. They weren't sure. And yet even that doubt had caused complications for me.

If Dr Menon believed strongly enough that I was a danger to myself, there was no way he would let it go. It would mean more visits from Social Services again. That wasn't the kind of attention I wanted. I had my reputation to think of. My business. My life.

And yet, my lip quivered. I wanted to confide in him. I wanted someone to know. To understand. To care.

I blinked furiously, trying to hold back the tears that threatened to start flowing at any second. I wasn't even sure why they were forming. I was stronger than that. My emotions were buried so deep within that I couldn't even remember the last time I'd cried. At least not in front of anyone else. My tears were saved for my pillow. It was the only confidant to my secret.

Until now.

'Lauren?'

He was waiting for an answer. An explanation.

My lips parted, but no words would come.

Maybe it was as simple as it being the first time in a really long time that someone hadn't believed my 'I'm fine'. Or more importantly, hadn't accepted it.

I wasn't sure everyone did believe it. Not always. But they let it pass. They didn't delve any deeper. They didn't care or just didn't want to know.

But he did.

He wasn't satisfied with my explanation. He didn't just roll his eyes, call me clumsy and move on with his day.

People had asked before. He wasn't the first. He wasn't even the most persistent. And yet there was something different about him, about the way he asked, the way he looked at me as though he could see into my soul.

It was ridiculous. I *knew* it was ridiculous. He was just another doctor. Curious. Concerned. He had a job to do. That was all it was. All I was.

And yet, I tried to recall the last time that anyone had looked at me that way. I knew pity. I'd lived with enough of it. But this was different. *He* was different.

'It was Josh.'

5

NOW

'Thanks for fetching my car,' I said, as Abhilash parked on the drive. 'And for driving me home.' I touched my fingers to the bandage on my head. 'My doctor wouldn't let me drive with a head injury.'

Abhilash chuckled. 'He sounds like a wise man, but you don't need to thank me, you know.' He turned the engine off and twisted in the driver's seat to look at me. 'I want to help you. I like to.'

I inhaled deeply, allowing the warmth of his tone, his presence, to wash over me. 'I just want you to know I'm grateful.'

He nodded. 'I know.'

I reached out and placed my hand on his shoulder, hoping my touch conveyed all the emotions that I couldn't put into words. He covered my hand with his and squeezed gently. 'Don't worry, Lauren,' he said, gazing at me earnestly. 'It's all going to be all right.'

A lump formed in my throat as his words took me back. Another time. Another doctor...

* * *

'You're going to be all right, Lauren.' An unfamiliar voice penetrated the darkness as I fought the drowsiness that made my eyelids heavy and uncooperative. I blinked as I peered around the unfamiliar room. A repetitive beeping grated on my nerves, increasing my determination not to give in to the desire to allow myself to drift back to sleep.

I was in bed, I realised as I tried to focus. But not my bed. Not my room.

The beeping seemed to intensify as my breathing quickened. There were wires and tubes connected to me. What were they? I didn't want them. I tried to sit up, but I felt too weak. A strange whimpering sound escaped my lips as I refused to give up. I focused my energy on my right hand and reached for the tube to pull it out of me.

'Everything's okay,' the voice said soothingly. My gaze drifted, following the sound. A man I didn't know smiled at me.

I grunted and resumed my quest to free myself of the tube.

'No, Lauren, you need to leave that where it is,' I turned at the sound of Mum's voice the other side of me.

The man lifted my right hand and placed it back at my side. I tried to pull my hand free, but he refused to let go. 'You're in hospital, Lauren. You were very sick. This tube is helping to make you better. Do you understand?'

I blinked again, focusing on his words.

Hospital.

I was in hospital.

I studied him cautiously. His funny blue clothes were like something I'd seen on TV. 'Are you a doctor?' My question was so quiet, so mumbled, for a moment I wasn't even sure he would hear it.

'Yes, I am. I did your surgery and came to check on your recovery.'

I frowned. I remembered being at home. My stomach had hurt. It *had been so bad. It wouldn't stop. 'I had surgery?' I tried to lift my head from the pillow to see my stomach but I was covered in a white sheet.*

He nodded. 'You were so brave and did so well.'

'I did?'

I glanced at Mum for confirmation and she nodded. 'He saved your life, Lauren.'

My eyes widened as I turned back and stared at the doctor.

'It's all going to be all right, now,' the doctor repeated. He smiled at me, his eyes locked on mine, full of warmth and certainty. It was calming. Reassuring.

At least to me.

'How can you be so sure?' Mum's anxious voice carried from the other side of my bed. 'I mean, I thought she was all right before and look where we are now. She just had a stomach-ache. It's not unusual for a ten-year-old. Just a tummy bug, that's all it seemed to be. There's one going around the whole school. But then she just collapsed.'

'You weren't to know,' the doctor said, soothingly.

'But I'm her mother. It's my job to know. My job to keep my child safe.'

I could hear the guilt causing her words to wobble. I felt bad for her. She was so distraught. So tormented. And yet, a tiny part of me felt vindicated. She should feel guilty. Remorseful. Scared.

I'd tried to tell her how much it had hurt. I'd begged her to make it better. To make the pain stop.

She'd told me to stop making a fuss.

I gritted my teeth.

I wasn't the one making a fuss now. I'd almost died. And yet, somehow it was all about her. Her guilt. Her pain.

'It was an easy mistake to make,' the doctor said, leaving my side, to go to her. 'Abdominal pain, vomiting and fever are all standard symptoms of a stomach bug. It's understandable that you didn't realise it was appendicitis.'

'But if I'd realised sooner...' Mum's voice was practically a wail. 'It wouldn't have perforated.'

'Lauren's appendix has been removed now. She's out of danger. And the peritonitis is being treated.'

'The what?' I asked.

'The pain in your tummy was caused by your appendix. When it burst, it caused an infection, but we're treating you with antibiotics.' The doctor nodded at the tube that ran into the vein in my arm. 'You're going to be fine.'

'But what if she isn't? What if...?' Mum chocked back a sob and the doctor's attention immediately refocused on her again.

He smiled gently as he reached for a box of tissues from beside my bed and handed them to her. 'Lauren's surgery went well and she'll make a full recovery. She'll be back home with you in a few days.'

Mum took a tissue and dabbed at her eyes. 'She just collapsed,' she repeated again.

The doctor pulled a chair from where it nestled against the wall and placed it behind Mum. 'Have a seat where you can be close to Lauren and I'll ask a nurse to bring you a cup of tea.' Mum sank into the chair obediently and the doctor placed his hand on her shoulder. 'You've had a terrible shock, Mrs Taylor. But everything's going to be fine now.'

Mum looked up at him. 'Thank you, doctor. You've been so good to us,' her voice rasped as she spoke. 'I was so scared I was going to lose my baby.' She sniffed. 'I can't lose her. She's all I have.'

'We weren't going to let that happen,' the doctor said and winked at me. 'Not on my watch.'

I felt a sharp stab of guilt in my chest. I'd been spiteful relishing in Mum's sorrow. Of course, she hadn't meant for me to suffer. She hadn't known I was so sick. Even the doctor said it was an easy mistake to make. She'd just been trying to do her best for me. Just like always.

The doctor gave Mum's shoulder a gentle squeeze before taking a

step back. 'I'll come back and check on you both later,' he said, as he
disappeared behind the curtain that was drawn around my bed.

I turned to Mum, her gaze still locked on the gap in the curtain
where the doctor had slipped through, a slight smile easing the panic
from her face.

* * *

I turned away, shoving the past into the recesses of my mind as I
rummaged in the glovebox. I pulled out my house keys and
phone.

'That's where you left them when you went out on the water
yesterday?' Abhilash arched an eyebrow. 'That doesn't seem very
safe.'

'True, but they were safer than me,' I added with a rueful
laugh.

Abhilash rolled his eyes. 'We definitely need to start taking
better care of you.'

'We?' I smiled. 'I like the way you say that. Like we're a
team.'

'We are,' Abhilash said. He sounded almost surprised, as
though I should know that already.

My smile widened.

We clambered out of the car and I pressed the power button
on my phone as I walked up the drive. 'The battery is dead,' I
said. 'I bet I have so many missed calls.'

'They can wait until tomorrow, can't they?' Abhilash said.
'Charge it in the morning. You should rest this evening.'

'But maybe there will be news about Josh...' My voice trailed
away.

'Do you really need to know, right now?' There was a touch of
hurt in Abhilash's tone. Josh wasn't supposed to mean anything to

me any more. He was my past. And a painful one at that. 'You need to focus on your recovery.'

I shook my head. 'You're right. It can wait.'

'I'm sure Josh will be found soon,' Abhilash added.

'I know,' I replied without hesitation. But that knowledge wasn't as comforting as Abhilash had intended. I swallowed. Josh would be found. I was certain of that.

Eventually.

I slid the key in the lock, pushed open the front door and stepped inside.

I paused. The house felt different. Empty. Abandoned.

And yet, there was something more as well. Something I hadn't felt in a long time. Something I had always longed for.

It felt like mine.

'Are you sure it's okay for me to be here?'

Abhilash's voice behind me pulled me from my thoughts and I turned back.

'Of course.' I held the door open wider for him and stepped aside. 'Come on in.'

He hesitated and cast a nervous glance behind him. I could feel the uncertainty radiating from him. It was the first time he'd been in my home.

My home.

If felt strange to think of it as mine. It had always been *ours*. Josh's and mine. We were a combined entity. Joined. Whole.

And now...

My gaze fell upon the bulging black bin bags that lined the hall. I swallowed. I'd done the right thing. Hadn't I?

Abhilash brushed against me as he joined me in the hall. His fingers wrapped around mine, sending tingles through my body. I turned to face him and allowed the door to close behind us, cocooning us inside.

'Are you hungry?' I asked, as I dropped my phone and keys on the little table by the door. 'I can make you something.' I took a step forward towards the kitchen, but Abhilash pulled me back.

'I'll make it. You're supposed to be resting.' He leaned forwards and his lips brushed mine. 'Doctor's orders.'

He started to pull away, but I reached up, threading my fingers through his short black hair. He kissed me again, longer this time, and I closed my eyes, savouring every moment.

'Yes, doctor,' I murmured compliantly as we finally separated.

'So, which way to the kitchen?'

I pointed to the door at the end of the hall.

'Great.' Abhilash kissed my cheek. 'You go and put your feet up and I'll start cooking.'

'No way,' I objected. 'I need to witness your culinary skills at work. The only thing Josh knew how to do was order take out.'

Josh.

An awkward silence descended around us.

I shouldn't have mentioned his name again. I'd spoilt the mood. Reminded us of the one thing we didn't want to think about.

'Do you think the police will want to talk to me again?' I asked the question that had been tormenting me.

Abhilash puffed out his cheeks and slowly let out a long deep breath. 'Possibly. I think I only stalled them at the hospital yesterday. Now you're home...'

My stomach stirred. No, I definitely shouldn't have mentioned Josh.

'Is that his stuff?' Abhilash asked, jerking his head towards the bags.

I nodded. It felt weird seeing all his belongings shoved into a few bags. That was all that his existence came down to. A few crumpled clothes tossed carelessly into bin bags. Perhaps I should have made more effort. I could have folded them at least.

But then what was the point?

'I should move them, I guess. They probably wouldn't look good if the police saw them.'

Abhilash shook his head. 'I'll do it.' He paused. 'Where should I put them?'

We stared at each other blankly.

'Do you think...' I licked my lips, my mouth suddenly feeling dry. 'Do you think they might ask to look around?'

'It's a possibility.'

We tiptoed carefully around the words neither of us could say. What if they didn't just ask? What if they didn't give me a choice?

'Let's eat first and we'll figure it out,' Abhilash said and I nodded as I followed him into the kitchen, a gnawing in my stomach telling me that this wasn't something we could figure out over a meal. It was too big. Too complicated.

Just like everything with Josh always had been.

6

THEN

I clamped my mouth closed as I stared at Dr Menon. I hadn't said that aloud. I couldn't have done.

The words had slipped out unguarded. I hadn't meant to say them. I'd needed to say something. But not that. Never that.

I couldn't accuse Josh.

And yet, I had.

'I don't know why I said that.' I fumbled over my words, my voice quiet and shaky.

'Is it true?' Dr Menon asked.

I froze.

To deny it now would make Dr Menon more convinced that his previous suspicion had been right. I would look more guilty. More unstable. But to confirm it would be to betray Josh even further. To blame him. The man who had stood by me through everything. Because of him I'd gained surrogate parents and even a brother. They weren't the same as the real thing. They couldn't be. But in a way, that's what made them better.

Josh didn't deserve this. Not from me. We had our problems. He wasn't perfect. But then, neither was I.

'Josh is...' Dr Menon's eyes automatically dropped to my left hand. 'Your boyfriend?' he asked.

I nodded as my thumb brushed across my finger and I felt the absence of the ring I so desperately wanted.

Dr Menon pulled up a chair and perched in front of me.

I waited for the doubt to show on his face. Blaming Josh had been foolish, not least because there was no way that Dr Menon would actually believe it. My file held too much history, too many suspicions, to cast doubt on the well documented theory that his colleagues had pursued over the years simply based on one flip-pant accusation.

'How long have you two been together?'

I frowned.

It wasn't the question I'd expected. It was so ordinary. So innocent. Harmless.

'Twelve years,' I replied. 'We started dating at school and bought a house together after uni six years ago.'

Dr Menon nodded silently, and I realised my error. He'd read my medical file. He knew my history. The pieces were fitting together in his mind like a giant jigsaw puzzle. One that I had never expected him to solve.

My chest tightened. What had I done?

'It's not what you think,' I told him. 'It's not all Josh.'

'I get it.' Dr Menon nodded. 'You feel responsible, as though somehow you could have prevented it. Or maybe you even feel like you deserved it.'

I shifted uncomfortably on the plastic chair. Dr Menon was so close to the truth. Too close. I was responsible. I always had been.

'Domestic abuse cases are always complex,' he added.

'Domestic abuse?' My heart pounded. 'No, that's not what this is. It's not how he is.'

Cold dread crept through my body. Why had I blamed Josh?

Why had I cared so much what Dr Menon thought of me that I would allow myself to betray the one person who had stood by me through everything that had happened?

It hadn't even made things better. I hadn't alleviated Dr Menon's fears. I'd just increased the scope. I'd entangled Josh in my mess now as well. Another cause for concern. Another safeguarding issue.

I'd always tried to protect Josh from the craziness of my life. Even when he, along with everyone else, had discovered the truth about Mum, I'd still shielded him from the details. It wasn't for her benefit. I didn't owe her that. I didn't owe her anything.

It was for Josh.

Details didn't help. They were things to dwell on. To analyse. They didn't erode the questions, they simply created more.

The questions were endless.

Unanswerable.

Intolerable.

My silence protected him. It's what I did. What I'd always done.

Until now.

'Every journey begins with a single step,' Dr Menon said softly.

I stared at him blankly.

'It's a quote by Lao Tzu,' he added, as though that was supposed to enlighten me.

I frowned. 'I don't understand what that has do to with a broken wrist.'

'Everything.'

'Ok-ay,' I dragged the word out. 'That clears that up, then.'

He chuckled.

I liked that sound. Deep. Rich. Warm.

'Maybe it's about avoiding the next broken wrist, or broken arm, or whatever it might be next time,' he said slowly.

A hollowness seemed to expand within me.

Next time.

He thought there'd be a next time too.

I knew it. I always knew it. It was inevitable. And yet, at the same time it was deniable.

I ignored that voice in my head that screamed at me that this was bad. That this wasn't how life was supposed to be. Pain. Guilt. Recurring hospital visits. But that voice was wrong. This was my life. It had always been my life.

'I know it might feel like you're trapped right now. But there's always a way out. A first step.'

I knew what he meant. Leave Josh. To him that was the answer. He thought it was so simple.

I'd *made* him think that.

But Josh wasn't really the problem.

I was.

I always had been.

This had been my life even before Josh. Another issue. Another hospital visit.

Dr Menon knew that. But he still didn't understand. He couldn't.

'I don't need to make a first step. I don't need a new start. I don't want one. Things are fine as they are.'

'Fine?'

'Good,' I corrected, silently cursing myself for my poor choice of wording.

He tipped his head to the left as he studied me, as though trying to read my thoughts. 'If you always stick with what you're used to, how do you know if there is anything better?'

I didn't need better. I didn't deserve it.

I just wanted Josh.

We were good together. We were complete.

'Josh loves me,' I said firmly. It was the one truth that I clung to. The one that had given me strength when my world had fallen apart.

It was all I had.

It was everything.

Dr Menon took a deep breath. 'Is that enough?'

7

NOW

My eyelids grew heavy as I pushed the remaining grilled chicken around on my plate, too tired to eat it.

'You should get some sleep,' Abhilash said. 'I'll check on you in a bit.'

'You don't need to do that. You should go home. I'll be fine.'

'You need someone to stay with you after a head injury.'

The hospital had already kept me in over twenty-four hours since the accident yesterday; surely I was out of danger now. I opened my mouth to question it, but Abhilash interrupted.

'You have your very own, personal doctor on hand. Will you please just let me do my job and take care of you?'

I clamped my mouth closed. I wasn't going to object. It was what I wanted. What I'd always wanted.

* * *

'Mum. Mum!' My cries got more desperate as the pain in my stomach intensified.

'I'm coming, baby. I'm coming.' I heard her footsteps as she ran up the stairs and swung my bedroom door open.

'It hurts so much, Mum,' I wailed as I lay curled up in bed, my arms wrapped around my stomach, tears streaming down my face.

For a second Mum froze in the doorway, her eyes wide, her face pale. She was scared. I could see it.

And then she nodded, as though jolting herself back into motion, back into control. She pulled her mobile phone from her pocket and stabbed at the buttons. 'Ambulance, please,' she said with a surprising calmness. 'My daughter is having severe stomach pains again.'

'Why does this keep happening?' I asked her, even though I knew it was futile. Parents were supposed to have the answers, and yet no one seemed to have the answers for this. Not Mum. Not even the doctors.

But they kept trying. They weren't giving up. They were fighting for me. That was something. In fact, right now, it was everything.

'She has a history of stomach issues following a perforated appendix two years ago,' Mum said into the phone, ignoring my question. She was in the zone. Focused. Organised. It was almost as though she couldn't see me now. She was fixated on the task at hand. Making the call. Getting to the hospital. Seeing the doctor.

Nothing else mattered.

* * *

I shook my head, pulling my thoughts back from the past. Abhilash's presence in my life, my home, was what I wanted. But it also came with risks. 'What if someone comes?' The question escaped my lips before I had chance to stop it.

'You mean what if Josh comes home and catches me here?'

'No.' I shook my head; he wasn't the one I was worried about. 'He won't.' The police, on the other hand…

Abhilash's forehead wrinkled. 'You seem very certain about that.'

I shrugged wearily. 'He can't.'

'Can't?' His gaze bore into me, instantly evaporating my drowsiness as I realised how that sounded.

'I have his keys,' I said quickly. 'He can't come back.'

'Oh,' the frown faded from Abhilash's forehead, but an uneasiness remained embedded in his features. 'You really don't seem worried at all.'

'Of course, I am,' I swallowed. 'I don't want anything bad to have happened to him.'

'I didn't mean worried for Josh. I meant you don't seem scared of him.'

'Oh.' I clasped my hands together, digging my nails into my palms as I debated how to respond.

'You're not scared that he might come back,' Abhilash continued. 'You're not worried about him finding me here. In fact, for a woman who has suffered from his violence for years, you really don't seem afraid at all.'

The chicken I had just eaten shifted uncomfortably in my stomach. It was the first time that Abhilash had ever doubted me. He'd always trusted me before. Always taken my word for things without question. But now...

I swallowed as bile rose in my throat. Was it that he didn't believe my accusations about Josh? Or that he questioned my role in his disappearance?

My right leg bounced up and down. If Abhilash doubted me then what chance did I stand with anyone else? What chance did I stand with the police?

'You don't know Josh like I do,' my words were terse and clipped. 'In fact, you don't know him at all.' Abhilash's question had put me on edge. He was the one person I never thought I would have to defend myself to.

'I know what he's capable of,' Abhilash said, fear resonating in his voice. 'I know what he's done to you. Can you blame me for being afraid of what lengths he might go to now that he feels rejected?'

My hands relaxed their grip as relief washed over me. He didn't doubt me. He was just scared for me.

He cared.

My stomach churned again. Only this time it wasn't fear. It was guilt.

'I'm not afraid of him. At least not in that way. It was never premeditated. Never intentional. It was impulsive. One split second when his anger just got away from him.'

'Or perhaps his fear,' Abhilash said quietly.

I stared at him with my mouth open. 'He hits me and he's the one who's afraid?'

'Maybe,' Abhilash's shoulders lifted slightly. 'Sometimes that's where the anger comes from. A fear of not being in control. Of losing something. Maybe of losing you.'

I scoffed. 'So, he hit me to keep me?' That was a ridiculous theory.

'It worked, didn't it? He hit you and yet you stayed.'

'Huh,' I grunted, unable to think of an argument.

'I'm not saying it's rational. It's a part of him he can't control. At least not without help.'

I laughed. 'Why would he get help? According to Josh, none of it happened. I fell. I hurt myself. He is always blameless.' I shrugged. 'Anyway, it doesn't matter now. It's in the past.'

'How can you be so sure of that?'

'Because he's gone.'

Abhilash drew back.

'I-I didn't mean that the way that it sounded,' I stammered.

He didn't speak. He just stared at me as though he was looking at a stranger.

My brain whirled. I had to fix this. I had to make him stop looking at me like that.

'Josh sulks when things don't go his way,' I said, reaching across the table to stroke Abhilash's arm. 'He lashes out. Then he withdraws.'

'But you said he didn't lash out when you broke up. You said he took it well.'

'He did.' I shifted on my chair, which suddenly felt hard and uncomfortable. 'I mean, he yelled a bit. But that was all. Then he left.'

'To sulk?'

'To regroup.'

'So, he *will* be back?'

I hesitated. It felt as though there was a double meaning to his question. I nodded slowly. 'Eventually.'

'And yet that doesn't worry you?'

I couldn't blame him for his nervousness. Given everything I had told Abhilash, I should be scared. And yet I wasn't. 'Not any more.'

'Why? What's changed?'

'I have.'

8

THEN

I clambered cautiously out of the taxi, conscious of protecting my right wrist even though it was now in a cast and the sling kept it close to my body. I closed the taxi door behind me and stood at the bottom of the drive, staring at the whitewashed three-bedroom house.

I was home.

The driver restarted the engine and I turned to watch as he pulled away from the kerb. I fought the urge to call out to him to stop. I wanted to go back to the hospital. To stay there. But I couldn't.

It was too soon.

I turned back to the house. This is where I belonged. And yet, even as I thought it I questioned how true it was. It was where I wanted to belong. But if I was honest with myself, it never had been.

Perhaps it was understandable. I'd spent so much time in hospitals that they felt more like home to me. I mattered there. More than I'd ever mattered anywhere else. Even here.

The question was, what to do about it? I was stuck. I knew

that. Living a life that felt incomplete. And yet, it was all I had. At least for now.

Good things come from a little bit of pain.

Mum's favourite saying sprang into my mind. She'd repeated it through my recovery after the burst appendix, and again through each set back. She was determined to keep me going. Not allowing me to wallow or give up. I was grateful to her for that. She'd taught me about perseverance. About inner strength.

Then again, her most powerful lessons hadn't come from her words, but from her actions. Those were the ones that I carried with me each day. The ones I would never be able to forget.

I shook my head, took a deep breath, and forced my feet into action. I couldn't stand on the drive all day reminiscing about the past. I'd already lost half a day at the hospital. Time that I should have been working. I gritted my teeth as I fumbled in my hand-bag, searching for my keys one handed. I'd worked too hard to build my business to let my clients think I was slacking off now.

Home might never have felt like somewhere I belonged, but my business did. I was good at that. It was the one thing that was truly mine. Josh had no part of it. He didn't want to. To him it was trivial. Just me and my laptop at our kitchen table didn't count as a real business in his eyes. Especially when that business was a social media consultancy.

Is that all you've got to do with your time?

His disinterest had hurt at first, but now I realised that it had been for the best. It was separate. Independent.

That was important.

I slid the key into the lock and paused as the accusation I had made to Dr Menon sprang into my thoughts. My slip had been weak. I'd allowed myself to panic and speak without thinking. I knew better than that. If Dr Menon deemed me to be in danger, he would raise another safeguarding flag and

Social Services would be back to poke their noses into my life again.

That was the last thing I needed.

* * *

My stomach tightened at the unmistakable crunching sound of a car pulling up on the gravel driveway. I froze, my left hand poised awkwardly over the mouse that it was unaccustomed to using, as I sat at the kitchen table. My gaze locked unseeingly on the computer screen in front of me.

A car door slammed closed.

I swallowed.

Josh was home.

I glanced across the kitchen at the digital clock on the oven. He was right on time. And yet, somehow, I still felt unprepared. I wasn't ready to face him. To see that pitying look. To hear his words of concern.

The key turned in the lock and the front door swished open.

I needed more time.

'Lauren?' Josh's voice called out from the hall.

I should answer. I should rush to him to greet him and welcome him home. It's what I used to do. Once.

I didn't move. Didn't speak.

'Lauren?' There was an anxiousness to his tone. Was he afraid that this time I hadn't come home? That this time had been too much?

'There you are!' Josh said, his words were breathy and hoarse as he entered the kitchen and his gaze fell upon me. 'Are you okay?' He crossed the kitchen in three easy strides to the kitchen table and then he was there. Right beside me. Leaning over me.

His warm breath brushing my cheek, his gaze fixed upon my wrist.

'You broke it, then?'

You.

The accusation jarred against me. He was like everyone else. Always assuming. Always blaming.

9

NOW

I studied Abhilash across the kitchen table. 'I was taught that life is pain. That love is pain. It was unavoidable. Acceptable. I never had anything or anyone I could count on. Not really. Not even myself.'

'And now?' he asked.

'I met you. You made me stronger. Braver. Different.'

Surprise flickered across Abhilash's face. 'I did?'

I smiled as I nodded. 'You did.'

Abhilash grinned. 'Well, I don't know how I did that. But I'm glad.'

We stared at each other silently as though neither of us knew what to say. But my revelation felt incomplete. He couldn't truly understand the impact he had made on me without knowing what my life had been like before him. The hopes I'd had. The dreams that had shattered. All of it had made me the person that sat before him now.

'We had so many plans when we bought this house,' I said, gazing around the kitchen. 'It was Josh's idea to move here. He said we should use the money Mum left me to do something good for me. For us. He was so excited. So certain.' I let out a deep sigh. 'He was mad at me because I didn't share his enthusiasm. To him, investing Mum's money was logical. It was just money. But to me...'

'It was a connection to the past. To her.'

I nodded as my heart swelled. 'Josh never understood that. Perhaps that should have been a sign. A warning that we weren't on the same page.' I shrugged. 'But Josh always knew how to talk me round. He called it *our* money and we were using it to build *our* future. Somehow calling it ours helped. It glossed over some of the darkness that it was tarnished with. But it never fully erased it.'

'You felt like she still had a hold over you?'

I smiled. 'I love how you just get it. You get me.'

He reached for my hand and squeezed. 'I do. I really do.'

'Well, Josh thought I was being ridiculous. And the logical part of me had to agree. I mean, it was a lot of money. We could never have afforded a place like this without it.' I shrugged again. It was a well-practiced move. Casual. Dismissive. Part of the pretence that things didn't matter. Didn't hurt. 'And, as Josh pointed out, we couldn't live with his parents for ever.'

'But you get on well with them, don't you? I mean, they took you in when you were fifteen after your Mum...' His voice trailed away, unable to say the word.

'Died.' I didn't have that problem. I didn't need tact. Not when it came to her. 'After Mum died.'

Abhilash nodded, but he looked uneasy. Perhaps I had been too blunt. Too cold. But then it was all she deserved.

'I love Josh's parents. They've always been so good to me. But like Josh said, as much as they loved me, I wasn't family. I would always just be a guest in their house.'

'He said that to you?' I heard the grimace in Abhilash's tone. I couldn't blame him. Even now Josh's words still hurt.

I nodded. 'A guest. After all that time, that was still all I was to them. All I'd ever be.' I tried to shrug, but this time I couldn't. 'He was right, of course. To me they were more like family than my own had been, but that didn't mean I was one of them. I was just someone they'd taken pity on. An obligation.'

'I'm sorry they made you feel that way.'

I frowned as I thought about how it had felt living in the Carter's house. 'They didn't,' I said. 'They never showed it. They didn't treat me like a guest. They treated me like a daughter.' It was what I'd needed. What I still needed.

'I didn't even realise how they really felt until Josh explained it to me. But then, I guess I wouldn't. As he said, his parents were good people. Very good. They would never have let on how much of an inconvenience I was. Not to me.' I paused, that revelation still hurt. Even now. 'Of course, once I knew, it was obvious that I couldn't stay there. But here,' I waved my hand around the room, 'this was our home.'

Our home.

It sounded warm and comforting. It sounded safe.

Not that it had turned out that way. Reality usually failed to live up to the fantasy.

'Josh told me we would get married, start a family, build a life together.' I clung to Abhilash's hand. It was like a lifeline as I drifted back into a time that I had tried to forget but knew I never would. 'He promised me that things would be different. That everything that had happened with Mum was truly behind me. I had him and he would never fail me. Not like she had.'

Abhilash stood up and walked around the table, without loosening his grip on my hand even for a second. He wrapped his other arm around my shoulders and drew me to him. 'I'm sorry that he didn't keep that promise.'

I shrugged weakly. I wanted to tell him that it didn't matter. That I was used to the disappointment. I wanted to believe that I didn't care. Not about Josh. Nor Mum. But it was a lie. People who didn't care simply let go of the past, of the pain.

I hadn't managed to let go of either.

10

THEN

My body tensed as Josh pulled me to my feet and wrapped his arms around my waist. I rested my left hand on his shoulder trying to reciprocate and appreciate the moment of intimacy, but it felt awkward and unfamiliar.

'I wish I could have come to the hospital with you,' he said apologetically.

I shook my head. 'It's fine.'

He hugged me tighter. 'I feel like I abandoned you.'

'Of course not.' The words danced off my tongue like the lyrics to a favourite song that I knew by heart. This was our pattern. Our routine.

'I should have been there for you.' Josh's voice was soft and desperate. He needed consoling. He needed my forgiveness.

And yet it was all distorted. The reasons. The apologies. Nothing was as it should be. Nothing was entirely real.

'You needed to get to work. It's fine,' I assured him. But then, it was fine. I didn't need him there. Not at the hospital. That was my place. Safe. Calm.

His presence there would be like two worlds colliding. Worlds that were best kept apart.

Josh nuzzled my neck. 'I'm so lucky to have such an understanding girlfriend.'

'I'm the lucky one,' I replied automatically. There was a time when I'd believed that.

Once.

I frowned. When had I stopped? I stared at the clock on the oven, as though it could help me identify the day. The hour. The minute. I wanted to pinpoint that moment. To go back to it. To change it.

I wanted to believe again.

To believe in him. In us. In something.

'Let's order a takeout tonight. We can eat watching a movie curled up on the sofa.'

'Really?' My voice echoed my surprise. We hadn't done that in months. Maybe longer.

Josh nodded. 'Just like old times. What do you say?'

My heart did a little somersault. I missed the old times. The times when we were passionate. Connected. I thought I was alone in mourning their loss. But maybe... just maybe...

'I'd like that,' my voice cracked, and I scolded myself silently. I should play it cool. Let things unfold naturally. But most importantly, not get my hopes up. I'd made that mistake before.

Josh nodded. 'Me too,' he said with conviction. 'It's been too long.'

I couldn't keep the smile off my face. Mum was right. Good things could come from a little bit of pain.

He stepped back and pulled his phone from his pocket. 'What do you feel like? Italian? Chinese?'

'Chinese,' I replied, 'if that's okay with you?'

'Whatever you want is okay with me.' Josh kissed my forehead, and my smile grew bigger.

I sank back into my chair as his fingers busily tapped on his phone. My gaze scanned the partly written email on my laptop screen as I tried to recapture my train of thought for the project I had been working on before Josh's arrival. It was almost complete. A couple more sentences and then I could hit send and be done for the day.

'Oh, you're still working.' The dejected tone of Josh's voice crashed down around me.

'I was just...' I hesitated. The email would take me less time to send than it would for Josh to place our order, and yet, somehow, I knew that wasn't the point. 'I was just packing up,' I said as I closed the email and clicked shut down.

Josh nodded and returned his focus to his phone and yet the vibe in the room felt different now. As though the warmth had dissipated.

I closed the laptop screen and rolled my eyes. I was being dramatic. Josh hated it when I did that. Overanalysed. Obsessed. And yet, it was who I was. Who I'd always been.

'Done,' he said with a nod. 'The food should be here within twenty minutes.'

'Perfect,' I replied, standing back up. I ran my hand across his chest. My action was instinctive and yet at the same time it surprised me. It was something I hadn't done for so long. At some point little touches like that had ceased to be part of how we were with each other. As though a line had been drawn between us and we each stayed on our own side.

For the most part.

I shook my head. Now wasn't the time to think about the past. For once in my life, I needed to focus on the now. 'Let's go and start the film while we wait.' I slid my hand across his shoulder, and down his arm to his hand, before linking my fingers through his. I tugged gently as I took a step towards the living room. My heart caught in my throat as I waited to see if he would follow. If he was still with me. Still happy.

He slid his phone into his back pocket, and I let out the breath that I hadn't even realised I'd been holding as he stepped forward to follow me, our hands still linked together.

There was still hope.

I sat on the sofa while Josh turned the TV on and loaded Netflix. He scrolled through the movies silently, his attention fixed on the screen. He'd always been like that. Completely focused. Absorbed. It didn't matter what the task was or how important or trivial it might be. Everything demanded his full attention.

Except me.

I shifted as the inescapable truth of that thought unsettled me. I'd held his focus at one point. I knew I had. I could still remember it. Remember how it felt. How *I* felt.

These days, mostly all I felt was forgotten.

A movie started playing and I realised that Josh had made his decision. He settled back against the sofa and lifted his arm as an invitation for me to snuggle against him. I shuffled into place. My place. It felt natural and right. Like coming home.

I stared at the TV screen, not even caring what we were watching. The movie didn't matter. Only this did. Us. Together.

Finally.

Josh's phone buzzed and he pushed me aside as he shuffled to retrieve it from his pocket.

'It's Paul,' Josh said, standing up. 'You don't mind if I take it, do you?'

I watched as he walked out of the room, closing the door behind him without even waiting for my answer.

I minded.

Of course I minded.

Sounds from the TV caught my attention where the movie was still playing, unwatched. Unseen.

Exactly as I felt.

11

THEN

'Why didn't you just leave?' Abhilash asked. 'The first time Josh raised a hand to you, why didn't you run? You'd been through so much with your mum, Josh had promised he would be different, that he'd keep you safe. But he didn't. So why didn't you leave the second you realised he'd lied?'

I shook my head. 'It seems so simple, doesn't it? So obvious. If someone hurts you, just leave. But in reality, life isn't that clear. Relationships aren't that simple. They're layered and complicated. Does one bad action undo years of good?' I shrugged. 'It's hard to say.'

'Okay, I get that. You have to weigh up the overall picture. And if it was a one-off maybe you could work through it. But it wasn't just one bad action. He hurt you repeatedly.'

'The first time it happened it was so fast. So unexpected. Like a brief flash of something he couldn't control. Just for a moment he became someone different. And then that person was gone. He was Josh again.' I shook my head slowly. 'I wasn't even sure that it had happened at all. I was on the floor. I'd fallen. My eye hurt. All the evidence was there and yet, it was as though my brain couldn't compute it. Josh couldn't have hurt me.'

'And the second? The third?'

'He was going through a lot. He'd been made redundant. He felt inadequate. Then he came home and I provoked him.'

Abhilash looked at me suspiciously. 'Provoked him how?'

'Just little things really. At least, they seemed it to me. I took too long to get ready, or I said the wrong thing when he just wanted to be left alone. I didn't pay attention to the signals. To his needs. I should have realised what he was going through. How much he was struggling.' I took a shaky breath. 'Just like I should have realised with Mum.'

'Just because they were having a tough time that doesn't excuse their behaviour. You don't exist to make them feel better. That isn't your role. It isn't your responsibility.'

'But that's what you do when you love someone. You support them. You help them. You make them feel better.'

'Not at the expense of your own happiness. Your own health.' There was a desperate edge to his voice. He was so anxious to reach me. To make me understand. 'They both hurt you. Badly.'

I nodded. 'I know. And I know it wasn't ideal. But,' the corner of my mouth lifted into a half smile, 'when you think about it, that just shows how strong their emotions were. How strong their love was. It was so powerful it couldn't be contained.'

Abhilash stared at me, his mouth opening and closing like a goldfish out of water, trying to breathe. 'You can't really believe that?' he said finally. 'Can you?' he added hesitantly. I could hear the fear embedded in his words. It horrified him to think for a second that I could not only accept that kind of treatment, but also condone it. It was sweet. Naïve, but sweet.

He believed love was good. That it led people to good choices. Good actions. That it meant they protected the person they loved.

He didn't understand that there was another side. That love could be darker. Painful.

I wasn't sure if I envied him for his ignorance. Or if I pitied him.

Because with the darkness came power. Intensity. Passion.

12

THEN

I clambered into bed and propped myself up on the pillows, listening to the sound of water running as Josh took a shower.

I rested my phone precariously in the fingers of my right hand. The cast on my wrist restricted my movement, but at least it was something. With my left hand I idly scrolled through Facebook. I had my own evening ritual too. I told myself it was work. That I was keeping up to date with my network. But really, I was trying to catch a glimpse of other people's lives.

Normal lives.

I wanted to know what it was like. What they were like. But social media only showed the surface. It didn't delve deep enough.

People only posted the parts they wanted others to see. Dinner at a nice restaurant. Sandcastles on the beach. Drinks with friends. Picnics in the New Forest.

I did all these things too. I put photographic evidence of them onto my social media channels just like they did. I was showing my friends, my clients, maybe even the world, that I was normal too. I was just like them.

Except, what if I wasn't?

Every like, every comment, was a form of validation. Acceptance. I was part of something. I belonged.

And yet, at the same time I knew, if I didn't post for a few days, no-one would probably even notice. They wouldn't miss me. My trivial little musings and staged photos didn't impact on their lives in any significant way. I was forgotten in the time it took to scroll to the next one, to hit the next like button, to type the next comment. It was all fleeting and superficial.

A post caught my attention and I stopped scrolling. I stared at the image of Paul and his girlfriend, Sasha, at a fancy-looking restaurant. No, not girlfriend: my attention locked on her left hand which she was holding up in front of the camera and the diamond ring which caught the light. She was his fiancée now.

The bathroom door opened and I looked up. 'Paul and Sasha have got engaged,' I told Josh as he walked into the bedroom, his brown hair tousled and damp from his shower.

'Hmm.' His faint murmur was only just audible.

My eyes narrowed as I studied him. 'Did you know?'

'Paul told me earlier when he called.'

'You didn't tell me.' I felt cold despite the heavy duvet. I'd been sitting right next to Josh all evening and yet he hadn't said a word. 'I'd have liked to have spoken to him to say congratulations. He didn't even message me.' My voice wobbled slightly as I spoke. Paul was practically a brother to me. He was family. Or so I'd thought. And yet no one had bothered to tell me his exciting news. I'd had to find out from social media just like everyone else.

Josh didn't even acknowledge my comment as he lifted the duvet and clambered into bed beside me.

I tried to ignore the heaviness in my chest. It wasn't as though he was intentionally ignoring my feelings. He was just... I studied him as he tapped the *do not disturb* icon on his phone, disapproval oozing from his features. He was just distracted, I realised with an uncomfortable sense of familiarity.

'All seems a bit fast to me. They've only been dating for a year,' Josh grumbled.

I shook my head. 'Sometimes that's all it takes.'

Josh grunted, unconvinced.

'So, how long do you think they should have waited?' I phrased my question cautiously and kept my tone light.

He turned, his gaze boring into me. 'You mean how long do I think *we* should wait, right?'

I shrugged, trying to look nonchalant, but we both knew he'd caught my feeble attempt at fishing.

He pumped the pillows behind him. 'You know we're not there yet.'

'Why not? We've been together since school. We've lived together for six years. How much longer do we need to wait?'

Josh sighed. 'As soon as Paul told me he'd got engaged, I knew it would get you started on this again.'

His dismissive tone hit a nerve. 'I think they are fair questions.'

I waited for a response, but none came. Clearly, he disagreed with me.

'When we bought this place after university we had plans, Josh. We wanted a three-bedroom house ready for the kids we were going to have. But we've never even furnished two of the rooms. They just stand empty. Abandoned. Like our dreams.'

'Why do you always have to be so melodramatic?'

'I'm not being melodramatic. I'm being honest. I want more than this. I want the whole package. Marriage. Kids. I want a guy that can commit to me.'

Josh scoffed. 'Good luck with that.'

I felt cold. 'W-what does that mean?' I couldn't breathe. He couldn't have meant it the way that it had sounded. But then, what other way was there?

He shrugged dismissively. 'Good luck finding that,' he said as he flicked off the light and shuffled down in bed.

I stared at him in the glow from my phone screen as tremors ran through my body. I couldn't stop them. It felt like I was being torn apart. My heart. My head. My body.

I didn't just want anyone to love me and commit to me. I wanted *him* to. I'd thought he did. Maybe not as much as I loved him. Maybe not always in the way that I wanted. The way that I needed. But it was a start. The rest would grow with time. We would get closer. Get married. We'd be together. Always.

Except he didn't want that. Not with me.

He thought no one would want that with me. That no one could.

'You're not going to start crying now, are you?'

I threw the duvet back, swung my legs out of bed and ran to the bathroom. I closed the door and leaned against it, needing its support. My world was coming unravelled and me along with it. Tears streamed down my face as I turned and stared at the door behind me. Everything I'd ever wanted was on the other side. And yet I realised now, that it was never going to be enough.

I was never going to be enough.

13

NOW

'Thank you for sharing that with me,' Abhilash said. 'I know it wasn't easy.'

I shook my head. 'No, it feels good to finally be able to talk about it. I've lived with the past alone for too long.'

Abhilash hugged me tighter. 'Well, you're not alone with it any more.'

I pulled back slightly so I could look at him. 'I know,' I whispered. 'And that means the world to me.'

He smiled and kissed me. We held each other for a few minutes longer before finally he stepped away. 'I should let you go and rest.'

I nodded reluctantly. I didn't want him to go. I just wanted to stay cocooned in his arms. But I wouldn't be clingy. Perhaps that was where I had gone wrong with Josh. I'd relied on him too much. Needed him too much.

I stood and picked up my plate to take it to the sink, but Abhilash took it from my hands.

'Leave that. I'll handle the cleaning.'

'I was just—'

'Rest,' he said.

I watched him manoeuvre around my kitchen, clearing the table and running the hot water to wash up. There was something almost mesmerising about it. He was simply doing ordinary things. Mundane little tasks. And yet, somehow, that was what made it special.

He was doing them for me.

Not because he had to. Not because I couldn't. But simply because he wanted to.

Abhilash turned and caught me staring at him. 'I'm going,' I said quickly, holding up my hands in surrender, before he could say anything.

His deep, rich chuckle followed me out of the room as I made my way up the stairs smiling. For the first time, the house finally felt like home.

It was a shame it was only temporary.

I walked into the bedroom and my smile instantly faded as a photo of Josh and me on the dressing table caught my attention.

Josh.

I didn't want to think about him right now. I didn't want to think about him at all. He was my past. And Abhilash was... I glanced back towards the stairs.

Abhilash was my now, I decided. Determined not to allow my thoughts to venture beyond that.

I picked up the frame, debating what to do with it. Perhaps I should have packed it with the rest of Josh's stuff. But then it wasn't really his. It was *ours*.

At least it had been.

It was the first photo we ever had taken together. Our first date in a way. Unofficially. Fourteen, yet even then we hadn't been carefree. Or rather, I hadn't been.

* * *

'I'm glad you could come with us today,' Josh said as we watched Emma pick up the bowling ball and swing it back and forth, preparing her aim.

'Yeah, me too.' I grinned at him and tried to ignore the churning in my stomach as I thought about how much trouble I would be in if Mum got back from her shift early and discovered I'd sneaked out.

Emma turned back to face us. 'I'm so bad at this; maybe you could show me how it's done?'

Jealousy prickled my skin as she gazed straight at Josh. I glanced at him, expecting him to leap from his seat, eager to help her, but his attention was still fixed on me, almost as though he hadn't even heard Emma's plea.

'I can give you some tips,' Josh's brother, Paul, said and rushed to her aid.

Emma smiled sweetly, but I caught the glare she shot in my direction before she turned her attention back to the bowling ball. Paul wasn't the brother she had hoped would be coaching her.

'I know your mum doesn't really like you hanging out with me,' Josh said, seemingly oblivious of the drama happening in front of us.

I shook my head. 'It's not you. We just have a lot going on right now. It's better if I stay home after school.'

'And at weekends,' Josh added. 'And sometimes even instead of school.'

I shifted awkwardly. 'Like I said—'

'I know, you have a lot going on,' Josh repeated back to me. 'But maybe I could help. If you'd let me.'

'I don't think you can. I don't think anyone really can.'

'I'd like to try.' Josh's knee brushed mine as he shuffled closer to me. 'You would?'

He nodded. 'I like you, Lauren. A lot.'

I swallowed. 'I like you too.'

'I know you get sick sometimes.'

The churning in my stomach intensified.

'You barely eat at lunchtimes.'

'You noticed.'

He smiled. 'I notice everything about you.'

My heart felt like it skipped a beat. He noticed me. Despite all the bad stuff that was going on in my life, he noticed me and wanted to be included.

'Food can make my stomach bad sometimes, so I have to be really careful what I eat.' I lowered my gaze. He was the first person I'd confided that to. Even Emma just thought I was a picky eater or on a new diet.

'That sucks.'

I chuckled at his understatement. 'Yeah, it really does.'

'Do the doctors have any idea what causes it? Or how to treat it?'

I scrunched my nose up. 'I had a perforated appendix. I had to have emergency surgery.'

'Wow,' Josh's eyes widened. 'That must have been so scary.'

I nodded. 'It was, but in a way it's been more scary since. I mean, the pain was horrendous. So bad that I passed out. But when I woke up, the surgery was done. I had to stay in hospital for a while to have antibiotics, but aside from that, it wasn't so bad. The doctor was so nice and the nurses looked after me. It was kind of fun in a way. Like being a princess or something.'

Heat crept into my cheeks. I couldn't believe I'd just admitted that. Josh would think I was so stupid now.

'Sounds kind of cool. Like when I had my tonsils out, everyone fussed over me for a couple of weeks afterwards.' He chuckled. 'I could have ice cream whenever I wanted.'

I smiled. I should have known that Josh would understand and wouldn't make fun of me. He wasn't like that.

'So how come it's more scary now?' Josh asked.

'Because the doctors knew what was wrong with me then. They knew how to fix it.' I let out a long sigh. 'After the surgery the doctors said everything was going to be okay. I was going to be okay. And I was, for a little while. Mum was super careful about my diet and wrote me notes to get me excused from PE. She was afraid of anything that might hinder my recovery. I thought she was totally OTT. But it turned out she was right. I started getting stomach cramps a few months later. It was just occasional at first. But now it's pretty much constant pain.'

'Can't the doctors do anything?'

'They're trying to. They've given me medications which are supposed to help, but they don't really work that well.' I shrugged. 'So they keep running tests. Lots of tests.'

'Wow, that...' Josh hesitated, as though searching for the right word.

'Sucks?' I suggested.

The corner of his mouth lifted in a half smile. 'Well, yeah.'

I nodded in silent agreement. He had no idea how much it did.

'But you feel okay today, though?'

I smiled at the note of concern in his voice. 'Yes, today is a good day.'

'Good.' He grinned at me. 'In that case, we should take a photo and preserve the memory.' He pulled his phone out of his pocket and leaned closer to me. I stared at our smiling images reflected on the screen and then suddenly Josh turned his head and kissed my cheek just as he pressed the button on his phone.

I stared at the image he'd captured. My eyes were wide with surprise as his lips brushed against my skin.

I turned to face him. A cautious smile rested on his lips. And I grinned. 'I'm going to need a copy of that photo.'

'Sure,' he laughed as he tapped on his screen, sending me the photo. 'How come I didn't know?'

I frowned. 'Huh?'

'About you being rushed into hospital for emergency surgery,' he clarified. 'I mean, that's the kind of thing friends tell each other, isn't it?'

There was a hurt tone to his voice that made my heart somersault.

He cared.

'It was a four years ago,' I tried to shrug, praying he couldn't hear my heart thudding with excitement. 'Before we moved here.'

'Oh right, in Manchester.'

A smile tugged at the corner of my lips. He'd remembered where I'd moved here from. But I shook my head. 'No, before that. We were in Birmingham back then.'

'Seriously? How many places have you lived?'

I shrugged. 'Three. No, wait, four. We've lived in Yorkshire too.'

'That's so cool. We've always lived in Bournemouth. We haven't even moved house. It's so boring.' He pouted as he kicked his toe against the table leg.

'Sounds kind of nice to me,' I said, trying not to let too much emotion sneak into my voice. 'Mum gets relocated a lot with her job. We go where she's needed. But it means constantly starting again. A new house. New school. New doctors.'

'Oh,' Josh frowned. 'I guess I hadn't really thought about that part of it.'

'It's not all bad,' I said, my voice barely a whisper. 'I like Bournemouth.'

'Yeah, there are some great things here.'

My gaze met his and I knew that neither of us were thinking about Bournemouth right then.

* * *

It had been a perfect moment. One that I thought I would treasure forever. I took a deep breath. I should have known better. Good things never lasted. There were always complications.

I opened the top drawer of the dressing table and shoved the picture frame inside. I paused and then flipped it over face down. I didn't need to see us. It wasn't like I could forget.

I closed the drawer, and my fingers instinctively traced the silhouette the frame had left in the thin layer of dust on the glass top of the dressing table.

Even his absence left a mark.

I jutted my chin forward and rubbed away the dust with the palm of my hand, removing all traces of what had stood there.

If only it was as easy to erase him from my mind.

14

THEN

After all these years of waiting. Of hoping. It was finally clear from the way Josh spoke that despite our plans, despite his promises, he would never commit. He would never propose. There would never be a wedding in our future. But worse than that, he didn't think I could have it with anyone.

Josh was right. Such a guy didn't exist. Not for me.

The power save caused the phone in my hand to switch itself off, plunging me into darkness. I sank down onto the cold, tiled floor and hugged my knees to my chest as I sobbed silently. Part of me longed for Josh to tap on the door, to ask if I was okay, to say he was sorry, that he hadn't meant it.

But I knew he wouldn't.

What had happened to us? What had happened to him?

There was a time when he'd cared. When he'd wanted that life with me. I'd thought he still did. I'd thought once things improved for him at work, once we were more financially stable, he'd be ready to start thinking about the future again. But perhaps that had been naïve.

We were on different paths. Living in the same house. Striving for different goals. We didn't fit. Not really. Not fully.

I'd created an entire business out of making things appear perfect, but perhaps I'd taken it too far. I'd applied it to real life as well. To us. I was still clinging to the dreams we'd had as teenagers, when Josh and I had plotted our escape. I frowned. No, not escape. Rescue. He'd been so determined to save me from the nightmare that I was living in, that maybe I'd got caught up in the romance of it all. I'd refused to let go even when the romance had faded and all we were left with was the harshness of a reality that didn't measure up.

And yet, the ache in my heart told me I still loved him.

Is that enough?

Dr Menon's question resounded in my brain. I'd said yes when he'd asked me. It was more than enough. It was everything.

But was it?

Was there more?

Or at least, should there be?

An image of Dr Menon flashed into my mind. His concerned expression. His gentle, probing questions.

Perhaps Josh was wrong. Perhaps there was someone else who cared.

I stood up and crept to the sink. I turned my phone back on and shone the light on the shelf behind the sink, searching for the prescription I had left there. I'd been so eager to get back to work, I hadn't found time to go to the pharmacy yet. I scanned the page, my eyes searching for one important detail.

Dr Abhilash Menon.

'Abhilash', I whispered, testing out the sound of it.

I perched on the side of the bath and returned to Facebook. It was just normal curiosity, I told myself as I typed his name into the search box. Everyone looked people up on social media these days.

I scanned through the list of profile photos and pressed *show more*. A longer list appeared and I hunched forward, squinting at one of the tiny pictures. Was that him?

I tapped on his name and waited as his profile opened. I smiled at the larger picture that was now easily recognisable.

I'd found him.

I scrolled down, studying his photos. He liked kite surfing. I nodded approvingly and kept scrolling. I wasn't even sure why. What was I looking for?

There were photos of him alone or in groups, but there was one thing noticeably missing: a partner. Or at least an obvious one.

I kept scrolling.

Was that what I was searching for? A sign that he was single? Available?

I shook my head. No, that was irrelevant. I didn't care if he was single or not.

I was in a relationship.

A long term one.

My gaze drifted to the bedroom door where Josh was probably already sleeping on the other side. I should be in there with him, snuggled up against his side, his arm wrapped around me, holding me close. It was where I wanted to be. The only place I wanted to be.

And yet...

I studied Abhilash's profile photo again. There was something about him. Something important. I'd shared a connection with him in a way that Josh and I hadn't in years.

The way he'd believed me without question was unexpected.

For once I wasn't defined by my past. My mother. He saw me for myself. He accepted my words. Accepted me.

I knew that there was nothing between us. Not romantically. There never would be. I didn't even want there to be. Not like that.

I just needed someone to see me. To know me. To like me for who I was. Not just how well I complied.

My finger lingered over the *add friend* button. Should I?

I nibbled my lower lip. It was a stupid idea. It's not like we were actually friends. I'd been nothing more than just another patient. He'd probably forgotten my name the moment I'd left the hospital. He had no reason to remember it. I hadn't impacted his life the way he had impacted mine.

Why would he accept a friend request from me? I was just going to embarrass myself. He'd laugh about me to his friends. I'd be the creepy, desperate ex-patient stalking him on social media.

But then, wasn't that exactly what I was? I shuddered and exited Facebook.

He wouldn't understand. I frowned. I didn't even understand. Our paths would probably never cross again. Not that I could discount the possibility of ending up back in hospital. It had happened before. Chances were, it would happen again. But even so, it was a big hospital, with hundreds of patients and many doctors. I wouldn't necessarily end up under his care again.

I caught a glimpse of my reflection in the mirror above the sink. Illuminated in the pale glow from my phone, the woman who stared back at me looked so small and sad. I tipped my head to the right. She looked lost.

But then that's exactly what I was.

I thought Josh was the only person who noticed my existence, but what if he wasn't? What if there was something more to me than he saw? More than I saw? Something that made a stranger care. Something that made my life important, even just in a small way.

It was foolish to think that Dr Menon was the key to figuring out who I was, but for some strange reason that was exactly how it felt.

I let out a deep sigh. Or perhaps he was just the trigger that made me realise there was even a question that needed to be answered?

It wasn't as though I expected anything from him. I didn't even need him to message me, or even to remember me. I just needed him to be there. For me.

In that moment at the hospital my well-being, maybe even my life, had mattered more to him than it had to me, maybe more than it had mattered in years. For the first time, I wasn't in it alone.

That's all I wanted from him now. All I needed. To not be alone. I needed to feel like that connection was still there. That I had a friend. Even if it was just a notification on an app on my phone.

Every journey begins with a single step.

The quote by Lao Tzu repeated in my head. I knew what first step Dr Menon believed I should make.

Leave Josh.

But it wasn't that simple.

He wasn't all bad.

And I wasn't all good.

I tapped the Facebook icon and Abhilash's profile appeared again. Perhaps this was the first step that I needed to make. So what if he thought I was crazy? So what if he and his friends laughed at me? They wouldn't be the first.

If there was even a chance that he might accept, no matter

how slim, wasn't it worth the risk? The worst that would happen would be that he rejected it.

I shrugged. I was used to that.

I clicked the *add friend* button and stared at the screen, waiting for a response.

I shook my head. What was I doing? I couldn't just wait here indefinitely. He was hardly going to drop whatever he was doing to immediately accept my request. If he even accepted it at all.

I turned the phone off again. It was done now. I'd made my decision. Whether he accepted or not was out of my hands.

Just like everything else in my life.

15

NOW

I groaned as I rolled onto my back in bed. I tentatively pressed my hand to my head, it still felt heavy and disorientated. I opened my eyes slowly, frowning at the filtered sunlight brightening the room through the closed blinds.

I heard noises drifting up from downstairs, and my body tensed.

Josh.

No, not Josh, I realised as memories of last night filtered back into my sleepy brain.

Abhilash.

A smile tugged on the corners of my lips. He'd stayed.

It wasn't the way I imagined us spending our first night together. Me upstairs and him down. But it was something. It was a beginning.

Now that Josh was no longer in the picture...

Light tapping on the bedroom door disrupted my imagination from drifting any further.

'Lauren?' Abhilash said softly as he pushed the door open a crack.

'I'm awake,' I called as I sat up and straightened the sheet around me. 'You can come in.'

The door opened slowly and Abhilash lingered on the landing, looking unsure of himself.

My heart soared at the simple reminder that he was the opposite of Josh. He never proceeded without invitation. Never assumed. Never pushed.

'I brought you some water and paracetamol.' I stared as he set the glass of water and packet of tablets down on the bedside cabinet beside me. 'I thought you might need them.'

I swallowed. Unable to take my eyes off them. It was such a simple gesture. Thoughtful. Kind. And yet, it brought back memories. Ones I didn't want to think about.

* * *

I sat at the breakfast bar, watching as Mum moved about the kitchen. The kettle boiled noisily, drowning out the sound of Wave FM playing on the radio. It was a normal Monday morning. Except nothing was normal about our lives.

I fidgeted with the waistband of my school skirt which no longer fitted and glared at the two little boxes of tablets that sat in the centre of the breakfast bar. Somehow, they had become the centre of our existence. Our everything.

Mum poured a glass of water and set it down beside them, before picking up the first box. She opened the box and pulled out the half-empty strip of foil-covered tablets. The kettle clicked off as it reached the boil, but Mum didn't seem to notice. Her attention was fixed on the medication. It was always fixed on the medication. It was her lifeline. Her hope. Her solace.

And my anguish.

'I don't want them,' I said, pouting.

'You need them.' Mum's voice was dismissive. She didn't even look up. To her there was no question. No doubt.

'They make my stomach hurt.'

'It's not the pills that make your stomach hurt. They are just paracetamol and anti-diarrhoea medication. They make you better. Without them, the pain would be intolerable. You know that.' She paused and looked at me. 'Remember how bad you felt before them?'

I scrunched my nose. I remembered.

'Besides, it's just temporary,' Mum said as she slid the glass of water closer to me.

'When is the next review with Dr Newman?' I asked, seizing on the slither of hope that she had thrown my way.

'Dr Clarke, dear. Don't you remember, Dr Newman referred us to a new doctor last time?'

My shoulders slumped. 'Oh yeah. Another one.' No doubt it would mean more questions. More tests. It always did.

Mum patted my hand. 'Don't be so pessimistic. They are doing everything they can, Lauren. You know that. You're a complicated case. It's taking a little bit longer to find a solution, but we will.'

We.

It was always 'we'. It was my body that was defective, but Mum and I were in this nightmare together. Every appointment. Every referral. Every test or scan. Every new medication and disappointing side effect. She never left me to handle it alone. Never got frustrated with each set back. Never got tired of taking care of me. Never resented me for disrupting both of our lives. She was just there with me throughout it all. Documenting every appointment. Every treatment. Researching. Questioning. Pressing the doctors to keep searching for a solution. She wouldn't let them give up on me, and she wouldn't let me either.

'We don't quit, Lauren. I didn't and neither can you. When things get tough, we stay strong. We endure,' Mum said with conviction.

I stiffened at her comment. I knew what she meant. What she had endured. Me.

Discovering she was pregnant had changed her life. I had changed her life. I knew she loved me. But at the same time, I also knew that some tiny part of her still resented me for that. She had lost so much and all she had gained was me. Somehow the scales didn't quite balance.

It was a debt that I could never repay. But I knew I would keep trying. She was right. We endured.

I popped the pill into my mouth and washed it down with a gulp of water.

We would endure this too.

* * *

'Thanks,' I murmured, forcing myself to look away. I refocused my attention on Abhilash and patted the empty space on the mattress next to me. 'Come and sit with me.' I needed a distraction. I needed him.

He hesitated for a second before complying. 'I just came to check on you before I leave,' he said as he perched on the edge of the bed beside me.

'You're leaving now?' My shoulders slumped.

'I need to get back to the hospital for my next shift.'

'Right,' I nodded automatically. 'Of course. I was just hoping we could have breakfast together before you left.'

'Sorry,' Abhilash looked sheepish. 'I hate to abandon you.'

My breath caught in my chest. For a moment he reminded me of Josh.

I feel like I abandoned you.

I shook my head. No. It wasn't the same. *They* weren't the

same. I forced a smile onto my lips. 'Not at all. I'm grateful for all you've done.' It wasn't fair of me to make him feel bad.

'Will you be okay here on your own?'

There was a weightiness to his question. Even when we didn't speak of him, Josh was always in our thoughts.

'I'll be fine,' I assured him with more conviction than I felt.

But it wasn't Josh I was afraid of. It was the emptiness. The silence. Because then there would be no escaping my own thoughts.

'I'll message you later to make sure you're okay,' Abhilash told me. 'And if you need anything, anything at all—'

'I'll call you, I promise.'

Abhilash nodded, leaning towards me. He wrapped his arms around me and I hugged him tightly, savouring the closeness. The connection.

I felt him shift in my arms and reluctantly I let him go. He needed to work. And I needed to let him.

If you love someone, let them go. Wasn't that the saying? If they were truly yours, they would return. It hadn't worked with Josh. At least not in the sense of him coming back to me. But then that hadn't really been the goal.

Abhilash brushed my cheek before kissing me. A long slow lingering kiss that sent tingles down my spine.

Josh had never kissed me like that. Not even in the beginning. Not even when he actually loved me.

'Bye,' Abhilash whispered breathlessly as he came up for air.

I nodded, not wanting to speak as I clung to the lingering memory of his lips against mine.

Letting go was hard. Especially with him.

I watched as he slipped out of the door and I stared at the empty space, willing him to come back, even though I could hear his footsteps retreating down the stairs. The front door opened and then closed with a clunk.

It sounded so definite. So final.

I shook my head. I was doing it again. Being melodramatic. Josh would tell me off if he was here.

The corner of my mouth lifted.

But he wasn't here.

Not any more.

16

THEN

I pushed open the door to the pub. My gaze scanned the empty tables. I was late, but by the looks of things, so was Emma. I went straight to our usual table. I was a creature of habit. There was something comforting in the familiar.

I started to pull a chair out but froze.

If you always stick with what you're used to, how do you know if there is anything better?

Dr Menon's question sprang into my head.

If I was happy with where I was then the existence of an alternative was irrelevant. But was I happy? I searched my emotions. What did happy even feel like? I wasn't sure that I remembered. Or perhaps I had never really known.

It felt like my happiness had been hinged on the future. When Josh and I were married. When I had a family of my own. I'd be happy then. I'd just been in a holding pattern. Waiting. And it didn't look like that was going to change.

I pulled my phone from my bag and opened Facebook.

I sighed.

Dr Menon still hadn't accepted my friend request. It seemed

now I was waiting for someone else too. So much for not caring whether he accepted or not.

I clicked on his profile image and studied his face. My stomach tightened. It felt like I was spying on him, but my curiosity wouldn't allow me to stop. I needed to know something about him. But what was I hoping to find? Something to reinforce the image I had of him, that he was the kind of guy I wanted as a friend? Or something to convince me that he wasn't? At least then I could give up waiting for his response. It didn't matter if he didn't accept if I no longer needed his approval.

I frowned. But I did need his approval. I really needed it to work out. I needed Dr Menon to accept my request. I needed to feel like I mattered to someone, even if it was just to a stranger.

I wasn't interested in him romantically. He was good looking. Charming. But so were other men. They'd never caught my attention. They never made me feel... I searched my emotions: what was it Abhilash made me feel?

Seen. Understood.

'Hey, Lauren.'

I set my phone down on the table as I jumped to my feet at the sound of Emma's voice behind me.

'Hi, Emma.' I gave her an awkward one-armed hug, before sinking back into my chair.

'Are you okay?' she asked, nodding at my cast.

'I'm fine,' I brushed her concern away. I didn't want to dwell on my broken wrist. I knew what would come next; questions about how I broke it. It was a well-rehearsed routine. She asked. And I lied.

'Who's the guy?'

I blinked as Emma broke protocol. I followed her gaze and realised she was looking at my phone. Heat crept into my checks as I stared at Dr Menon's profile page displayed on the screen.

'No-one.'

Emma's eyebrows arched and I knew I'd said the wrong thing. 'No-one? So that totally explains why you're checking out his Facebook page.'

I reached for my phone, but Emma was quicker and snatched the phone off the table.

'He's cute.'

I sank back down into my chair as I searched my mind for a response. But what could I say? I couldn't deny it. But it seemed risky to agree. I had a boyfriend. I wasn't supposed to notice other guys.

The corner of Emma's mouth twitched as she watched me squirm. 'So, come on then, who is,' she glanced back at the screen as she sat down opposite me, 'Abhilash? And more importantly, how do you know him?'

'I don't.' I cringed. 'Not really.' I shuffled awkwardly in my chair.

She edged forwards in her seat. 'But you want to?'

'No.' I rolled my eyes. 'He's the doctor who treated me a couple of days ago at the hospital. I was just...' my mind went blank. What was I doing?

'Checking him out?'

'It's not like that.'

Emma leaned forwards and whispered across the table. 'Did something happen between you and your doctor?'

'No, of course not.' I bristled at her accusation. She should know me better than that. 'He's just a friend. Not even a friend.'

'Not a friend? But you've sent him a friend request.' Emma looked bewildered as she pointed at the pending status.

I snatched my phone out of her hands and pressed the power button, plunging the screen into darkness, silently cursing myself for not having thought to do so sooner. 'It was a mistake.'

Our eyes met and I had the sinking feeling that she knew I was lying.

'Is everything okay between you and Josh? I mean, I was only kidding about you hooking up with your doctor, but...'

I drew back. 'But what?'

'Something's going on, isn't it?'

'I wouldn't cheat on Josh.'

'No.' Emma shook her head. 'I know that. But are you still happy together?'

I hesitated. 'I'm not sure.' It was the most honest thing I'd said to her in years.

Emma leaned forward and patted my hand. 'You know I'm here if you want to talk about it.'

I shook my head. 'I can't.'

Her brow creased. 'Can't?'

I stared at her. She was right to question it. 'Can't' didn't seem the right word. She was my best friend. My only friend. Of course, I should be able to talk to her about anything. Even about Josh. It's what friends did.

But it's not what *I* did.

Ever.

Emma withdrew her hand and leaned back in her chair. I'd shut her out and hurt her feelings.

Guilt chafed at me. She didn't realise I'd never let her in the first place. I'd always held her at the periphery of my life. I confided in her, but never about the really big stuff. The stuff I couldn't talk about. The stuff I couldn't put into words.

It wasn't that I didn't trust her. It was more that I didn't trust myself.

'You know Josh adores you.' There was a harshness to her tone. 'Do you know how rare that is?'

She thought I was being disloyal. Perhaps I was. I'd tried to befriend another guy when I had a boyfriend. Josh wasn't a bad guy. We'd just lost our way a little, that was all. He still loved me. And yet, here I was, desperately waiting for acceptance from someone I barely even knew.

'You did well to snare him early.'

I jolted upright as though I'd been hit with a bolt of electricity. 'Snare him? You make it sound like I chased after him and trapped him.'

Emma laughed. 'More like lured him in.'

I blinked. 'Seriously?'

'Oh, don't get all hurt and offended. You know what I mean.'

'No, I don't.' My words were clipped and too loud. I glanced around as the bartender turned in our direction, but I didn't care.

'Come on, Lauren. You have this innocent "rescue me" vibe going on and you know how to work it.'

My heart beat faster as I struggled to control my breathing.

'Josh was the hottest guy in our year. Everyone had a crush on him,' Emma continued.

I arched an eyebrow. 'Even you?' It was something I'd always suspected, but I'd never had the nerve to ask before. It was like an unwritten rule to our friendship: don't accuse your one and only friend of having a crush on your boyfriend. Regardless of the answer, there was no way that conversation would end well.

There was a flash of something unreadable across Emma's face. Was it anger? Hurt? Or maybe guilt?

Emma rolled her eyes as her expression relaxed. 'You know he's not my type.'

The only thing I knew for sure was that people were never as transparent as they appeared. There was always more to them. Another layer. Another lie.

'You have this way of always trying to make everything more than it is. Like you want everything to be perfect. But sometimes people are just what they are. Your doctor is just your doctor. And every relationship has ups and downs. I just think you should be more appreciative of what you've got, that's all.'

I bristled inside. I didn't need Emma to tell me to be grateful. I was. I knew how to focus on the positives. I had a home. A boyfriend. A business. I counted my blessings every day. Even on the bad days.

Just like Mum had taught me.

'Not many guys would have stuck with you through everything that happened. They just don't need that kind of drama. And his family were great to you too.'

I nodded. She was right. They were. The Carters weren't like most people. They didn't just talk about doing the right thing, but then duck out when it turned out that the right thing was actually messy and complicated. They followed through. They helped. They cared. Just like Josh had. Once.

Did he still?

'You and Josh aren't even married yet, and they already treat you like the daughter they never had.'

Yet.

I swallowed. 'Josh doesn't want to get married.' I mentally kicked myself as soon as the words had left my mouth. Emma wasn't the person to confide in. Not about this. Not about anything concerning Josh.

Her eyebrows wrinkled. 'You mean right now?'

I hesitated. I knew I shouldn't tell her. She'd probably be glad. And yet, I needed to tell someone. 'I mean at all.'

Her eyes widened. 'Oh.' And then she shrugged. 'Does it really matter though? I mean what difference does a ring and a bit of paper really make? You two have been together so long already, it's probably not even worth the hassle.'

She was so dismissive. Just a ring. A hassle. Nothing important.

But it was important.

To me.

'Besides, he could change his mind,' Emma continued. 'Especially now Paul's getting married. He might decide he wants a big party too.'

A party. That's what Emma thought would change Josh's mind. Not the prospect of exchanging vows. Not committing to each other in front of family and friends. But a party.

Even if she was right, was that a good enough reason to get married?

Or didn't it matter? I'd still be Mrs Josh Carter. Wasn't that the most important thing?

I drummed my fingers against the table. Maybe I shouldn't give up so easily. Perhaps Emma could see what I couldn't. I was too close. Too desperate.

Or perhaps she just didn't know Josh, or I, as well as she thought...

'So, maybe you shouldn't stalk cute doctors.' Emma laughed.

I squirmed in my chair. It was too late. That was exactly what I'd done. I'd become obsessed. He'd shown me a little bit of kindness and I thought it meant something. Not that he felt anything for me. Not that he wanted me. But that maybe, just maybe, it meant I was worthy of being noticed. Of being cared about.

It had been foolish. I'd known it at the time. But now, somehow, it seemed worse. I hated myself for my weakness. But I was always the same. Whenever an idea lodged itself in my brain I had to follow it through, regardless of how ill-conceived that action was.

For a little while, sending Dr Menon the friend request had

helped. I'd felt calmer knowing I'd done everything I could. It was out of my hands. He would either accept it or he wouldn't.

So why was I checking my phone every few minutes, waiting for a notification from him? If it really didn't matter, then why couldn't I let it go?

And if it did matter, then what did that mean?

'What can I get you to drink?' I asked Emma, eager to distract both of us from questions that I most definitely was not ready to face.

17

NOW

I reached for my phone on the bedside cabinet and froze as my hand touched the wood. I turned and frowned. My phone always went everywhere with me. It was how Josh stayed in contact throughout the day.

I shook that thought away. Things were different now. I didn't need to hear from Josh.

They can wait until tomorrow, can't they?

Abhilash's question replayed in my mind as I remembered setting the phone down in the hall as we'd come in. I'd intended to charge it later, but I must have left it downstairs, its battery still dead.

It was the longest I'd gone without my phone by my side in years.

I was finally free. And yet somehow, I still didn't feel it.

I pushed the sheet aside and swung my legs out of bed. What now?

I had the house to myself. There was no time limit. No watching the clock waiting for Josh to return. Not now.

Not ever.

That thought was so liberating. And yet, at the same time, so isolating.

There was an eeriness to the silence. As though something was missing.

I'd known this feeling before.

I'd felt the same way after Mum's death. Lost. Untethered.

It wasn't as though I wanted either of them back. I was glad they were gone. And yet, somehow that didn't eliminate the void that their absence created in my life.

I wasn't good at being on my own.

* * *

'Do I really have to stay here alone?'

Mum chuckled. 'You're not alone. Not here. The hospital is full of people. Just look around you.'

I gazed around the ward. Every bed was occupied.

'That's not what I meant,' I grumbled. They weren't friends. They weren't even company. They were just patients. Strangers.

'Oh, come on, Lauren. You can't be grumpy. Not when you have all these lovely nurses and doctors looking after you every moment. They are so good to you.'

I snorted. 'Why don't I go home, and you can stay here if you like it so much then?' I was being spiteful. I knew it. And yet, I couldn't stop myself. She didn't understand what it was like. Being here all the time. Poked and prodded.

'I wish I could,' she said, stroking my hand.

The regret in her voice cut into me. Of course, she would switch places with me if she could. She was my mum. It must be torturing her to see me like this and not be able to help. Bringing me here was the only thing she could do for me. And I was making her feel bad about it.

'I'm sorry,' I murmured.

'*You don't have to apologise. Not to me. I know how hard this is on you. How unfair. It breaks my heart to see you like this. But I know, I absolutely know, that it's all for the best.*' She leaned forwards and hugged me. I buried my head in her shoulder, inhaling the fruity scent of her shampoo. I felt safe nestled in her arms. Loved. Protected.

I wasn't alone.

* * *

I stood up abruptly. A feeble attempt to put space between me and the memory. It didn't work. It never worked. The past always followed me.

I'd been so wrong about Josh. Just as I had with Mum. They had both deceived me. Both made promises they never intended to keep.

And I had fallen for it both times.

I was gullible.

I frowned. No, not gullible. Trusting. That wasn't a bad thing. Just misguided. I would be more careful about whom I placed my trust in now.

My frown dissipated as I thought about Abhilash. He was different. He was trustworthy. I was sure of it.

And if he wasn't... I shrugged. I knew how to deal with that.

18

THEN

I stretched, arching my back, as I cursed myself for my bad posture. Spending all morning hunched over my computer wasn't good for me.

Not that I should complain. After all it was my choice to work. Josh didn't expect me to. He didn't even want me to.

I rolled my shoulders, cringing at the grating sound that emanated from them. I should at least buy a proper desk and an ergonomic chair. It would be an investment. One I could have made months ago.

And yet, I hadn't.

Even now I could feel hesitation welling inside me. It wasn't the cost. I could afford it and more besides. And we had the space. Two bedrooms sat empty upstairs. It didn't look like they would be needed for their intended purpose anytime soon. If at all. So why not turn one of them into an office space?

I nodded in agreement with my own reasoning. It was sound and logical. I knew that. But somehow it still felt like too much of a leap.

There was something safe about sitting at the kitchen table, dabbling in a bit of social media, playing at running my own business. Beyond my clients, no one expected much from me. In fact, no one really knew what I even did.

I celebrated each contract, each success, silently. Privately. Not because I didn't want to share it. But because I knew that this way it meant I could also handle any failure privately too.

And it would fail.

It was inevitable.

Josh had told me so.

I knew what it was like to be on public display when life self-combusted. I'd lived through it before. I wouldn't do that again. The pressure had been too much. For me. For Josh. It was where our problems had started. I frowned. Or perhaps, it was just what had made them noticeable.

But we'd ignored them.

We'd carried on as though they didn't exist. Too afraid to acknowledge them. Too afraid to face the repercussions of what that would mean. After all, what was the alternative? He was all that I had. The link to my new life. My new family. Without him it would all disappear.

I took a deep breath. The past had taught me a lot. And I was smart enough not to make the same mistakes Mum had.

Subtlety. Discretion. They were the key. Everything had to be kept in balance. Kept hidden.

I glanced at the clock. It was almost 1 p.m. Time for lunch. My stomach growled as if in agreement.

The chair scraped across the kitchen tiles as I stood up. My mouth was already watering at the thought of coffee and cake at Café Riva. Perched at the top of the cliff at Fisherman's Walk, it had delicious cakes and a stunning view. It was tempting to go there every day. But for the sake of my waistline, I limited my treats to Friday lunch times.

I grabbed my keys and phone and headed out of the door. I weaved my way through the streets towards the seafront. I might have had reservations about buying the house, but the proximity to the beach was the one thing that made it worth it.

My pace slowed for a second as it struck me that Josh should have been the one thing that made it worth it. That made everything worth it.

I shook my head. He was. Of course, he was. The beach was just a high second.

I snapped a quick photo of the outside of the café before stepping inside and joining the queue that almost reached to the door.

My attention returned to my phone as I opened Facebook. Despite having spent the whole morning working on social media accounts, I still couldn't resist the temptation to post an update.

Friday cake time at Riva

I typed, tagging the café and attaching the photo I'd just taken.

As soon as I'd finished, my finger automatically went to the search box. I didn't even think about what I was doing. It had become my daily ritual. His name appeared in the list as the last search.

Abhilash Menon

It had been three days since I'd sent the friend request. Surely, he must have seen it by now? I sighed. I'd known it was a long shot. I'd known he probably wouldn't accept. And yet, instinctively I still dived for the phone every time it pinged. Just in case.

No matter how many times logic told me I wouldn't get a response, some part of me refused to give up.

It had become a fixation. Something I clung to. A hope. A need.

The question that still baffled me though was why?

I loved Josh. I wanted a life with him. To marry him. So why did the acceptance of an ill-advised friend request by a guy who was practically a stranger matter so much?

I should forget all about him. Just like he'd forgotten about me.

I should. But I wouldn't.

Not yet.

I tapped on his name.

It wasn't as though I was doing anything wrong. His status updates were public. If he'd wanted to keep me out, he'd have made his account private. Leaving it open to everyone was an invitation to look inside. To view his life. Him.

It was the same with my own account. I shared posts publicly, enabling my clients to catch a glimpse of my life. My world. It helped build connections. Trust. But what they saw was only a tiny fragment of a bigger picture. They knew the parts of my life that I was willing to share. The edited version.

Perfect conditions for kite surfing today!

I stared at the picture. Abhilash was laying his yellow kite out on the beach, preparing to surf. I pulled the phone closer to me. Behind him, the cliff lift at Fisherman's Walk was visible.

I checked the time stamp. He'd posted it five minutes ago.

My head jolted up as I looked out of the window. He was close.

Very close.

19

NOW

I watched the charging symbol on the phone screen:

1%... 2%...

I pressed the power button and waited impatiently as the screen loaded.

Notifications pinged rapidly: WhatsApp messages, text messages and missed calls. So many people had tried to reach me. I felt a warm glow. So many people cared.

I opened WhatsApp and read the first message.

Are you okay? Any news on Josh?

I moved to the next.

I heard Josh is missing, have you heard anything yet?

I scrolled through them. Each of them asked about Josh. I was a passing thought, if I was even mentioned at all. Josh was the focus.

My jaw clenched. It was always about Josh. Even now. Even when he wasn't here.

I lingered on the final message.

We heard you'd been discharged from the hospital, we'll call round this afternoon to check in on you. Hope you're okay xx

I smiled; at least Josh's parents cared about me. They had always cared about me. Maybe not as much as I wanted them to, but it was something. They'd stuck by me through everything that had happened before. They would stick by me this time too.

I didn't need Josh. I had them. I had family.

If I handled things right.

* * *

The sound of my phone ringing pierced the silence in the house. I snatched it up and glanced at the screen. I didn't recognise the number. It wasn't one in my contacts. My breath caught in my chest as I pressed the answer button.

'Ms Taylor?'

It wasn't Josh.

I froze for a second as I tried to identify the strange, unsettling feeling that had descended on me. Was it disappointment?

Or relief?

'Ms Taylor?' The man repeated.

There was something vaguely familiar about his voice and I felt sure I'd heard it somewhere before.

'Yes,' I replied cautiously.

'This is PC Smith. We met at the hospital on Sunday.'

My stomach plummeted. The police were calling me. There

was no situation when that would be a good thing. I knew that from before.

'I remember.' I clamped my mouth closed before I could say any more. I wanted to ask why he was calling. What had he discovered. But I knew it was always best to say as little as possible. Especially to the police.

'We'd like to ask you some more questions.'

'Okay.' It wasn't surprising. Josh was still missing. Of course, they would want to speak to me. Abhilash had cut them off at the hospital, but I was home now. I was well enough to talk to them. To help them.

'We'd like you to come down to the police station.'

My chest tightened. The police station.

Again.

* * *

'Am I in trouble?' I looked at Mrs Carter, searching her face for clues as I sat beside her in the small room.

I'd never been inside a police station before. I'd never expected to be in one now. And yet, here I was.

'No, Lauren. PC Collier just wants to ask you a few questions, that's all.'

'But why didn't Mum bring me? Why would she make me come here alone?' I was only fifteen; surely Mum should have come to the police station with me?

Mrs Carter shook her head. 'Your Mum couldn't make it. But you're not alone; I'm here.' She winked at me conspiratorially as if to show we were a team. United. Together.

I felt the knot in my stomach loosen slightly. Josh's mum was nice. I liked her. She was different to my Mum. Calmer. More easy going. She'd even talked Mum into letting me go round to their house after school every now and then. And she always invited me to stay for dinner.

Not that I ever accepted. As Mum pointed out, the last thing I needed was to have a bad stomach after eating Mrs Carter's food and offend her. She and Josh wouldn't invite me back again if I did that.

I turned back to face PC Collier seated the other side of the table. She didn't look like a police officer. She looked like an ordinary person. 'Why aren't you wearing a uniform?'

She smiled. 'I'm a protection officer. I work for the Public Protection Unit. We're a special team that don't wear uniforms.'

I nodded approvingly. 'I hate wearing my school uniform. I can't wait until I start sixth form next year and can wear whatever I want.'

She chuckled. 'I don't blame you.'

'So, who do you protect?' I was intrigued now. My nerves at being in a police station had been surpassed by my curiosity. None of my friends had been inside a police interview room. For once, I had done something they hadn't.

'We protect anyone who needs our help.'

I nodded. I liked that. 'Kind of like a doctor, then?'

'Kind of. Just without all the medical stuff.'

I scrunched my nose. 'Yeah, that can be gross.'

'You've spent a lot of time with doctors, haven't you?'

'Yeah, looooads of doctors.' I dragged the word out. There had been so many. Weird that she would know that though.

'Only in the last few years?'

I nodded. 'I had a burst appendix when I was ten. I had surgery and they said I'd be okay, but...' I shrugged.

'So, you started getting sick straight after the surgery?'

'No, not right away.' I frowned, trying to remember four and a half years ago. 'I got better to start with. The doctors were really pleased with me. They said I was a star patient.' I beamed with pride at that memory.

'And after you left the hospital?'

'I continued to get better. Mum was so obsessed about it.'

PC Collier shifted forwards. 'In what way?'

'I don't know, like, being super careful about what I ate. Lots of fruit and vegetables. And everything had to be organic. She was always Googling the best diet or new vitamin supplement. I think it really scared her when I was rushed into hospital in the ambulance. She wanted to make sure I stayed healthy after that.'

'But you didn't.'

I frowned as I studied her. It hadn't sounded like a question. More like a statement.

'No, I started getting tummy upsets. Like, really bad ones. Mum took me to the doctors straight away the first time it happened. The GP gave me some pills and they helped. But then it happened again. And again.'

'What did your Mum do?'

'She took me back to the GP each time. But he said it was fine. Probably just a tummy bug. But I kept getting them. More and more often. And more painful each time.' I shrugged as though it wasn't a big deal. But it was. The pain had been unbearable sometimes and I was always tired. 'Mum said it wasn't normal for a child to be so sick all the time, not when she was already so careful about what I ate. So she took me back to the doctor again.'

'Then what happened?'

'Mum thought I had Crohn's disease. She'd done all this research and thought it was a possibility after a burst appendix. The GP didn't seem convinced, but he referred me to a specialist to check it out. I had to go to the hospital for some tests, but the results were all normal. When we moved from Birmingham to Yorkshire because of Mum's job, she said it was for the best. We could see new doctors. Better doctors. And we started again with all the tests.'

'That must have been unpleasant for you.'

I nodded. 'It was awful. The blood tests and stool samples weren't a big deal, but the endoscopies sucked.'

'And the results from all these tests?'

'They were normal,' I sighed. 'Always normal.'

PC Collier nodded.

'Mum was annoyed that they wouldn't start treatment for Crohn's, but the doctors said they couldn't. Not without a confirmed diagnosis. They were so confused. I overhead the nurses talking once, they said the gastroenterology consultant was going to meet with someone from paediatrics as well as my GP to discuss my case and try and get to the bottom of what was going on.'

'And did they?'

I shrugged. 'Mum got moved again right after that.'

'I see.'

I stared at PC Collier. There was something about the way that she said those two little words that made my skin prickle.

What was I doing here? Talking to her? Answering all these questions? My medical history might be fascinating to the doctors, but she was a police officer. She wasn't interested in all this stuff. Or she shouldn't be.

We protect anyone who needs our help.

PC Collier's earlier words circled in my mind.

'Am I who you're protecting?'

My question hung in the air as PC Collier and Mrs Carter looked at each other.

'Do you need protecting, Lauren?' PC Collier asked.

'That's not an answer,' I objected. And yet, even as I said it, I realised that it was.

* * *

'You can have a solicitor present if you wish to do so,' PC Smith continued.

I blinked as my brain tried to catch up. 'A s-solicitor?' I stuttered over the word. Why would he suggest that? I hadn't needed one last time.

Not even later.

'We will be conducting the interview under caution,' PC Smith said flatly.

Under caution.

I wanted to object. To tell him he was overreacting. I would talk to them. They didn't need to caution me. But I couldn't. The words wouldn't come.

This was bad. Very bad.

20

THEN

The wind whipped my long blonde hair into my face as I strode down the zig-zag chine towards the beach. The hot cup of coffee and a paper bag containing my much-longed-for cake more of a hindrance than a desire now. I'd contemplated stepping out of the queue and running straight to the beach, but common sense stopped me.

I wouldn't chase after him. I wasn't that desperate.

Besides, taking my coffee and cake down to the beach gave me a more legitimate reason for being there rather than trying to pass myself off as a sunbather wearing a smart business suit on the windy beach. I cursed myself for not having thought to change before I left home. If I hadn't had a video call with a new client earlier, I would have looked more casual.

My gaze scanned the beach as I walked. I was searching for him before I was even aware of it. From the photo Abhilash had posted, he had to be here somewhere in the array of coloured kites that lined the beach.

I wouldn't approach him. I couldn't. I shouldn't. That would be too bold. Too forward. I was more subtle than that. I would just walk past.

Slowly.

If he saw me. If he waved. If he smiled. Or even if his eyes simply showed even the slightest sign of recognition, then I'd acknowledge him. I'd stop and speak. Say hello. Comment on the weather. Ask how he was. Anything. Everything.

As long as he noticed me.

Remembered me.

I sighed heavily. This wasn't healthy. Wasn't normal.

I should give up now. Turn back. Go home. It wasn't too late.

And yet, I kept walking.

My gaze locked onto a bright-yellow kite. It was the only yellow one on the beach. I squinted, trying to identify its owner, but they were all dressed in black wetsuits, making them hard to identify from this distance.

Surfers were starting to carry their boards to the water, as their kites lifted into the air. I quickened my pace to a half jog as I neared the end of the chine and veered across the promenade on to the sand. If he took to the water before I got there, I'd miss my chance.

But my chance for what?

I headed towards the sea. My best bet was to stroll casually along the shoreline and let Abhilash come to me. If I positioned myself right, he'd have to walk past me to get into the water. I squinted at the yellow kite. Assuming, of course, that was his kite and he wasn't already surfing.

'Lauren?'

I stopped and pivoted in the soft sand.

'Hey, I thought that was you.' Abhilash grinned at me.

'Oh hi, A... er, Dr Menon?' I'd spent days thinking of him as

Abhilash, but to call him by his first name without invitation was impolite. Let alone too revealing of my stalkerish behaviour.

'Please, call me Abhilash. It's my day off.'

I smiled and nodded.

'I'm not delaying you, am I?' he asked, a tiny frown creasing his brow. 'You looked like you were in kind of a hurry.'

'Oh, no, I was just, er, trying to burn off a few calories in preparation for all the extra ones I'm about to indulge in.' I gave a feeble chuckle as I lifted my coffee and paper bag to demonstrate my point.

How long had he been watching me? Had he seen me frantically scanning all the surfers? Had he realised I was looking for him?

Then again, if he was preparing to surf, how had he spotted me at all? Shouldn't he have been focused on his kite? I glanced back across the beach at the single yellow kite left abandoned on the sand.

'I was just about to take advantage of the ideal surfing conditions today,' Abhilash said. 'It makes a change for it to coincide with my day off.'

'Great, it looks like fun.'

'You've never tried?'

I shook my head. 'Not got round to it yet.'

'You should.' His eyes lit up as he smiled. 'It's incredible.'

I nodded again.

'I can give you some pointers if you like.' His eyes widened, as though he'd just realised what he'd said. 'I mean, erm, if you wanted to learn,' he added.

He seemed flustered.

At the hospital he'd been so calm and reassuring. But then we both knew our roles there. Out here it was undefined.

'That would be great, thanks.' I tried not to sound too enthusiastic. He probably hadn't really meant it. Just one of those things that get said in the moment but would never get put into practice.

Although, he didn't seem like someone who was insincere.

We smiled awkwardly at each other. Now that I was here face to face with him, I realised that I hadn't got as far as figuring out what I would actually say if I did meet him.

Why hadn't I thought of that sooner?

'So how is the wrist?'

I glanced down at the cast and scrunched my nose. 'Uncomfortable. Hot. Itchy. But otherwise, all good.'

He laughed. 'Taking it all in your stride, I see.'

'Is there any other way?'

'Maybe.' Our eyes met and I could practically feel his penetrating stare boring into my soul.

I knew what his maybe meant. Leave Josh. Avoid any more broken bones. To him it was that simple. It was only complicated to me.

'How are things at home?'

'Quiet.'

'That's good.'

I nodded again. We were playing a cryptic game. But then there were no clear guidelines for what to say in this kind of situation. No one teaches you how to have conversations about the things that are the most important. The most difficult.

But then, why did it feel like this was important?

'Do you want to sit down for a bit? Eat your lunch? Have a chat?'

I nodded instantly before my thoughts had even caught up to allow me to voice my agreement. My excitement.

Excitement.

My brain registered that emotion. It felt out of place. Excessive. And yet, the feeling remained.

'Let's sit on the wooden breaker,' Abhilash said, signalling ahead. 'Save you getting sand all over your lovely suit.'

'Okay,' I managed to murmur, as heat crept into my cheeks. He liked my suit. He'd noticed what I was wearing.

Just like Josh used to.

We walked side by side to the breaker as clarity seeped into my brain. Suddenly it all made sense. It had been so long since Josh had paid any attention to me, I was excited at being noticed and treated with consideration. It was flattering. It was what I needed. What I craved.

Even if it was by the wrong person.

I sat down and perched my coffee beside me. I opened the paper bag and held it out towards Abhilash. 'Would you like some coffee and walnut cake?'

He shook his head. 'No thanks, I'll eat after I've surfed.'

I nodded as I broke a piece of cake off and popped it into my mouth. I chewed slowly, searching my brain for something to say. This is what I'd wanted. What I'd hoped for. And now that I was here, we were just sitting in silence.

'How are you managing at work with your cast?' Abhilash asked.

'Great,' I said, a little too enthusiastically. 'Well, I mean, it's fine. A little tricky given I'm right-handed, but I run my own social media marketing business, so the boss has been very supportive.'

Abhilash chuckled. 'I'm glad.'

'Plus the cast is proving excellent material for Instagram. The response has been fantastic. Which in my line of work is critical.'

'Who knew a broken wrist could be good for business,' he said, shaking his head.

'Good things come from a little bit of pain.'

Abhilash stared at me, his eyes wide. 'You really believe that?'

I shrugged. 'It's what Mum always said.'

Abhilash looked horrified. He probably wondered why I still paid attention to anything she'd said.

Sometimes I wondered the same thing myself.

21

NOW

The phone felt heavy in my hand as I hung up. Why had I charged it? I rolled my eyes. Leaving my phone switched off wouldn't have helped me avoid the police. Not for long. If they couldn't reach me by phone they would simply have turned up on my doorstep.

I shuddered at that thought.

I'd had enough police in my home the last time. Snooping through everything. Invading my privacy. Dissecting my life. No, it was best to go to them.

Not that the police station was somewhere I wanted to return to either. At least I'd had Josh's mum with me back then. Janice had been by my side every step of the way. She hadn't said much. She wasn't allowed to. But she'd been there. That was enough. That was everything.

I tapped the screen and pulled up her number. She probably wouldn't be allowed in the interview with me this time now that I was no longer a minor. But she could still go with me. Even just knowing she was sitting outside waiting for me would help.

My finger hesitated over the call button. There was just one problem. This wasn't the same as last time.

* * *

'You should have told me, Lauren,' Josh said.

I shook my head. 'I couldn't. I couldn't tell anyone.'

'I'm not anyone.' The anguish in Josh's voice tore into my heart. I'd hurt him. I hadn't trusted him with the biggest secret I had. And he knew it. He felt it.

'I'm your boyfriend, it's my job to protect you. I failed.'

'No, you didn't—'

'You made me fail.'

I flinched at his accusation.

'I know what everyone's saying about me.'

'About you?' I frowned. All the gossip was focused on me. Wasn't it? My life had been exposed. My weakness. My naivety.

'You made me look stupid. Everyone thinks I let you down. That I failed you. They think I should have intervened. But how could I when you didn't tell me? You shut me out. You hid the truth from me.'

'I didn't know. Not for sure.' My voice faded. 'She's my mum,' I whispered. Despite what the police said, it still didn't feel true. It didn't feel possible.

And yet, I knew it was.

'And I'm your boyfriend,' Josh said.

My boyfriend. Those words had power. Strength. Mum might have abandoned me but I wasn't alone. I was still loved. Still wanted. Still part of something.

Josh pulled me towards him and wrapped his arms around me. 'You have to tell me everything from now on, Lauren.'

'I promise.' My voice was breathless as my lungs fought for breath *in his embrace. I could feel the strength of his love for me. The intensity was almost overwhelming. So powerful that it hurt.*

It was how I knew he loved me.

'I'm going to take care of you now. I'm going to take care of everything,' Josh whispered.

Before it had all been about my mum. This time it was about her son.

Would Janice still be in my corner?

I threw my phone on the sofa. I knew the answer to that.

The Carters had already done so much for me. More than anyone could be expected to. Especially for someone who wasn't family.

Who was never going to be family.

I drummed my fingers against the leather sofa. If not Janice, then who? I was still too dizzy and nauseous to contemplate driving and taking a taxi didn't appeal. I couldn't go alone. Not back there.

I sucked in a deep breath. Abhilash was at work; I couldn't call him. Which left only one person...

22

THEN

'Tell me about your mum.'

My shoulders slumped. I shouldn't have mentioned her. I knew better than that. It was a door that should remain firmly shut. At least to other people. 'It's all in my records.'

'I don't mean that. I mean the other stuff. The good stuff.'

I blinked. It wasn't a request I'd expected. No one ever asked about the good times. The normal times. They only wanted to know the bad parts. The details. The how. The why. They weren't questions I liked to dwell on. Mostly because even now, it didn't make sense. Not fully.

It just hurt.

'You do have some good memories, don't you?'

I nodded slowly. 'Yeah, lots of them, but...' My voice trailed away. They were all tarnished now.

'It was just the two of you?'

I nodded again. 'I never knew my dad. They were in college when Mum got pregnant.' I shrugged. 'He wasn't ready to be a dad.'

'I'm sorry.'

Silence fell between us. What else was there to say? He'd made his choice. Part of me didn't blame him. He was just a kid himself. The thought of becoming a father must have been over-whelming. And yet, I was the one who still had to live with the knowledge that he didn't accept me. Didn't love me.

All I'd had was Mum.

Until I didn't even have her.

'What was she like?'

'Amazing,' I said wistfully, as I remembered the woman who had once been my whole world. 'We were so close. I guess because we were all each other had. My dad wasn't the only one that didn't want anything to do with me. Mum's parents didn't either. Apparently, they were really old fashioned. It was bad enough that Mum was pregnant at seventeen, but then when she told them she and my dad weren't getting married, they flipped out. They told her if she was old enough to create a life, she was old enough to deal with the consequences that came with it. So she did.'

'Good for her,' Abhilash sounded impressed. I had been too. Once.

'I was her everything. She put me first. She protected me.' I let the memories wash over me. That feeling of safety. Of love.

I missed that feeling.

It had been taken from me. Stolen along with everything else. My memories were all I had left. And even they weren't real.

'It was all a lie, though.'

Abhilash shook his head. 'I don't believe that.'

I stared at him, stunned by his naivety. 'How could it be anything else?'

'I think she probably did love you, but she wasn't well enough to love you in a healthy way.'

'You're condoning her actions?'

Abhilash flinched. 'Never. What she did was so wrong. So bad. I don't even know how you could begin to forgive that. But...'

I inhaled sharply, waiting for the accusations. The blame.

'I can't help wondering what must have happened to her to feel that her actions were acceptable. Necessary, even.' Abhilash stared at the waves to the side of us. 'She must have been in a place of such desperation. That doesn't condone it. It never could. But I just wish she could have got the help she needed sooner.' He turned to face me, his expression sad and regretful. 'For both of you.'

And there it was.

The blame.

He hadn't come right out and said it, of course. That wasn't his way. He was tactful. Compassionate. But beneath his words the accusation resonated. Because I knew what had happened to her. I knew where that sense of desperation had originated.

Me.

It always came back to me. I was the reason for everything. The reason she dropped out of college and got shunned by her family. My birth. My existence took everything thing she had loved away from her.

All she was left with was me.

And I wasn't enough.

23

NOW

I paced the hall, my stomach somersaulting every time I heard a car engine. I was supposed to have been done with trips to the police station after the last time. I'd worked so hard to put it all behind me. Pretend it hadn't happened. And yet the memories remained. Lingering just out of sight.

It's all going to be fine, I told myself for the tenth time, twisting my bag strap between my fingers as it hung from my shoulder. It would be standard procedure for the police to talk to those who were closest to the person who had disappeared. It was just a missing persons case.

Just.

I cringed at my poor choice of wording. I would have to be careful of that in front of the police officers. But it was true. That's all it was. There was no body.

This time.

I peered out of the little window in the front door at the sound of a car pulling up in front of the house. I glanced at my bag, checking my phone was inside it as I opened the door and stepped outside. But Emma was out of the car and halfway up the drive before I had even shut the door behind me.

'Oh, Lauren, I've been so worried about you.' She flung her arms around me and hugged me tightly.

'You were?' The question slipped out as I tried to keep my balance.

Her arms fell to her sides as she stepped back, a pained expression on her face. 'Of course I was.'

'Sorry,' I was instantly contrite. 'It's just I've received so many messages asking about Josh, and I know you've always—' I caught myself, just in time, before I said she had always had a crush on him. It was the truth. But I knew better than most that the truth shouldn't always be spoken. 'Been close.' I finished feebly as I closed the front door.

'You and I are close too,' Emma said, linking her arm in mine as we walked towards her car.

'Yeah, I know.' Except, I didn't. There had always been a gulf between us, even at school. We were friends, but at the same time we were rivals. We both wanted the same thing.

Josh.

I might have won him but that didn't mean Emma had ever fully got over her crush. He was the one that got away. And I was the one who stole him.

At least that was the impression she'd always given me. The reality was that Josh had never been interested in her. He'd confided in me once that even without my presence he would never have dated her. But again, that was another truth that didn't need to be shared.

'Everyone's been calling to ask about you.'

'About me?' Or about Josh? I added silently.

'Do you remember Tim Harris?'

I shrugged, not even attempting to remember. He was irrelevant. Everything was irrelevant today. I had bigger things to think about.

We will be conducting the interview under caution.

'You must remember him. Josh used to hang out with him a lot, before we all split up to go to different unis.'

I tried to concentrate. 'Yeah, vaguely.' But I didn't. What did I care about some random kid from secondary school who I hadn't even seen in ten years?'

'Well, even he called to ask about you. He was really interested. Which proves what I always suspected.'

'What's that?'

'That he had a crush on you.'

I rolled my eyes.

'Not that you'd have noticed. You only ever had eyes for Josh. But clearly, he's still harbouring feelings for you. He was so concerned and focused on you he didn't even ask if Josh had been f-found.' Her voice cracked. Tim wasn't the only one still harbouring feelings of unrequited love.

I opened the passenger door as Emma walked around to the other side. 'I just can't get over Josh being missing. It's so awful.'

We were back to Josh. Again.

I flopped onto the seat. It was always about him.

I was still on the periphery. Of his life. His family. His friends.

I glanced at Emma as she clambered in beside me. Despite her claims, it was clear that Josh was the only reason she was here.

'The thought of him out there somewhere in the water.' Emma twisted in her seat and stared in the direction of the sea, even though it was out of sight behind rows of houses.

'He isn't in the water,' I said, clicking my seat belt fastened.

Her head snapped back, and she stared at me. 'But you were on the jet-ski together.'

I shook my head. 'I was alone.'

She frowned. 'Paul told me you were together.' It wasn't a question, but an accusation. Paul's version of events outweighed mine. She'd never even liked Paul. 'He showed me Josh's text.'

'Ah,' I said as understanding dawned on me. That explained it. It wasn't that Emma believed Paul over me.

She believed Josh.

24

THEN

'Well, I guess I should get out on the water.' Abhilash jerked his head towards the kite surfers who were following the westerly current towards Bournemouth pier.

'Right.' I nodded, not wanting our conversation to end but at the same time having no idea how to prolong it. We stood up and I picked up my empty coffee cup.

'It was good to see you again,' Abhilash said, giving me a smile that told me he really meant it. Regardless of whether he realised I'd been looking for him or not, he did seem genuinely pleased to chat with me.

'If you ever need someone to talk to...' He let his statement hang unfinished. But I knew what he meant. If I wanted to talk about Josh.

'Thanks,' I replied, surprised to discover that I was actually grateful for the offer. It wasn't what I'd come for. At least, I didn't think it was. But somehow, knowing that there was someone willing to listen, to not judge, it made me feel a little less alone.

He shifted his weight from foot to foot, sinking in the damp sand. 'Bye then,' he said, but he hesitated a moment longer before heading back up the beach towards his kite and board. I stared after him. Had it been my imagination, or had he been reluctant to leave?

I rolled my eyes and scolded myself for my wishful thinking.

My eyes widened as he glanced back over his shoulder, and I realised I'd been caught watching him. He waved and I lifted my hand in a feeble half wave back to acknowledge him, whilst wishing I hadn't been quite so obvious.

The majority of my interactions with other people were done online, via email or WhatsApp messages. I was clearly out of practice with the social etiquette of real-life encounters. Then again, what was the etiquette when it came to stalking your doctor?

I winced. Quite simply, it would be *don't do it*. So clearly it was too late for me then.

I headed up the beach towards the promenade and threw my cup in the bin. I started to turn back to the chine when I heard a ping from my bag. I unzipped it, reached inside, pulled out my phone, and flicked the screen on.

I froze.

Abhilash accepted your friend request.

I read it again.

He'd accepted.

I glanced back over my shoulder, my eyes scanning the beach behind me, half expecting to see him watching me. Or perhaps more accurately, I wanted to see him.

Another ping drew my attention back to the phone in my hands.

Abhilash is waving at you.

My jaw dropped open. Abhilash hadn't just accepted the request; he was communicating with me in Messenger.

My hand trembled as I clicked to wave back.

I waited.

I was vaguely aware that I was still standing in the middle of the path. But I didn't move. I couldn't. I wasn't sure I even remembered how.

Dots flashed on the screen...

Abhilash is typing…

What would he say? What could he say? I'd literally only just left him. We'd exhausted all the customary small talk. What else was there?

Unless it was to tell me to stay away from him...

I shook my head. No, that couldn't be it. He wouldn't have answered if that was the case. He would simply have blocked me.

Hey, I was so surprised to see you.

I puffed out my cheeks as I let out a deep breath of relief. I hadn't creeped him out. I'd merely surprised him.

I chuckled. I couldn't blame him for that. It was a big beach. The chances of us being in exactly the same spot at the same time had to be fairly slim, right? At least under normal circumstances.

But these weren't normal circumstances. I'd had an advantage.

Heat crept onto my face. I'd stalked him. Literally, this time. Not just online. I'd followed him in real life now too. That couldn't be good. Not for either of us.

And yet, it hadn't all been down to me. Luck had played a role too. A big role. If he hadn't been at Fisherman's Walk at the same

time that I was at Café Riva... if he hadn't posted his location on
Facebook...

I'm really happy that we ran into each other. And I meant it, I'm here if
you ever need someone to talk to.

It was good to see you too. And thanks.

I couldn't restrain the grin that stretched across my face. He
was happy to see me. Really happy.

Josh used to be happy to see me.

That thought was like a bucket of icy cold water thrown
over me.

What was I doing? Getting excited about messages from
another guy. Analysing his messages, making assumptions on
how genuine his words were like I knew him.

Talk soon. Bye.

I stared at the message.

Soon.

I stared at that word. Did that mean he wanted to keep in
touch? Or was it just a line to sign off with? Polite. Meaningless.
Empty.

Only time would tell.

I slipped the phone back into my bag with a sigh. I'd never
been very good at waiting. I wanted to know everything immediately. I wanted to understand. To plan.

I needed that consistency. That structure.

I wanted things to be simple. To be right or wrong. Good
or bad.

And yet, they never were.

I took a step forward but stopped again. Something about the timing felt odd. It seemed too coincidental for him to have discovered my friend request the moment I walked away. So did that mean he'd already seen it? Had he ignored it? Ignored me? But then, why respond now?

In fact, why respond at all?

25

NOW

'What's going on?' Emma demanded.

'I don't know. All I know is that Josh wasn't with me.'

'Then why am I taking you to the police station?'

'I was his girlfriend. We lived together. Of course the police would want to talk to me.' I repeated the same rationalisations that I had been trying to convince myself of ever since PC Smith's call.

'Was?' Her eyes narrowed suspiciously. 'You think he's dead?'

'No, that's not what I meant.'

'You're already talking about him in the past tense.'

'I'm talking about *us* in the past tense. There's a difference.'

'You broke up?' Her eyes widened as realisation dawned on her. 'Because of that doctor?'

I inhaled sharply. 'I should call a taxi,' I said, reaching for my bag to retrieve my phone. It's what I should have done in the first place. It would have been simpler. What had possessed me to call Emma for a lift?

'No,' she said forcefully, ramming her seat belt into the clip. 'I said I'd drive you.' She jabbed the key into the ignition and started the engine. 'And I will.'

She pressed the accelerator sharply, jolting us forwards as she pulled away from the kerb. I glanced back as the house faded from view and for the first time ever, I found myself wishing I could stay there.

'I want to know the rest of the story,' Emma demanded.

'He's just a friend.'

'He's your doctor, Lauren. Not your friend.'

'Why can't he be both?'

'That's not how it works. It's not right.'

'We haven't done anything wrong. It's not like he's my GP or consultant or anything. He just treated me once in the ED. That's all.' Technically it was twice now, but I wasn't about to enlighten Emma of that fact.

'And then you stalked him on Facebook.'

'I was curious.'

'You were obsessed. You've been acting weird ever since you met him.'

'You're being ridiculous.'

'Am I?'

I tried not to squirm. She was right; I had stalked him. I couldn't explain it. I felt a pull towards him, right from the start. But I'd never planned on becoming romantically involved. It had just sort of happened. It was a sign of how strong our connection was. Everything had evolved from there.

'He was your doctor. He treated you when you were injured. Looked after you. Helped heal you. You seem to think that means something more than it does. It's like you're trying to turn it into some sort of perfect relationship. Just like you did with Josh.'

'That's not true!' I objected.

Was it? The silent question resounded in my head. Maybe at

one point I'd believed Josh was perfect. That we were perfect. I'd tried so hard to sustain that image, not just to everyone else, but to myself too. I wanted it to be real. I needed it to be. But its perfection was artificial.

Abhilash was different though. I knew his flaws. Even the ones that he couldn't see, at least, not yet. I knew what we had was complex and precarious. It wasn't perfect. I wasn't trying to make it perfect.

I was just... I puffed out my cheeks and let out a deep breath. What was I trying to do? Not make things perfect, but I was trying to make things better. That wasn't a bad thing. It was natural. Normal.

I folded my arms across my chest. It didn't matter what Emma or anyone else thought. Abhilash made me laugh. He made me happy. Safe. That's what people who cared about you did. It's what Josh should have done.

'What's in it for him?'

I shook my head. 'I don't understand.'

'He's a doctor, Lauren. He meets people all day, every day. Rich women. Interesting women. Beautiful women. So why you?'

I shrank back. I wanted to crawl away. To hide. Emma was right; I was none of those things. But it wasn't her place to say so. She was supposed to be my friend.

'Maybe it was my scintillating personality,' I said, suddenly feeling bolder. I wasn't going to sit here and let her tear me down.

Enough people had done that to me already.

'Or maybe it was your medical file.'

I frowned. 'What does that mean?'

'You're vulnerable. An easy target. Especially to a doctor.'

'I'm not!' My objection resonated around the car; it sounded so firm and certain. And yet inside I knew it was true: I was an easy target.

I always had been.

'Come on, we all know about the unexplained injuries. The hospital visits.' She glanced at me. 'Josh told me they sent social workers to check on you last year.'

'I...' Josh had told her? He'd talked about our problems to other people? I was stunned. Josh never talked about our problems. Not even to me.

'Given your mum's obsession with doctors—'

A chill ran through me. 'It's not like that.'

It made sense now. Josh hadn't talked about our problems. He'd talked about mine. The ones everyone thought I had. The ones he *made* everyone think I had.

'We're worried about you, Lauren. We're worried that this obsession with your doctor is a sign that you are deteriorating. We just want to help you.'

'We?'

'Josh and I.'

'You've talked to Josh?' I glared at her. 'About Abhilash?'

'Of course I have.' She rolled her eyes. 'I'm your friend. It's my job to look out for you.'

'Whose friend?' I snapped. 'Mine? Or Josh's?'

'Both.'

I snorted. Her loyalty was divided. But worse still, it was weighted towards Josh.

'What your mum did. What she put you through. It was awful. I mean, I know I used to moan about my mum when were we kids, but it was all normal stuff. Just mild teenage rebellion. But yours...' she puffed out her cheeks as she exhaled. 'That was messed up.'

I clenched my fists, digging my nails into my palms, desperate to stop my mind drifting back to the past. But it was no good. Memories of that first visit to the police station had already been brought to the surface thanks to PC Smith's call. I couldn't bury them now. I couldn't avoid them.

* * *

'Concerns have been raised about your medical treatment.' PC Collier said.

'You mean from when I was admitted last week?'

PC Collier frowned. 'You're aware of the concerns?'

I had the feeling I had said the wrong thing. I knew something she didn't expect me to. But then again, what did I really know?

'The doctor last week kept asking me about my medication. What I take. What the pills looked like.'

'Do you know why? Was there something in particular that had triggered these questions?'

'I was feeling better.' I paused. 'No, actually I was feeling good.' I shrugged. 'For me, anyway.'

'You'd been admitted for severe stomach pains, right?'

I nodded. 'Yeah, but they couldn't find the cause. They kept me in though because the doctor said I was malnourished and dehydrated.'

'That doesn't seem to concern you.'

I shrugged. 'It's not the first time. My stomach hurts so much that I don't eat a lot. And whatever I do eat...' I wasn't sure how to finish that sentence. It was bad enough to talk about this stuff with the doctors, but to a police officer and Josh's mum... I ran my sweaty palms across my thighs, feeling uncomfortable.

'Doesn't stay in your system very long?' PC Collier asked.

I nodded and smiled. I liked her polite way of phrasing it.

'But the hospital always seems to have better medication. Whenever I have to stay for a few days, my stomach settles. I asked the doctor why I couldn't be on the same stuff at home.'

'And what did he say?'

'*That I already was.*'

PC Collier tapped her pen on her notepad thoughtfully. 'So, let me make sure I understand this properly. You're saying you have the same medication in hospital as you do at home, but you only get sick at home?'

I nodded.

'*Is it possible that you forget your medication sometimes when you are at home? Or maybe take more than you're supposed to?*'

'*No way. Mum is like, obsessed about it. She makes sure I take the right dose at the right time, every single day.' I groaned. 'Whether I want to or not.*'

'*You don't want to take your medication?*'

I shook my head.

'*Why not?*'

I scrunched my nose. She would think I was crazy. Or just being difficult and making a fuss. That's what Mum thought.

'*Lauren?*'

'*Sometimes it seems like I kinda feel worse when I take them.*'

'*The pills have side effects?*'

'*No, it's more like they don't do what they are supposed to, or maybe...' I rolled my eyes. 'Never mind. It's stupid.*'

'*No, Lauren, carry on. Finish what you wanted to say.*'

I squirmed. 'It just seems like they do the opposite of what they are supposed to.'

'*Oh my...' Mrs Carter gasped beside me. 'Is her mother giving her the wrong medication?*'

'*Mrs Carter,' PC Collier's tone was abrupt. 'You are here to support Lauren, not to participate in the conversation.*'

'*But can't you check?*'

'*They already did.' Both women stared at me, surprise etched onto their faces. 'Some people came to the house. I was upstairs, and Mum thought I hadn't heard. But she was really loud. She was so cross that* they had turned up without an invitation and demanded to see my medication.'

PC Collier nodded. 'They took a sample and had it tested. It was the correct medication.'

I nodded. 'Of course, it was. Mum wouldn't give me anything that was bad for me.'

'You're certain of that?' PC Collier asked.

I didn't know what was going on, but whatever it was, Mum wasn't involved. She couldn't be.

'She's my mum.'

26

THEN

I rolled onto my side as soon as I woke up, being careful to keep my cast out of the way as I reached for my phone. It had become my routine now. The little red notification determined the mood for the start of my day.

My eyes widened as I saw it. The little three above the WhatsApp icon. Three messages. From Abhilash? My heart pounded as I tried not to get my hopes up. They might not be from him...

I tapped the screen and grinned.

They were all from him. Every single one.

It had been a risk asking for his phone number. He could have said no. It wasn't really necessary; we'd been chatting through Facebook messenger for days. We could have stayed like that.

But on Facebook, I was just one of his hundreds of 'friends'. His phone number was something that was restricted to the closest ones. The real ones.

And now I was part of that group.

Hey, how are you doing?

I smiled as I read the first message he'd sent at midnight.

Sorry, I've just realised the time. You're probably sleeping. I'm on the night shift and forgot that my breaks don't coincide with normal people's lives.

I glanced at the time stamp. He'd sent it one minute after his first message.

Just got home and wanted to say hi before I sleep. Catch you later. Have a good day.

I read the final message and smiled. There was a time when Josh used to do that. To message during the day or call at lunch just to hear my voice. A time when he used to miss me.

It was different now. He barely called, and certainly not to chat. He still messaged, but he didn't even wait for my reply. At best, it felt like he was ticking me off his to-do list. I sighed. And at worst, it felt like he was reminding me where I was supposed to be. What I was supposed to be doing.

Waiting for him.

I closed my eyes as the memories overwhelmed me. The saddest part was that it worked. I was waiting for him. Even before I'd started my business, I'd kept my phone with me every second of the day. I didn't want to miss his call, his text. No matter what I was doing, I always answered it immediately. The phone barely passed the first ring before it was pressed to my ear.

I'd seen him only a few hours before when he left for work and would see him again when he got home, and yet I waited in anticipation for his calls and texts as though I hadn't seen or heard from him in days.

But then, in a way it felt like I hadn't. Just because I saw him each day, it didn't mean he was present. There was a distance between us even when we sat side by side on the sofa.

I opened my eyes and re-read Abhilash's message. I started to type a reply but stopped. He'd sent his last message two hours ago. If I replied now, I could wake him. But if I didn't, he might think I was ignoring him. That three messages through the night were too much.

I nibbled my lip. Were they too much?

I drummed my fingers against the phone. What was normal? Or better still, *who* was normal?

We all had our quirks. Abhilash's was sending messages in the middle of the night. But was that so strange? He was on a break. He messaged when he thought about me.

He'd thought about me.

The realisation seeped into my brain.

I didn't care what time he messaged. Or how often. I didn't care if it was too soon. Or if I didn't really know what it meant.

All that mattered was that he'd thought about me.

But at the same time, I knew that that was the one thing that shouldn't matter. I had a boyfriend. He was the one who was supposed to think about me. Miss me.

It will all end in tears.

Mum's warning resounded in my ears. She used it a lot. Anytime I wanted to go somewhere or do something. She was the voice of caution that still echoed in my head. She was probably right. At least this time.

But somehow, that wasn't enough to deter me.

27

___

NOW

'There was never any proof,' I said quietly.

'Just because the police couldn't find anything, that doesn't mean she wasn't guilty.' Emma replied, flicking the indicator on and swinging the car round the corner too fast.

'The police didn't even arrest her.'

Emma scoffed. 'If she was so innocent, how come you made a miraculous recovery after they got involved?'

I didn't respond.

'Because your mum was on best behaviour then, that's how,' Emma answered her own question. 'She knew they were watching her. And with Social Services coming round to check on you at random times, she had to be careful. She had to change.'

I closed my eyes. Mum had changed. The suspicions, the accusations, they changed her. They crushed her. I'd watched it happen. She seemed to withdraw into herself a little more each day.

I'd done that to her.

The doctors had only started questioning the medication I

was given at home because I'd made some stupid comment. Everything had escalated from there.

I'd betrayed her.

I'd destroyed her.

'She had to see the doctor after everything happened. She was suffering from depression.'

Emma shot a quick glance at me. 'That wasn't your fault, you know.'

I shrugged. Of course it was my fault.

'You weren't responsible for what she did.'

'I told you, there was never any proof that she did anything.'

I held my breath, waiting for Emma to object again. She was right of course. The police didn't have enough evidence for an arrest, but they'd still believed Mum was guilty.

We all had.

Eventually.

'I didn't mean that,' she slowed down as we approached the police station and parked beside the kerb. She shifted the gear stick into neutral and twisted in her seat to look at me.

'I meant, it's not your fault that she killed herself.'

28

THEN

My feet slowed their pace as I approached Café Riva and doubts crept into my mind. After a week of messaging, Abhilash and I had decided to meet again. A planned meeting this time. No stalking would be required. And yet somehow that made me feel even more uneasy.

I couldn't pass it off as a chance encounter. This was intentional. Agreed. But that was okay, wasn't it? It was just coffee with a friend.

It sounded so innocent. So normal. Not that it eased my guilty conscience.

It felt as though I was betraying Josh. Cheating on him. Where did that line lie? The one between an innocent coffee and something more?

It felt hazy and ambiguous. But perhaps the fact that I was even asking the question was a sign that line was a tightrope, and I was walking it.

I rummaged for my phone in my bag. There was still time to call it off. To cancel. To revert to my quiet obedient life as the respectable girlfriend who never strayed.

And yet I kept walking.

My stomach did a little somersault as I saw Abhilash standing at the entrance, a tiny bouquet of miniature roses in his hand.

He'd bought me flowers.

Buying flowers is such a waste of money.

Josh's voice resounded in my head.

I pushed that thought away. Surely it wasn't a waste if they brought someone joy?

Not that Josh had ever tested that theory.

'Hey.' Abhilash's eyes lit up as he saw me. 'It's good to see you.' He shuffled awkwardly as though unsure how to greet me.

'You too,' I replied with a smile as I debated what was appropriate. A handshake? A hug?

'These are for you,' he said, handing me the flowers.

'They're beautiful, thank you.' Heat crept into my cheeks. 'But you didn't need to bring me flowers.'

It's just coffee, I repeated to myself. But somehow it sounded more like a question than a statement now.

'They grow in our garden,' Abhilash replied as though dismissing his gift. 'It didn't feel right to come empty handed.'

I smiled again. Economical and thoughtful. Josh could learn a thing or two from him. 'Well, I appreciate them, thank you.'

It was just a shame I wouldn't be able to take them home.

'Lauren, are you okay?'

'Huh?'

'You seem to be trying to strangle the roses.'

I looked down at my hand gripping the stems so tightly. 'Sorry, I just thinking about—' I clamped my mouth shut.

'Josh?'

I nodded hesitantly. I shouldn't be thinking about him. Not now. Not when I was with Abhilash. 'It's just that Josh gets kind of jealous. He doesn't like it when someone, *anyone*, gives me flowers.'

'Anyone?' He studied me, waiting for an explanation.

'About six months ago, I had a delivery. I was cooking Sunday dinner at the time, so Josh answered the door. He came into the kitchen carrying this huge, beautiful bouquet of yellow roses.' I held my hands up, trying to demonstrate the size. 'It was incredible. I was so excited. But also surprised. Josh had never bought me flowers before, and it wasn't even my birthday or our anniversary. It was only when my gaze lifted from the flowers to his face that I realised...'

'They weren't from Josh,' Abhilash said, his eyes wide.

'No, and he was really mad about it. He dumped them on the worktop. I wanted to put them in water. They were too beautiful to be treated like that. But I didn't move. I couldn't. I asked him who they were for, silently praying that there had been a mistake and they had been delivered to the wrong house.'

'But they hadn't?'

I shook my head. 'No, there hadn't been a mistake. At least not by the delivery driver. They were for me. Josh pulled out a card and read it to me: "Lauren, thanks for everything, Graham".'

'Who's Graham?' Abhilash inquisitively.

I let out a rueful chuckle. 'That's what Josh wanted to know too. Except he didn't ask as nicely as you. But the only Graham I knew was a client. I was so relieved. I mean, he was *just* a client. A really happy one. He'd been my first client, the one who had got me started with my whole business, and for the first time he was actually making a profit. He said he had me and my marketing campaign to thank for it.'

'That's impressive.'

'Josh didn't think so. In fact, he didn't even believe me. Didn't think that my little hobby business was capable of making that kind of difference. That *I* was capable. He wanted to know what else I had been doing for this "client".' I put air quotes around the word. 'As Josh pointed out, his clients didn't send him gifts. He worked hard for them, but the most he got was a thank you. So what made me different? What made me deserving of elaborate bouquets of flowers that a husband would only buy for his wife for a special occasion? Or...' I took a deep breath. 'For his bit on the side.'

'Wow,' Abhilash took a step back. 'He said that to you? That's so... that's just...' he shook his head, unable to finish his sentences. 'I'm sorry, perhaps the roses were a bad idea.' He lifted his hand as though he wanted to take the roses back.

'No,' I said as I pulled them close to my chest protectively. They were mine. He'd given them me. He couldn't take them away. Not now.

Abhilash smiled, but the concern didn't lift from his brow. 'But if Josh sees them...'

He was right. I couldn't let Josh see them. At least if I gave them back to Abhilash, he could keep them for me. It was better than throwing them away. 'Can I at least keep them for a little longer?'

'Of course,' Abhilash nodded firmly. 'And don't worry; next time, I'll bring you a plant instead. Something you can put in the garden where he won't notice it.'

I blinked.

Next time.

'Coffee and cake?' Abhilash asked as he held the door to the café open for me. I nodded as I stepped inside, while my brain was still fixated on the meaning of the flowers.

What were we doing here? Could I still claim that we weren't doing anything wrong? That we were just two acquaintances meeting for coffee?

I played with a rose petal as we joined the queue and Abhilash peered into the cake cabinet. Didn't the presence of roses change everything?

Whilst I'd been trying to convince myself that this was nothing, it hadn't occurred to me to consider what Abhilash might think our outing meant.

'Hmm, the millionaire's shortcake looks delicious.'

I grinned. All thoughts of flowers faded from my head. 'That's my favourite.'

'Really?' He smiled as I nodded. 'We seem to be in sync again.'

My stomach did another little flip. It seemed to have a habit of doing that when Abhilash was around.

Shouldn't it be Josh who gave me butterflies in my stomach?

I felt my smile fade as I realised that he never had. His touch didn't make my skin tingle. His kiss didn't curl my toes. I'd always assumed they were exaggerated concepts only found in romantic movies. And yet, somehow, Abhilash seemed to be evidence of the contrary.

29

NOW

I followed PC Smith into the small interview room. My legs felt like lead. Each step was heavy and reluctant. I didn't want to be here. Not again.

'Take a seat,' PC Smith said. I turned my head, surveying the room. Not that there was much to see. Just four chairs and a table. I squinted. It even looked like the same table from the last time I was here.

I shuddered, pushing that thought away. I mustn't let myself think about it. Not now.

'Are you cold?' he asked, looking surprised. I couldn't blame him. It was hotter than normal for September.

I shook my head but didn't elaborate as I sank into the chair he indicated. He didn't need to know about the ghosts that still accompanied me. At least, not more than he already knew from his files.

'Thanks for coming in,' he said as he sat on the other side of the table.

I nodded, even though we both knew from the tone of his

phone call two hours earlier that my attendance wasn't really optional.

The clunk of the door opening caught my attention, and I looked up as woman entered. She nodded at me before sitting beside PC Smith. Her presence caught me off guard. I'd assumed that PC Jennings, the female office from the hospital, would be joining us. Instead, I was faced with this stranger.

Except... I squinted as I studied her face. She didn't entirely seem like a stranger.

Our eyes met and I froze. There was something about her. Something familiar. Something that made the air feel heavy in my lungs.

My gaze flicked to her smart grey suit. This wasn't just the routine interview by a couple of uniformed officers to tick the necessary boxes that I'd hoped. This was different. This was more.

'Let's get started,' PC Smith said. 'Lauren Taylor, this interview is being recorded. You're not under arrest and are free to leave at any time. You may have a solicitor with you if you wish. You do not have to say anything, but it may harm your defence if you don't mention when questioned something which you later rely on in court. Anything you do say may be given in evidence.'

'Do you understand, Ms Taylor?'

My stomach contracted. 'Yes,' I replied because it was obvious that's what I was supposed to say. But I didn't understand. I didn't understand anything that was happening right now. How had it come to this? Why was I here under caution?

I wanted to ask. I wanted to know. And yet, at the same time I was afraid to.

* * *

'What did I tell you about being too chatty?' Mum gripped my hand as we walked along the hospital corridor towards the car park.

I winced, clutching my stomach as I struggled to keep up. 'I'm sorry, Mum. I only asked the doctor why I wasn't getting better.' It was a fair question. An important one.

'I told you, leave that to me. Keep quiet. Don't ask questions. Just tell them it hurts. Always tell them it hurts.'

Mum's voice echoed in my memory. She was right. Keeping quiet was always better. Safer.

The police couldn't have anything on me. They couldn't know.

No one knew.

Only Josh.

'This interview is being conducted by PC Smith and DC Collier from the Public Protection Unit,' PC Smith continued.

Public Protection Unit.

His words repeated in my head, as my gaze darted back to her. She was one of them. The PPU.

I felt myself rocking back and forth in my chair. I knew I should stop it. I shouldn't let them see my reaction. But I couldn't.

I'd encountered the PPU before.

Why hadn't it occurred to me that PC Smith would connect the dots back to my past? I was known to them. There was history. Records. My life had been scrutinised and dissected.

Collier.

I suddenly realised what PC Smith had called her. The name was like nails screeching across a blackboard. Piercing and chilling, it sent vibrations through my body.

I knew her.

But worse still, she knew me.

30

THEN

'Do you want to talk about it?' Abhilash asked as he carried our coffees to a bench at the top of the cliff a few metres away from the busy café.

'About what?' I asked, forcing my tone to stay light, despite the sinking feeling in the pit of my stomach telling me that I already knew what he wanted to talk about.

'Josh.'

It was such a simple reply. But talking about Josh wasn't a simple conversation. Not if I was honest. Of course, I could stick with the script. Say how good things were. How much we loved each other. How happy he made me. It wasn't a lie. But it was only part of the story. A fragment of our time together.

The rest was messy. Complicated. Painful.

I sank down onto the bench. 'He's going through a tough time right now.'

'You don't have to defend him, you know. Not to me,' Abhilash said as he sat beside me and handed a coffee to me.

'I'm not. I'm just...'

'Defending him to yourself?'

'That's not fair. Josh isn't a bad guy. We have a good life together. He loves me.'

Abhilash nodded. 'I'm sure he does. But does he love you in a good way? A way that doesn't make you afraid of him? That doesn't cause you physical pain?'

'Sometimes that's what love is: when you feel it so strongly that it's overpowering.' Mum had taught me that. Love hurts when it's real.

Abhilash tipped his head to the left. 'But, Lauren, don't you see, that's not a healthy kind of love.'

Perhaps he was right. But it was all I had. All I'd ever had. 'You don't know him like I do. After everything that happened with Mum, he was there for me. It felt heroic. My very own Prince Charming coming to my rescue. At least, that's how I saw it.' I sighed. 'Josh saw it differently. He thought I'd shut him out. That I hadn't trusted him enough. That I should have confided in him. Turned to him for help. But I didn't know I needed help. Not from my own mother.'

Abhilash studied me, absorbing everything. 'Is that what went wrong between you two?'

'Maybe.' I frowned, trying to pinpoint the reason. The cause. 'It's as though he's spent the last eleven years trying to redeem himself. To be the hero he thinks he failed to be before.'

'It's an admirable idea,' Abhilash said. 'Except, he's not saving you. He's hurting you.'

'I guess that trying to be a hero is like trying to be perfect. Impossible. Every minor stumbling block seems like a humungous failure because he's set himself an impossible target. Sometimes that frustration boils over.'

'At you,' Abhilash said sadly.

'I think he still blames me. I shut him out. I made him fail. And every setback since, every problem, he views as a further sign that he is failing to live up to his own high expectations for himself.'

'And somehow he thinks that's your fault?'

'Maybe it is.'

'You don't really believe that, do you?'

I shrugged. The truth was that it was hard not to believe it. First Mum, then Josh. My love hadn't been enough for either of them. Not as it was. Not as I was. They needed more. They tried to teach me. To change me.

Abhilash placed his hand on my arm. 'I'm worried about you, Lauren.'

I stared at his hand as my heart raced at his touch.

What was I doing? Complaining about Josh to another guy. It wasn't right. It wasn't fair. Not to Josh and not even to Abhilash. None of this was his problem. I wasn't his problem.

'You don't need to worry about me,' I assured Abhilash, as I met his eyes. 'I'm fine. I have a good life with Josh. In fact, I should just be grateful and stop complaining. You have better things to do with your day than sit here listening to some stupid woman whine.'

'You're funny, smart and interesting. Even though you're stressed and feel bad about yourself. You aren't moaning. We're just talking. It's what friends do. They share their problems.'

'Problems,' I scoffed. 'I have my own business, a nice home and a long-term boyfriend, who will *hopefully* marry me someday. They are hardly problems.'

'Is that what success looks like to you? A decent job. A house. A husband.'

I stared at him blankly. 'What else is there?'

'Happiness,' Abhilash replied.

Happiness.

That *was* happiness, wasn't it? Love. Security. They were the things I craved. They made me happy.

And yet, for some reason as my gaze drifted back to Abhilash's hand on my arm, I couldn't help wondering if maybe I was missing something.

'If you dwell on regrets about the past and worry about the future, you're missing out on the present. The now. And that's the only thing we really have any control over. So live in the present.'

Was Abhilash right? Was I missing out on what mattered because I was so focused on making a perfect future that would outweigh the past?

'You carry this guilt with you for everyone that surrounds you. But the truth is, everyone has their own problems and we must all be adult enough to solve them ourselves or ask for help, not make them someone else's issue.'

I nibbled my fingernail. What he was saying made sense. And yet, something inside me still screamed at me that I had let Josh down. I had failed him.

'Josh's disappointment with his life, with himself, isn't your responsibility. It isn't your guilt to carry,' Abhilash urged.

'You don't understand,' I shook my head. Abhilash didn't know enough to judge Josh. To judge our relationship. He didn't know what Josh had done for me. What it had done to him.

I'd created the view that Abhilash held of Josh. One sided. Bad. But there was so much more. I searched for the words that would explain it. That would help him to see Josh more clearly. But then perhaps Abhilash's opinion of Josh didn't matter. Nor did his views on our relationship. At least they shouldn't.

He wasn't anyone to me. Just an independent third party who only knew tiny fragments about me and my life.

A jarring realisation struck me. Perhaps that was exactly why it did matter. Because he was independent. Because he could see what I couldn't. Or perhaps more accurately, what I wouldn't.

He was voicing the doubts that had been stirring under the surface of my own consciousness for a while. Doubts that I refused to listen to. Because everything I had hinged on those doubts being wrong.

They had the potential to throw my relationship with Josh, my entire life, into question. I wasn't ready to face that possibility.

Yet, by seeking out Abhilash, the one person who had any knowledge of the issues Josh and I were facing, perhaps some part of my brain, my being, was trying to tell me something. Perhaps, ready or not, those doubts wouldn't be quietened any longer.

'What if I'm wrong?' I voiced the question that had tormented me silently for years. 'I know Josh. The real Josh. This other side of him, it doesn't fit. It's hard to understand how he could change so much. I mean, maybe I imagine it. Maybe I overreact. Maybe I cause it. No one else ever sees that side of him. It must be something to do with me. My fault. My inadeq—'

'No.' Abhilash shook his head firmly. 'Just no.'

'He loves me,' I repeated.

'Then why does he treat you like someone he hates?'

'He doesn't.'

Abhilash studied me silently, his expression neutral as though he was waiting for me to hear the lie in my own words.

'He doesn't,' I urged, but my voice sounded less certain. There was a quiver to it that seemed to emanate from somewhere deep inside me. A doubt. A fear. 'He's always so upset afterwards. So desperate. So broken. How could I let him suffer like that? To hurt? Especially when I knew I could take that pain away. I could make it better. Make us better. I could fix it.'

'By forgiving him?'

'By loving him.' I let out a deep breath. 'It wasn't easy. Comforting him when my ribs ached or my lip bled. But I did it for us. I told him it was okay. That we were okay. It was a lie. I knew that. I knew that it wasn't okay. Not even close. But I also knew that it could be. It would be.'

'How did that even happen?' Abhilash shook his head in disbelief. 'How did it become about him? How he felt bad. How he needed comfort. He needed forgiveness. What about you? What about what you need?'

'I needed him.'

That was all there was to it. No matter how many excuses I made, how much blame I absorbed. There was only really one reason I stayed. I needed him. I needed that feeling of belonging. To him. To his family. I didn't want to be alone. Adrift. I needed connection. Stability. I needed him.

I frowned as I realised that Abhilash was nodding, a small smile curving his lips upwards.

'What?' I asked, bemused.

'Do you realise what you said?'

I stared at him blankly.

'You said needed, as in the past tense.'

My mind raced as I tried to recall what I'd said. Was he right? 'It must have been a slip of the tongue.'

'Are you sure about that?'

I hesitated. Was I sure? About anything?

Was it a mistake or was my subconscious trying to tell me something that I wasn't ready to accept?

Yet.

'You need to make a change, Lauren. You know the way that things are isn't working. It's time to do something different. I know it's scary—'

'I'm not a coward,' I bristled. How dare he assume that I was weak. Afraid.

'I know that. I know the kind of life you've lived. Or at least I know enough to know that not everyone could have overcome it the way you have. But that doesn't mean you're not stuck.'

'I'm not stuck,' I protested.

Was I?

Had I stayed with Josh to protect myself? Had I stayed in a bad situation because at least I knew how to handle that?

'Different means making a decision for yourself. Taking a chance. Risking failure. Risking being alone. So you stay where you are. You're better off there, right? Unhappy, but safe?'

I ground my toe into the soft dry sand, unable to meet Abhilash's eye. How did he do that? How did he express how I felt when I hadn't even realised it myself, let alone been able to put those emotions into words?

'Except, you're not even safe. Are you?'

He reached out and lifted my chin until our eyes met.

'No,' I whispered. 'I'm not.' My vision blurred as tears started to form in my eyes. Normally I would have held them back. Regained my composure. My act. But what for? Abhilash saw the real me through it all anyway. The only person I was fooling here was myself.

It was time that stopped.

I took a deep breath. 'I've never been safe.'

It felt strange to say those words aloud. To recognise my life for what it was, one dangerous trap after another.

They'd both loved me. They'd both hurt me.

And I'd let them.

'I've never been alone before.'

Abhilash studied me. 'Yes, you have. You might have been surrounded by other people – people telling you they cared, that they would protect you – but the truth is, really you were always on your own.'

31

NOW

'Ms Taylor, are you all right?' I heard DC Collier's voice, but it was distorted and distant as the walls closed in around me. 'Lauren?'

The informality of her using my first name broke through the haze. It's what she used to call me. I'd been too young for her to call me Ms Taylor back then.

'Do you remember me, Lauren?' Her tone was soft and gentle. Just like before.

* * *

'Are you all right, Lauren?'

I nodded silently, while inside every fibre of my being screamed no, I wasn't all right. How could I be?

I stared at PC Collier. My world had crumbled since the last time I'd been here. I wanted to blame this place. To blame her. But the reality was the police weren't at fault for any of it. All they and Social Services had done was to expose the truth. Not that any of them knew anything for sure. At least, nothing they could prove.

But it had been enough.

Enough to destroy my life. To destroy my family.

Before them I'd had a home. A mother. Now I had neither.

'Can you tell me how things had been at home since we talked six months ago?'

I glanced at the video camera in the corner of the room, conscious that every reply, every movement, was being recorded. There had been no camera last time I was here. It was a sign that things had changed.

Mum had been alive then.

'It's standard practice for an ABE interview regarding a death,' PC Collier said, following my gaze to the camera.

'ABE?' I asked, as my mind raced, desperately trying to decipher its meaning. And more importantly, what that meant for me...

'Sorry,' PC Collier said. 'It stands for achieving best evidence. It's just so we have a more formal record.'

I nodded. It made sense. But I still didn't like it.

'Things at home were...?' PC Collier prompted, returning to her unanswered question.

'Fine,' I lied.

PC Collier angled her head to one side. 'You didn't notice any changes? Everything at home felt the same as it always had?'

I hesitated. She didn't believe me. I couldn't blame her. We wouldn't be back here if everything had really been fine after our last conversation.

But then again, if everything had been fine, we would never have met in the first place.

'You carried on with your medication, the same as before?' PC Collier prompted.

I nodded. 'Yes, Mum gave it me every day, just like normal, but...' I twisted my hands together.

'Go on, it's okay,' Mrs Carter said softly beside me.

'I felt good. I felt well. I thought the medication was finally work-

ing. But when I went for my next appointment with the doctor, he said I didn't even need it any more.'

'So, you've stopped taking the pills?'

'He reduced the dosage at first, but yes, now I've stopped taking them completely.'

'And how do you feel?'

'Great, I don't have any stomach pain at all.' I was conscious of how flat my voice was. I felt good and yet I sounded miserable. The two didn't coincide.

'You don't seem very happy about that.'

'I am. It's just,' I scrunched my nose up, 'it doesn't make sense, does it? I was so sick for years. I tried so many medications to make me better and nothing worked. And yet now, suddenly, I'm like, totally fine. And I don't need any medication at all.' I picked at the edge of the wooden tabletop. 'I know I'm just a kid, but even I know that illnesses don't work like that. You don't get better instantaneously without surgery or medication. You don't just wake up one day and be fixed. Not unless...'

'Unless what, Lauren?'

'Unless you were never really ill to begin with.'

PC Collier said nothing. She didn't need to. I could read her expression as clearly as if she had spoken aloud.

'You thought it was Mum, didn't you? That she was doing something to my medication?' The questions had tormented me for months. Constantly circling in my brain. Making me wonder. Making me doubt.

'I had my suspicions, yes. It was possible that your mother suffered with something called Fabricated or Induced Illness. FII for short. It's a very rare form of child abuse, where a parent, typically a mother, causes or exaggerates her child's illness to get attention.'

'You suspected her of that, but you left me there alone?' I stared at her, my eyes wide. 'In that house. With her.'

'Without any evidence, I couldn't get you removed from your moth-

er's care. Having the safeguarding team make unannounced visits, putting a flag on your address so the PPU would be notified of any 999 calls, and contacting all the hospitals in the region to be on alert, was all I could do to protect you. You were never alone, Lauren.'

I nodded slowly, cocooned in a sense of calm. She hadn't abandoned me. Neither had the doctors. They were still trying to help. Quietly. Subtly. But they were there in the background. Protecting me.

'It worked,' I said. 'The visits,' I clarified when PC Collier frowned. 'Mum hated them. She was really indignant about having strangers barging into her home, checking up on her, judging her parenting abilities.' I took a deep breath. 'I felt really guilty for that at first.'

'Why?'

I stared at the table, studying the grain of the wood. 'It was my fault. If I hadn't asked the doctor why I couldn't have the same medication at home as I did in the hospital, your investigation would never have started.'

'Yes, it would.'

My head jolted up, and I stared at her.

'Questions had already been raised. I'd already become involved in your case before your last admission to hospital. I was investigating your previous addresses. Talking to your doctors there. Your neighbours.'

'You were?' The investigation had been bigger than I'd realised. Unless...

I bit my lip. What if PC Collier was just telling me that to make me feel better? To ease my guilt? She was nice. She wouldn't want me to blame myself for what had happened. But it could still have been my fault.

PC Collier's brow creased as she looked deep in concentration. 'Why "at first"?'

'Huh?'

'You said you felt guilty for that "at first". Why only at first?'

I swallowed. 'W-well, I mean, I f-felt guilty until I got better.' I cursed my stutter. 'When the doctors stopped my medication and I was okay, I started to have doubts about her. About what she had done.'

'And how did you feel then?'

I held my body rigid. Conscious that every movement, every reaction, every word was being recorded.

'I was confused. I couldn't understand how she could do that to me. I kept thinking I must be wrong. It wasn't possible. I was a bad person, a bad daughter, to even contemplate it for a second. But as impossible as it was, there didn't seem to be any other explanation.'

'Did that make you angry? Your own mother may have poisoned you, and not just once, but over a sustained period.'

Angry.

The word circled in my brain.

I'd been beyond angry. I'd hated her. I'd wanted to punish her. To make her suffer like she had made me. I'd wanted her to feel that same agonising burning pain in the pit of her stomach. To know what it was like to live with the fear that she wasn't going to get better. That she was going to die.

I shook my head. 'I was scared.' It wasn't a lie. I had been scared.

Of her.

And for her.

* * *

I nodded, unable to speak. It was pointless to deny that I recognised her. My reaction had already betrayed me.

I cursed myself silently as I dug my fingers into the soft flesh of my thigh, out of sight beneath the table. I was better than that. More careful. More concealed.

'It's good to see you again,' she continued. 'It's not often that I get to see the children I have worked with when they are grown up. See how their lives have gone. What they have become.'

She was the same. Warm. Friendly. The kind of person that was easy to talk to. Easy to open up to.

It's what made her so dangerous.

She was waiting for a response. But what was the right one? The expected one? I was sitting in a police station. My boyfriend was missing. It wasn't the right time to assure her how well things had turned out or how much my life had changed.

Besides, I wasn't sure that it had.

32

THEN

'I checked out your business online,' Abhilash said as we carried our coffee and cakes down the chine towards the beach. It was our ritual now: coffee at the beach at least once a week.

I swung my head round to the right and I stared at him. 'You did? Why?'

Abhilash chuckled. 'I guess I was curious about it. About you.'

I turned away as heat crept into my cheeks.

'It's incredible.'

I scoffed. 'It's nothing. Just a hobby.'

Abhilash rested his hand on my arm and stopped walking. I paused beside him, staring at his hand on my skin.

'Don't do that.'

My gaze jolted up to meet his. 'Do what?' I asked, praying that my voice sounded more innocent than I felt.

'Don't dismiss your hard work as irrelevant. You've built your own business. A successful one. That's not nothing. That's something incredible. And you should feel proud of yourself and all you have accomplished.'

I was proud.

But I was proud silently.

Privately.

A little voice in my head told me that I'd done something good. Something right. No matter how many times Josh criticised me, that little voice still persisted. It wouldn't be drowned out.

But in its certainty that what I was doing was good and worthwhile, that little voice carried with it one huge implication: for me to be right, that meant Josh was wrong.

It was the only time I'd doubted him. The only time I'd questioned his opinion. I never voiced my concerns. Never spoke them aloud. Until now. And yet, even that silent thought felt like a betrayal. Josh deserved better from me.

Abhilash nodded towards the breaker, and we perched against the wood. 'If it's so unimportant then why do it? Why not just close it down and admit defeat?'

His question startled me. 'I-I don't have the skills to do anything else,' I stuttered over my words. He sounded like Josh. Harsh. Critical. My heart sank. I should have known better. I should have known that he wouldn't be any different.

'So don't do anything. You said Josh doesn't expect you to work.'

'But I like it.' My voice was so tiny and weak, almost as though I was afraid to be heard. Afraid to admit that I enjoyed my work. That I liked what I did.

'Why?'

I shrugged. 'I don't know.' I felt bullied. Pressured. Why was he doing this?

'Yes, you do. Why?' Abhilash repeated.

'Because it's mine.' It felt like a betrayal to Josh. I wanted something separate. Something private. Something mine. Just mine.

I frowned. Was that why I hadn't quit? Josh's disapproval had always been enough to dissuade me of things before. His approval was everything. He was my compass. He kept me on course. And yet for the first time his disapproval wasn't enough to stop me.

Abhilash smiled. 'See, it is important.'

I stared at him. His tone was so different now. Lighter. Friendlier. Normal. Like he usually was.

'W-what...?' What had just happened?

'I'm sorry if I was being tough, but I wanted you to realise that your business matters. You matter.'

I blinked. I was wrong. Abhilash wasn't like Josh. He'd been doing it on purpose, trying to provoke me, to make me face the truth.

'Don't let anyone make you doubt yourself,' Abhilash said. 'Just because Josh doesn't have faith in your abilities, that shouldn't hold you back. You need to stop letting other people's words have such power over you. You take them on board as though they determine your worth. But you shouldn't let anyone have that power. Only you.'

I shook my head. 'It's not that easy to ignore everyone else's opinions.' I took a swig of coffee from the paper cup.

'Fine, then listen to mine. You're amazing.'

I spluttered on my coffee.

'I'm serious,' Abhilash objected. 'Even though you've had all these struggles in your life, you've overcome them all and achieved success.'

A wave of guilt washed over me. He was right. I had a successful business. A nice home. A good life. I had so many things to be grateful for. And yet, I felt sorry for myself. Despite everything I had, I still wasn't satisfied.

But the truth was it was only part of the story. I hadn't overcome everything...

33

NOW

'I was surprised when PC Smith contacted me,' DC Collier said. 'I was fairly new to the PPU when we met before. Yours was one of my first cases. Certainly the most complex one I had worked at that point. I guess that's why it stayed with me all these years. I never forgot. But then, I don't suppose you did either.'

I shook my head. To her it had just been a case. To me it had been my life.

'You're still with the PPU, then?' I asked, attempting to steer the conversation onto safer ground.

'Yes. It's not a role that is suited to everyone. Some find it too difficult, too emotionally draining to stay too long. But others, like myself, can't bear to leave. Too many people need our help. I'm a DC now, so I guess must be doing something right.' She smiled, and I could sense the pride she took in that promotion. Not in the job title, but in the sense that it was a sign she was making a difference.

'Not that every case ends well.' Her smile faded. 'Or some-times fully solved,' she added as her eyes met mine.

I was conscious of my heart beating. It felt stronger. Faster. I fought to maintain the appearance of calm whilst inside panic bubbled in the pit of my stomach.

There had always been a lingering question over Mum's death, at least to DC Collier. She'd been careful. Subtle. But I could sense it. The doubt. The suspicion.

* * *

'How was your relationship with your mum in the days before she died?' PC Collier asked.

I kept my gaze fixed on her, conscious that I shouldn't keep looking at the camera in the corner of the room. It might arouse suspicion. 'Quiet,' I replied. 'I had so many questions about my illness, but I was too afraid to ask them. Part of me couldn't bear to make that accusation out loud, especially to her. And another part was scared that if I did, she might confirm it. Maybe not with her words, but maybe her actions would give her away. Maybe I might actually be right.'

'So what did you do?'

'Nothing.'

'You were afraid that your mother had been poisoning you, and you decided to do nothing?'

'There was nothing for me to do. Josh was handling everything.'

'Josh?' Mrs Carter exclaimed beside me.

'He was as scared as I was about me staying in that house with her. Maybe even more so. He was disappointed in me that I hadn't told him what was happening. That I hadn't let him fix it earlier. That I hadn't let him help me.' I shook my head. 'The thing is, I didn't know I needed help earlier. I wasn't even entirely sure that I needed it then. Not 100 per cent.'

'And how exactly did Josh decide to help you?' PC Collier asked.

'By rescuing me. From her.'

* * *

'Given our history, I wanted to be involved in Josh Carter's missing person case. It felt important for me to be here.' DC Collier said, pulling me back to the present.

I didn't respond. What could I say? It wasn't as though I was happy to see her. Her presence in Josh's case wouldn't help. It would just muddy the waters. All she wanted to do was dig up things that had been left to settle undisturbed for eleven years.

'You and Josh have been together a long time,' she said. 'If I remember correctly, you had been dating for about a year when everything with your mum came to a head.'

I nodded.

DC Collier let out a breath. 'That's a long time to be together. Especially for a school romance. I guess that everything you went through together brought you closer.'

I knew what she was hinting at. I was right: she wasn't here to solve Josh's missing person's case. Or at least not just his case.

She was here for answers to Mum's death too.

'How is your relationship? Are you two still as close as you were back then?'

I hesitated. If I told them that Josh and I had broken up, they would want to know why. That would lead to more questions. More suspicion.

'We saw the bags of Josh's clothes in your hall,' PC Smith said.

I blinked. I'd been so focused on DC Collier, I'd almost forgotten he was there. In my surprise, it took a second before the meaning of his statement registered in my brain.

'You've been in my house?'

'Yours and Josh's house, yes. His parents let us in on Sunday afternoon when you were in hospital,' PC Smith clarified.

'They had no right to do that.'

'Checking the home of a missing person is one of the first things that we do, especially when there is a concern for their safety.'

'But Josh hasn't been missing that long yet.' I cursed the 'yet' I'd added on the end of my sentence. Did that make it sound like I didn't expect him to be found?

'We needed to make sure that the coastguard weren't wasting their time if he had simply made it home.'

'Oh,' my shoulders sagged. 'That makes sense.' It did. At least from their perspective. And yet, it still felt wrong. It was my home and they had been snooping around. Searching through our belongings. Our lives.

I felt violated.

Seen.

And it was all for nothing. They were looking for him in the wrong places.

'Does that mean that Josh's parents saw the bags of his stuff too?'

PC Smith frowned. Perhaps from his perspective it was a strange issue to focus on. But to me it mattered.

They didn't need to know that Josh and I had broken up. Not yet. And certainly not like this.

These things needed to be handled carefully. With the right timing. The right message. It was the only way that I stood a chance of remaining part of the family. I might only be on the outskirts, but that didn't mean I was prepared to give it up. It was better than the alternative.

It was better than nothing.

34

THEN

I lowered my eyes and stared at the cast on my right wrist as thoughts of Josh raced in my head.

'Lauren?' I looked up and saw Abhilash's eyes darting back and forth from my face to my hands. 'Does your business have something to do with what happened to your wrist?'

'I, er...' I tried to shrug but my shoulders felt heavy. I inhaled deeply. I'd already told Abhilash it was Josh who had caused my injury. It was only natural that he would be curious about the details.

I swirled remaining coffee in the bottom of my cup. 'Josh doesn't approve.'

'And how does he show that disapproval, Lauren?'

'Little ways. At first.'

'Go on,' Abhilash said softly.

'He told me I was wasting my time. He wanted me to give up. I thought it was because it was such a crazy idea; I thought he was trying to protect me from failing. Just like he always did.' My gaze met Abhilash's. 'Now I wonder if really he was just trying to stop me from succeeding.'

'Just like he's always done?' Abhilash asked and I turned away.

'It's as though I've been living my life through a mirror. Everything's flipped around. People are the opposite of who they claimed to be. Good is bad. Love is...'

'Hate?' Abhilash finished for me.

'Hmm,' I shook my head. 'I'm not sure if it's hate. Not exactly. I think Josh loves me. Just like Mum did too. But that kind of love is turbulent and destabilising. When it's good, it's intense and powerful. It makes you feel like you can overcome anything. Nothing is impossible. It's just that sometimes you have to put up with a bit of pain first.'

'There's one thing I'm curious about: why didn't you shut your business down when Josh disapproved?'

I tipped my head to the right as I contemplated his question. 'I've wondered that myself. Many times. To be honest, I'm not sure. I thought about it. I knew it would be easier. Safer. But...' I shrugged. 'Something always stopped me.'

'Do you think you saw it as a way out? If you made it a success, you'd have your own money? Your freedom?'

'I'm not sure I was thinking that far ahead. I just wanted to make what we had work. I wanted to be better. To be stronger. Perhaps the business was my way of doing that. If I could make just one thing in my life work...'

'Then there was hope for everything else?'

'Perhaps.' I shrugged. 'Or perhaps it was just stubborn pride. I wanted to know if I was smart enough. Capable enough to put my degree to use even after all these years.'

'I think you got your proof.'

'Yeah, I think I did.'

I shifted my right arm awkwardly in its sling. 'I thought it would prove it to Josh too. I thought that he would be excited when he realised how well the business was doing. How well *I* was doing. I thought he'd be impressed. Proud.'

'But he wasn't?'

'I'd told him I'd been adding to our savings, but I guess he hadn't paid attention. Or maybe he just thought it would be trivial amounts. When he realised...' I jutted out my bottom lip and blew a long deep breath causing my fringe to flutter. 'He was definitely not proud of me, that's for sure.'

'That's so unfair.'

I shook my head. 'It's my fault. I should have thought about how it would make him feel. He'd been working hard for years to provide for us and then I come along thinking that a few months of my little hobby business is somehow equivalent and made him feel as though what he was doing wasn't good enough.'

'But it's not as though you were saying that, were you?'

'Well, no, but that's the message I was sending him.'

'According to who?'

'Josh,' I bit back the 'obviously' that threatened to spill from my lips. It went without saying it was Josh, didn't it? After all, he was the one who my thoughtlessness had offended.

'You do realise how crazy that is, right?'

I blinked. 'Crazy?'

'You've created your own successful business. From scratch. All by yourself. And you used that to contribute to your shared savings, so you could *both* benefit. Most people would see that not just as a huge achievement, but also a supportive thing to do for your relationship as a couple.'

'But I undermined him.'

'How?'

Why was Abhilash asking so many questions? Why couldn't he just understand? I did. I knew what I'd done was bad.

Doubt niggled at me somewhere deep inside.

Wasn't it?

'By being good at something?'

I shook my head. 'No, you're missing the point.'

'Am I?' Abhilash tipped his head to the right. 'Or maybe that *is* the point.'

'No, Josh doesn't resent me for being good at my job, he resents me for—' I clamped my mouth closed.

'Resents you for what?'

'Nothing. I don't know why I said that.'

'Yes, you do. What does Josh resent you for?'

My lips parted and then closed again silently. I was wrong. Of course, I was wrong. I *had* to be wrong. But sometimes it felt as though Josh resented me for... 'Everything,' I whispered.

I waited for Abhilash to correct me and tell me I was being foolish. Josh was my boyfriend. He loved me. He didn't resent me for anything.

I felt Abhilash's hand rest on top of my mine. 'I'm sorry,' he said softly.

I realised then that he wasn't going to correct me. He couldn't.

There was nothing for him to correct.

35

NOW

'Lauren?' DC Collier prompted. 'What's the situation between you and Josh?'

I took a deep breath. There was no way they were going to let me distract them from their questions. And pretending everything was fine between us was no longer an option. Not now they'd seen Josh's stuff in bags. I had to give them an explanation.

'We broke up.' I was suddenly conscious of my expression and body language. What did they reveal?

I was supposed to be sad after a breakup, wasn't I? Did I seem sad?

'When?' PC Smith asked.

'Saturday evening.'

'The evening before Josh disappeared?' PC Smith asked as he looked at DC Collier.

I nodded, even though neither of them really needed an answer.

I knew what they were thinking. The timing was suspicious. Could our breakup have been a motive to want to harm Josh? Or was I lying about breaking up with him simply to provide an excuse for his bags being packed if something sinister had happened to him?

It wasn't ideal for them to find out like this.

But then again, nothing about this situation was ideal.

'And who instigated this breakup?' PC Smith asked.

'I did.' I steeled myself for their next question.

'Why?' I stared at PC Smith. Even though I'd been expecting it, his question still made my chest tighten. 'Why after all these years together did you break up now?'

'We wanted different things from the relationship,' I said cautiously. It was true. We did. Very different things.

'Okay,' DC Collier said. 'So, talk me through Sunday morning.'

I blinked. The shift in the direction of questioning threw me. I'd expected them to be more intrusive. Digging into the minutia of our relationship. What different things? Why now? Why not before?

I was glad they hadn't asked. Hadn't pried. Mostly because I wasn't sure I could answer. Not fully.

And certainly not without looking more guilty.

Yet the fact that they hadn't also felt troubling. It was too easy.

And I knew, nothing was ever easy.

I licked my lips. 'It's like I already told PC Smith at the hospital. I took the jet-ski out just like normal.'

'Just like normal?' PC Smith asked.

'Yes. Well, no,' I stammered. I scolded myself silently. They had barely started with their questions, and I'd already slipped up. 'Josh and I usually go together.'

'But not on that occasion?'

His face was neutral, but there was something about the tone of his voice that oozed disbelief.

I swallowed. 'No.'

'So the morning after you broke up with your boyfriend you decided to go for a ride?'

'It helps to clear my head.'

'Did you have his permission?'

I blinked.

'The jet-ski was purchased by Josh. He is the registered owner. You claim you and he had broken up and yet you took his jet-ski out without him.'

'No, it's not like that.'

'So, Josh gave you his permission?'

'It's mine. I mean, he bought the jet-ski with *my* money.'

PC Smith arched an eyebrow. '*Your* money?'

'Well, he paid from our joint account, but it was money I'd earned from my business.'

'Did Josh often make such extravagant purchases with *your* money?'

'No, this was...' My voice trailed away.

'This was what?' PC Smith asked, leaning forwards.

'Different.'

I'd thought we would use the savings to prepare for starting our family. Instead, Josh had gone out and bought something expensive and impulsive. Perhaps it was intended to be a peace offering. An extravagant gift we could use together to make amends for his initial reaction. Or perhaps it was a way of reminding me that my job, just like his purchase, was unnecessary and frivolous.

'So you view it as yours?'

'We agreed. He's going to sign it over to me.'

'This was part of the arrangement when you broke up?'

I nodded.

'What about the house? As it's Josh's stuff in bags and not yours, it seems you plan on staying there.'

'That's mine too. We used my inheritance from Mum to buy it.' As soon as I said it, I regretted it. I'd brought Mum back into the forefront of their minds again. Her death. My inheritance.

'Josh doesn't seem to be left with very much that's his...'

PC Smith's statement hung in the air. I knew what he was doing. He was trying to prompt a reaction. To throw me off balance. Put me on the defensive. It was a game to him. Part of the challenge.

But it was a game I was far too familiar with.

I was good at judging the timing. Of knowing when to speak and when to stay quiet. Sometimes I got it wrong. It wasn't an exact science. People were always unpredictable. Even people I knew well.

'Of course, if Josh chose not to go along with this *arrangement* of yours, it would be you that lost out, wouldn't it?' PC Smith prompted.

'Tell me more about this business of yours,' DC Collier chimed in. 'It's quite an impressive accomplishment to be earning enough for extravagances like a jet-ski.'

'It's just something I run from home. A social media marketing consultancy.'

'We spoke to Josh's parents,' DC Collier said. 'Your business is new. It's only been running for a little over a year.'

'Almost two,' I corrected.

DC Collier nodded in acknowledgement. 'Even so, the Carters seemed to think it was more of a hobby than a proper business.'

I recoiled at his words. *A hobby*. The Carters thought of my business in that way too. Just like Josh. I was trying so hard to be part of their lives, their world, and yet perhaps to them I was as trivial and unimportant as my little business.

'You weren't even working before that,' PC Smith continued,

seemingly oblivious to my reaction. 'Josh was supporting you both. And according to them, he still was.'

'That's true,' I conceded. 'Josh paid the monthly bills.'

The corners of PC Smith's mouth twitched. He thought they had me. He thought they'd won.

'I didn't really talk much about my business. I mean it was years since I graduated, and I didn't work afterwards. It felt like a huge gamble. I was nervous that it might fail. If no one knew about it, then at least I could fail in private.'

DC Collier nodded. 'I can understand that.'

She was playing the role of good cop. Friendly. Sympathetic. Understanding. She was using our history to build a rapport. She wanted to establish a sense of trust. Where I would feel safe enough to let my guard down.

But her plan was flawed.

I never felt safe.

I'd never *been* safe.

'Why didn't you get a job after university? You're a smart young woman. No children. Not much of a social life. And no outside interests or hobbies. At least as far as the Carters know.'

The Carters.

They were pitting them against me. Pumping them for information about me when I wasn't around, wasn't even conscious, to defend myself.

They were making them into a single entity. *The Carters.* An elite group which I had never fully belonged to.

I gritted my teeth as resentment intensified inside me.

Because of Josh.

'With the house paid for and Josh working full time, there wasn't really a need for me to work as well.' I was surprised how level and calm my voice sounded. I was rational and logical. At least on the surface.

'Weren't you bored?' DC Collier asked.

Very. The answer resounded silently in my head. But boredom wasn't the worst part.

'And lonely?' She added.

I fought to keep my expression neutral. It felt as though she had read my mind. My feelings. My loneliness.

'Was that why you had so many visits to the hospital?'

I struggled for air. It had only been a matter of time before that question would be asked. I didn't know the form it would take. But I knew it would come.

It always did.

And yet, somehow, I was always unprepared for it.

36

THEN

'I haven't been up here for ages,' Abhilash said as we stood at the top of Hengistbury Head, looking across at the Isle of Wight.

'Can you see the polar bear?' I asked him, and he swung his head to the right to stare at me, a bewildered expression on his face.

'Did you just say the "polar bear"?'

I laughed. 'How long have you lived in Bournemouth?'

'A couple of years.'

'And you've never noticed the polar bear?'

He was still staring at me, clearly doubting my sanity at this point. 'No, I think I would remember something like that.'

I pointed at the Isle of Wight. 'Can you see the white chalk exposed on the side of the cliffs?'

'Y-e-ah...' Abhilash replied, still dubious.

'That's the polar bear.'

'So you weren't talking about a real one then?'

Now it was my turn to stare at him, stunned. 'I know this is England, and the winters can get cold, but not that cold.'

Abhilash gave me a playful shove. 'Hey, you can't blame me. You're the one who randomly started talking about polar bears.'

I rolled my eyes. 'Tell me you can at least see it now?'

He frowned as he studied the cliffs in the distance.

'Look,' I pointed to the top left of the cliffs. 'His head is over there, and you can see his legs. Kind of.' I scrunched my nose. 'You have to sort of squint a bit I guess from this angle. He's much clearer from—'

My words evaporated as Abhilash caught hold of my left hand as I was pointing. He guided it down, his fingers entwining with mine. I stared at him, not entirely sure what was happening. We were just talking about the polar bear and now, somehow, we were holding hands, staring into each other's eyes.

I'd been disappointed when he'd arrived each week empty handed, without any flowers. It was silly of me to expect them. To hope for them. We both knew I couldn't take them home. But he'd talked about buying me a plant; I guess that was all it had been though: talk.

I thought it was a sign that he was shifting our relationship back into the friend zone. Not that we had ever really left it. Its definition had just become a little blurry for a while. That was all. Flowers had a way of doing that. Of making something seem like more than it was.

But now... I stared deep into his eyes, trying to read his thoughts, his feelings. What was I to him?

And perhaps, more importantly, what was he to me?

It felt as though everything around us froze. We were all that existed. We drew closer to each other, and then his lips were against mine. Soft. Tender. I closed my eyes, lost in the moment. All I knew was that I didn't want it to end.

But it did.

We parted as slowly as we had met as our gazes reconnected.

We'd kissed.

Had he initiated it? Or had I? I shook my head as reality seeped back into my thoughts. Either way, it didn't matter. It was still wrong.

'We can't do this.'

'Why not?'

'I have a boyfriend.' My voice rose slightly at the end, making my statement sound more like a question.

'Do you?' Abhilash asked.

I nodded. 'You know I do. Josh.' I thought saying his name would make it feel more absolute.

It didn't.

I glanced down at our hands aware that we were still connected. Still holding on.

What was it about him? What drew me to him like a moth to a flame? It was bad for me. Dangerous. I had a boyfriend. One I loved. One I would lose if he saw me here with another man. My whole world could burn to the ground if I got caught. And yet, I was still here, mesmerised by the glow of the flame.

'You mean the guy that hits you? The guy that puts you in hospital?'

I pulled my hand free. 'He's not always like that.'

'Okay,' Abhilash turned away and leaned on the wooden railing. 'Tell me what he's like when he isn't hurting you. Tell me how amazing he is that all the bad stuff becomes irrelevant.'

'He...' Words failed me.

I wanted to tell him stories of the sweet, kind, caring man Josh was. But the memories of that man were so distant, so faded that I could barely even remember them.

He had been attentive and thoughtful once, though. I knew he had. It's what had drawn me to him. I'd thought it would always be like that. Warm. Safe. Exciting. But that was the fantasy.

Reality wasn't like that. Things weren't always good. Couples weren't always completely in sync.

Relationships took work. Give and take. Ours wasn't perfect. But no-one's was. Not really.

My career was based on helping businesses put on a show for the outside world. To highlight their admirable qualities and downplay the negatives. The internet had exaggerated it to a whole new level, but it was no different to what we did in real life too. Put on makeup to hide the tear stains before going out of the house. Tell everyone that we're fine even when we're not. Keep our emotions in check when we're around other people, until we can get home and scream, yell, or cry. We all do what gets us through. It's an act. Ours was no different to anyone else's.

'At least tell me why you love him.'

'Because he's always there.'

'That's your reason?'

I nodded slowly. 'No matter how bad things get, no matter what craziness happens in our lives, he's always there. He never leaves me. Never abandons me.'

Abhilash shook his head. 'Just because he's physically present, it doesn't mean he hasn't abandoned you.'

Fast-paced music emanated from the phone in Abhilash's pocket. I stepped away as he reached for it, allowing him space to take his call.

'Where are you going?' Abhilash asked, his voice etched in surprise as he rejected the call and the music ceased.

'Don't you need to answer that?'

He gave me a lopsided grin. 'Not right now; I'm with you.'

My heart felt like it skipped a beat. He'd hung up for me. I had his attention. Undivided. Focused. 'But it could be important.'

Abhilash shrugged, 'It was my brother. I can call him back later.'

It was the first time he'd mentioned a brother. We'd been so focused on my family and my relationships that we hadn't talked very much about his. 'Do you have a big family?' I asked as I leaned against the railing.

'My parents, an older brother and lots of aunts, uncles and cousins.'

'That must be nice,' I heard the envious tone in my voice. A big family meant you always had someone. You would never be alone. Never be abandoned.

'It's loud. Chaotic. And amazing,' Abhilash said with a wide grin. He scrolled through photos on his phone until he found the one he was searching for. 'This is my family,' he announced proudly, as he angled the screen towards me. 'We took this photo on their last visit here.'

I studied the people that were staring back at me. I could see the likeness between Abhilash and his brother. They both had their father's features. I felt a familiar ache in my chest as I wondered if I shared anything with my own dad. His eyes? His smile?

'My brother and I are incredibly close. We talk every day, despite the physical distance.'

'What do you talk about?' I asked cautiously.

'Everything,' Abhilash replied. 'Well, almost everything.'

I nodded. There was a caveat. *I* was the caveat. The thing that wasn't discussed. No one knew about me. But then, no one in my life really knew about him either.

Perhaps it was part of what made us special. What we had was just for us. Private. Safe.

Other people had a way of interfering. Of messing things up. It was better this way.

Just us.

'It's a lovely photo,' I told him earnestly. 'Your parents look so happy. So proud.'

He nodded. 'They are. They were excited to be here, and it was so good to see them. I miss them a lot.' His gaze drifted to the screen and he looked at his parents affectionately. 'I can't wait to see them again soon.'

Soon.

That word made my stomach churn. It held implications. Ones I wasn't ready to face. Not yet. I needed more time.

We needed more time.

I'd noticed the way his eyes lit up as he talked about his family. He loved them so much that he would do anything for them. That kind of love was special and rare. But it was also dangerous.

He just hadn't realised it yet.

* * *

It was great to see you again today.

I smiled as I read Abhilash's message as I sat on the sofa in my living room. I tucked my feet underneath me and snuggled against the cushions.

You too.

Every day I know you a little more.

I winced.

I'm not sure that's a good thing. You're getting to know more of my problems. Usually that's when most people run away.

I'm not most people.

I smiled.

No, I guess you're not.

I might not be able to take you lifelong with me, but I'll never run away from you. I'll never abandon you.

I knew what he meant. I knew why he might not be able to take me with him for life. What obstacles stood in our way. *Who* stood in our way.

But I also knew that was why he needed me so much. Because I could see what he couldn't. I could see those obstacles for what they really were.

Something to be overcome.

My smile grew bigger. His words gave me hope. He wouldn't abandon me. And yet, at the same time, nerves churned in my stomach.

Perhaps he should.

37

NOW

'I know what you're thinking,' I said bluntly. 'And you're wrong.'

'What am I thinking, Lauren?'

I hesitated. Perhaps it wasn't the wisest move to call her out into the open. DC Collier's questions had been subtle and gentle, but their meaning was obvious. Now though, she had put me on the spot. Made me be the one to explain.

She was smart.

Maybe too smart.

'You think that I'm like Mum. That I seek out attention from doctors. You think that because she suffered with FII, I might do too.'

'It's a possibility, isn't it?' DC Collier asked, clearly already aware that it was.

She wasn't alone. I knew the risks too. The psychologist I'd seen after Mum's death had explained them to me. They'd been worried. No, not just worried. Scared. Given what I'd been through and the way that Mum died, they monitored me closely. Stuff like that changes you. It would have been impossible for it not to. Not that there was any proof of what Mum had done. No proof that she even had Fabricated or Induced Illness. Not for sure. She didn't leave a nice neat little trail for the police to follow to determine her guilt. Not even in death.

But there was enough suspicion.

They knew.

And so did I.

'Do you suffer with FII?'

I snorted at the bluntness of her question. 'Why bother asking the question when we all know you won't believe the answer?'

'Why wouldn't I believe you?' DC Collier asked, and I realised my error.

I'd been arrogant and hostile. And it had come back to bite me.

Why shouldn't she believe me? If I was telling the truth...

'It's the typical assumption, given Mum's history,' I said quickly. 'It's impossible for me to disprove. All I can do is deny it. But we both know that's exactly what she would do too. What she *did* do.'

'Yes,' DC Collier said slowly. 'It is a tricky one, isn't it?' She tapped her pen on her notepad as she seemed lost in thought.

The action was so simple and yet such a poignant reminder.

PC Collier tapped her pen against her notepad. I'd thrown her by mentioning Josh. He hadn't factored into her equation.

Until now.

'As the days passed, Mum's indignation at all the visits seemed to fade into sadness,' I said, skipping over my mention of Josh.

Now wasn't the time to elaborate. Everything needed to be handled the right way. In the right order. Plant a seed of doubt and move on. I tried not to smile. Mum had taught me well.

'She even went to the doctor herself,' I continued. 'He prescribed anti-depressants. I think she'd had them before too, when I was much younger.'

PC Collier nodded. 'Yes, I've reviewed your mum's medical notes. She had several bouts of depression over the last fourteen years.'

'Fourteen years?' My eyes widened. I hadn't anticipated that. I thought I'd figured it all out. But there were still pieces I didn't know. Still secrets Mum had kept. I ran my fingers through my hair as I realised the significance of this revelation. 'I'm fifteen.'

'We don't know that there's any correlation,' PC Collier assured me, instantly realising what I was thinking.

I scoffed. The timing was too coincidental for my presence not to have at least been a factor. Even if I wasn't the cause directly, I was the reason she was so alone. Why she had no one else.

I'd deprived her of attention. Of love. Perhaps it made sense that she would use me to try and recapture a tiny fragment of what she had lost because of me.

'How did she seem the day that she died?'

I blinked as PC Collier's question disrupted my thoughts.

Desperate. The words sprang into my head, but I gritted my teeth, preventing myself from saying it aloud.

It was the wrong answer.

Everything needed to have been normal. Nothing to arouse suspicion.

'Quiet,' I said. It wasn't a lie. Everything in that house had become quiet. We moved through the days barely speaking.

The silence was almost worse that everything that had come before. Mum had cared then. She'd talked to me. Hugged me. Paid attention to me.

And then, suddenly, nothing.

I really was alone.

* * *

'I guess the *simple* solution, if you want us to believe that you didn't harm yourself, would be for you to explain how you keep sustaining so many injuries.'

Simple.

There was nothing simple about that explanation.

38

THEN

I drummed my fingers on the kitchen table as I stared at the laptop screen. The words blurred as my thoughts drifted back to Abhilash and our encounter at Hengistbury Head. I hadn't felt this excited about anything in a long time.

And yet, at the same time, it was wrong. Very wrong.

I'd kissed another guy.

I pushed that thought away, refusing to allow my brain to contemplate what that meant. I had a boyfriend. One I loved completely. Unconditionally. That didn't change just because he wasn't going to put a ring on my finger.

Did it?

But then it wasn't about the jewellery, or the big wedding and the white dress. It was more than that. I wanted that commitment. That certainty that we were united. Legally. Totally. I would be a Carter. I would be one of them. I would belong.

Instead, I was just me.

An unwelcome thought gnawed at the back of my mind. Was it really Josh that I loved? Or just what being with him could give me?

Josh had been a part of my life even through the worst times. He'd been my lifeline when the rest of my world had disintegrated around me.

His family had taken me in. Given me a home. Support. Love. Losing Josh would mean losing everything. Everyone.

Could I really walk away from all of that?

I couldn't tell his family the truth about Josh. I couldn't destroy the image they had of their son. Not that they would ever believe me, even if I tried.

I clung on at the periphery of his world. The Carters were welcoming. Caring. But at the end of the day, they were Josh's family, not mine. Josh was the link that held our chain together; without him, I would be completely detached.

We don't quit. When things get tough, we stay strong. We endure.

Mum's words came back to me. She might not have been the best role model. At least not with her actions. But I couldn't dispute that she made a good point.

I was giving up on Josh too easily. Refocusing my attention on finding someone who appreciated me, instead of simply reminding Josh why he'd chosen me in the first place.

If I wanted to be a Carter then I needed to fight for it. Whatever it took.

I slammed the laptop closed and packed it away in the cupboard out of sight. Work could wait. I had more important things to do this afternoon.

I had to endure.

* * *

'Wow, what's all this?'

Josh stood in the kitchen doorway, his eyes wide as his gaze focused on the carefully laid table bathed in a golden glow from the flickering candles.

'I thought we should do something special for a change.'

His eyes narrowed. 'What's the occasion?'

I shrugged. 'It's Friday night.'

'That's not an occasion. That happens every week. But this doesn't.' There was a guarded tone to his voice. He was suspicious of my actions. Had we really come to this? Where doing something nice was assumed to have ulterior motives?

Then again, if I was honest with myself, it did.

'True.' I walked to the fridge and opened the door. 'But perhaps it should,' I added, pulling out a bottle of prosecco.

Josh laughed as the tension eased from his expression. 'I'm not going to object to that.'

'I thought we could spend the weekend together too. Now we're into the summer, maybe go to the beach together tomorrow. If you have time?' I added cautiously. I mustn't push too hard.

Josh nodded. 'That's a great idea. We live so close and yet we barely spend any time there these days.'

I nodded. There were a lot of things we didn't do any more. At least, we hadn't. 'It's time we changed that,' I announced with a grin.

His fingers brushed mine as I handed him the prosecco. I stared at my hand as he moved away. His touch didn't have the same effect as Abhilash's. It felt flat. Ordinary.

'Did you go out today?' he asked as he stepped back and pulled the foil from the top of the bottle.

A chill ran through my body as I took the salad from the bottom drawer of the fridge, but I knew it had nothing to do with where I was standing. I pondered my answer. I should tell him. 'Just for coffee at Hengistbury Head.'

Josh chuckled. 'Did you and Emma set the world to rights?'

His assumption that I'd gone for coffee with Emma threw me. I hadn't said I'd met anyone. I could have gone alone. Couldn't I? That was reasonable. I usually did.

And yet to correct him would be to invite more questions, or to force myself into telling a lie.

But then was telling him I'd gone alone really any worse than letting him assume I'd met Emma?

'I'm glad you two are still close. It's sad that you've never really had many friends.'

Guilt cut into me like a knife penetrating into my heart. He was concerned about me. He cared that I was alone. That all I really had was him.

I pivoted to face him, nudging the fridge door closed with my elbow. 'I don't need friends. I have you.'

I had everything I'd ever wanted. A home. A family. Love. How could it not be enough?

How could I risk losing it?

For what? For Abhilash?

Was he any better?

On the surface he had so much potential. But I knew better than to blindly trust. I'd been deceived too much for that.

I'd come to accept it. It was part of life, how people behaved. But Abhilash had made me question it. Was it possible that I deserved more?

Josh and I were the perfect couple. At least on the surface. But people are like icebergs. There's so much more to them than can been seen from the surface. So much that they keep hidden from everyone else. And sometimes, even from themselves.

Josh was no different.

Nor was Abhilash. He had his flaws too.

But then again, so did I.

* * *

'That lasagne was amazing,' Josh said as I cleared the plates.

'I'm glad you enjoyed it,' I grinned at him. Cooking with a broken wrist hadn't been easy, but it was worth it. 'I hope you saved room for dessert.'

'Absolutely!' Josh replied, cranking his neck to watch as I pulled a tray from the oven and cut two generous sized pieces of brownie. I slid them onto plates and added a scoop of vanilla ice cream to each.

'Is that your homemade chocolate brownie?' Josh asked, licking his lips.

'Sadly no, I couldn't manage it with my wrist, but next time I'll make it myself.' I set the plates down on the table as I sat back down opposite Josh.

He grinned at me. 'That would be awesome, Lauren. You haven't baked in ages.' He grabbed his spoon and shoved a piece of brownie into his mouth. 'Hmm,' he murmured closing his eyes. 'Not quite as good as yours, but still delicious.'

I beamed with pride as I scooped a piece of brownie onto my spoon. I was right. This is what we needed. We could be like we used to be. I just had to remind Josh what that was like.

'See what you can do when you're not wasting your time playing around with all that social media rubbish.'

I froze.

Social media rubbish.

That's all it was to him. Even now. Even when I had proved what it could be.

'But I'm doing well with it, Josh.'

Josh scoffed as he took another bite of brownie. 'It's a fad. You've been lucky so far. That's all.'

I set my spoon back on my plate, no longer hungry.

'I could get a proper job,' I said quietly. I loved what I did. Running my own business. Building something from nothing. But Josh was right; it was risk. There was no certainty in it for the long term. My clients could easily decide to replace me with an in-house team, or the smaller ones might just learn from watching what I had been doing and replicate it themselves.

There was no pension. No holiday pay or sick leave. I was out on my own with no safety net.

And yet, there was a reason why I had started it.

'Y-yeah, maybe,' Josh said. But there was a hesitancy to it.

'That didn't sound very convincing.'

Josh lowered his gaze and studied the remainder of his brownie intently.

I drew back. 'You don't think I could find a job.'

'It's not like you've ever actually worked before.'

'I work every day.'

He arched an eyebrow. 'It's not really the same thing though, is it?'

'I told you I should have got a job straight after uni.'

Josh shook his head. 'And I told you, you didn't need to.' He reached across the table and rested his hand on top of mine. 'You still don't.' My eyes met his and he smiled. 'Like I told you back then, I want to take care of you, Lauren. That hasn't changed.'

I squeezed his hand. 'It hasn't?'

Josh shook his head. 'You just need to let me.'

I nodded slowly. Perhaps he was right. I was the one that was getting in our way. My business absorbed my time and energy. It distracted me from us.

And yet, to simply leave everything to Josh wasn't fair. I didn't want to be a burden. I wanted to be a partner. 'But ever since you were made redundant—' I clamped my mouth closed. I knew better than that. We never talked about the redundancy.

He snatched his hand away and sat bolt upright in his chair. 'We hit a rough patch. That's all. I handled it. I got a new job, didn't I?'

I nodded enthusiastically, preventing myself from pointing out that it didn't pay anywhere nearly as much as he had been earning before.

He didn't need that reminder.

We didn't need it.

I watched his shoulders rise and fall as he sucked in a deep breath and let it out slowly. 'Excellent, I'm glad that's settled then.'

I nodded again. Except, was it settled? Had it ever been?

39

NOW

'Okay then,' DC Collier said, when I didn't respond. 'If you're not ready to talk about your injuries, let's talk about Josh.'

I gritted my teeth. That topic wasn't any better.

'I think we misjudged you,' PC Smith said as he watched my reaction. 'We thought it was all about the money. What you could gain financially with Josh out of the picture.' He shook his head. 'But we were wrong. Money isn't what matters to you, is it? So what does? Love?'

I nibbled the inside of my cheek. I had a bad feeling about where this was going.

'You went through a lot when you were a kid. It was just you and your mum. She was the only person who loved you. And then,' he shook his head sadly, 'you realised that even she didn't love you enough, did she?' A chill seemed to seep into my bones. I'd been too confident. Too smug. I thought I'd outsmarted him. That he was clueless, fumbling in the dark. But there was more to PC Smith than I'd realised.

'I'm loved,' I replied. 'I always have been.'

'Just not in the way you want, though. Right?'

I jutted my chin forward defiantly. 'We don't get to choose how people treat us.'

'But we do get to choose how we treat them,' DC Collier said. 'Tell us about your relationship with Josh.'

I glared at her. They were a tag team. Two against one. I was outnumbered.

Not that it mattered. Even one on one, I'd never done well. People didn't play fair. I'd learnt that the hard way.

'You'd been together a long time. He'd helped you with every-thing with your mum.' I caught the emphasis DC Collier placed on "helped". She thought he was involved with what happened to her. She thought we both were.

But she still couldn't prove it.

My heart swelled as I thought about how angry Josh had been when he discovered what Mum had done. He'd been so protec-tive. He would have done anything for me.

I'd felt it then, that passion, that love he had for me. It had been invigorating. Despite everything that had happened. Despite Mum's betrayal, with Josh by my side, I was strong. Invincible.

'So, why after all that time together did you break up now?' DC Collier continued.

I sighed as she intruded on my memory of Josh. The Josh I used to know. The Josh that had loved me.

Almost the right amount.

'People grow up.' I shrugged. Dismissing her question as though it was irrelevant. But we all knew it wasn't. 'They change.'

'Did you change? Or did Josh?'

I frowned as I contemplated my answer. Had Josh changed? Or had he always been the same? I wasn't entirely sure. Perhaps it wasn't about him at all. Perhaps it was me. My standards had changed. What I was prepared to accept, to live with, had shifted. I wanted more. I wanted better.

I wanted Abhilash.

'We'd always had our problems. I think I just wasn't ready to face that before. I wasn't prepared to risk losing him.'

'And now you are?'

'Now I know I deserve better.'

'Better than...?' DC Collier let her sentence hang in the air. She was leading me. Trying to find out what broke Josh and I up.

I cursed my slip. I'd just walked into telling her that Josh wasn't good enough. But if I told her why, I would be giving her even more reason to distrust me.

'Josh was a threat to you, wasn't he?'

I stared at PC Smith. He knew. It was impossible. No one knew what Josh was to me. Only Josh. And he'd never talk. He couldn't.

And yet, somehow PC Smith knew.

'I don't understand.' I was playing for time. Acting ignorant. One question circled on repeat in my brain.

How? How could he know?

40

THEN

I watched them as they waded into the water. The couples. The guys holding their girlfriends' hands, helping them over the pebbles that dug into their feet, making it hard to walk without stumbling. Hugging and kissing as they submerged into the cold water. Their heads close together. Talking. Laughing.

There was nowhere else they wanted to be than right there. In that moment. Together.

It was perfect.

I wanted that. Every part of me longed for it. Ached for it. That closeness. That bond. That love. I let out a wistful sigh. That perfection.

But it took effort to create it. To mould it into shape. To make it solid and real.

I looked across at Josh lying less than a metre away on his beach towel, and yet he seemed so far away.

'Let's go and cool off in the sea,' I blurted the suggestion out. It wasn't as though I could swim. Not with my cast. But we could paddle. We could be together.

Josh glanced up from his book and looked first at me and then at the water. I waited for his no. The water was too cold. He was comfortable lying on the soft sand. He wanted to finish his book. They were all valid reasons. All ones I had heard before.

'Okay.'

A shot of adrenaline jolted into my veins. He'd said yes. He wanted to paddle. With me.

We would be like those other couples. Close. Connected. Everyone would think we were perfect too. There was hope for us yet. This was just the start. Sharing things together. Little moments.

Like we used to.

He put his book down and stood up, straightening his towel on the sand as he waited for me.

He'd waited for me.

The event was so unusual that my brain savoured it, embedding that fact deep into my memory.

He did still care.

I scrambled to my feet and we started walking towards the shore. His stride was longer and he edged ahead of me. I did a little jog as best as I could as we reached the pebbles that had been washed up onto the sand. *My little run.* That's what he used to call it. Affectionate. Cute. It had been an inside joke. One of many.

He didn't notice.

He reached the water before me and waded in. It didn't matter. It didn't mean anything, I told myself as I focused my attention on tentatively tiptoeing over the pebbles beneath my feet and bracing myself against the cold water.

There was a time when he'd have noticed. Helped.

I shook that thought away. I was reading too much into trivial little things. The important thing to keep focused on was that he'd come with me. He wanted to be with me.

I looked up at the sound of a splash and realised Josh had dived in, immersing himself in the salty waves. He'd always been like that. No fear. No hesitation. Straight in. Whereas I was always the one dawdling on the side-lines trying to summon my courage to follow.

Josh swam a few strokes. He needed to, of course; the water was cold. Movement was necessary. I waited. Expecting to see him circling back towards me.

He didn't.

I watched the arch of spray fly from his arm with each powerful stroke of his front crawl as he swam further and further away. I waded in deeper, the icy water reaching my knees and then my thighs.

I stopped. What was I doing? I couldn't chase after him. Not with my cast. But I knew without it that is exactly what I would have done.

What I'd always done.

With a sigh I turned my back on Josh and waded slowly towards the shore. I clambered over the pebbles, not even caring as they dug into the soles of my bare feet.

As picked up my towel, I wondered if Josh would even notice that I had left the water. There was a time when he would have done. But then, there was a time when our conversations had held his full attention without his gaze being locked on the TV screen or his phone. A time when he'd accepted what I said without scorn or disapproval. A time when I'd mattered. Or at least, I'd felt as though I had.

We used to have passion. Desire. Fire. Now there was just co-habitation.

I was clinging on. Hoping a ring would solve it. Solve us. But the truth was we were beyond saving. A ring was a promise of more than he could give me. Perhaps it always had been. Perhaps that was why in all the years we had been together, he'd always said 'someday'. It was a dismissal. Avoidance. He'd never commit. Never give an indication of how far away 'someday' might be. Perhaps he'd always known that it wasn't our destiny.

He wouldn't allow it to be.

Perhaps we weren't meant to have lasted, not beyond school or university. We'd been teenagers when we fell in love. We thought it would last forever, but even forever had a time limit.

People changed. Love changed. Mum was enough evidence of that.

The question was, what was I going to do about it?

It was obvious now that Josh wasn't my future but leaving him would destroy everything. I wouldn't just lose him. I would lose his family too.

I'd been clinging on to the edges for so long, fighting to establish a place for myself. Breaking up with Josh would relegate me to the role of ex-girlfriend. Demoted further out of the family. They wouldn't keep in touch with someone who was no longer part of their son's life.

There had to be another way.

A way to be free of Josh, but to keep the people that mattered. His family.

My family.

41

NOW

'Josh was a threat to you,' PC Smith repeated. 'Because he knew, didn't he?'

My mouth opened and closed as I fought for air. His question threw me. It wasn't the accusation I had been bracing myself for.

I frowned, searching my brain, what could Josh have known?

Abhilash.

His name sprang to my mind.

It was the only secret I had from Josh. *He* was the only secret I had.

One I thought that I had kept well. But I hadn't counted on one thing...

Emma.

I closed my eyes as I recalled our conversation as Emma drove me here. I should have known, of course Emma would have told Josh about Abhilash.

'I see from your reaction I'm right.' The smug tone was back in PC Smith's voice.

Panic bubbled in my chest. I couldn't get Abhilash tied up in my mess. It wasn't fair to him. It could jeopardise too much.

'Did he want you to get help?' DC Collier asked.

I blinked. 'Help?' I stared from one to the other. 'Help with what?'

They exchanged a confused look. My reaction had clearly surprised them. They thought I knew what they were talking about.

'With your, um, mental health,' PC Smith said hesitantly.

'My...?' It took a moment for the magnitude of what he'd said to sink in. 'Oh, you think I did something to Josh to prevent him getting me help for FII.' It wasn't a question. I didn't need an answer. It was obvious. They thought the same as everyone thought.

That I was like Mum.

If she could harm the one person she loved, then so could I.

'We're aware of the safeguarding procedures that have been put in place,' DC Collier informed me. 'Your medical history. Your repeated hospital admissions.'

'Josh figured it out too, didn't he?' PC Smith asked, but his tone was less confident now. 'He wanted you to get help. Psychiatric help.'

I stared at him, speechless.

'If you are deemed to be a risk to yourself or to others...'

I nodded. 'I know the drill.'

'Up until now, there have only been speculations. But if Josh had discovered what was happening, if he was going to expose the truth—'

I laughed.

Loud unrestrained, impulsive laughter.

It wasn't wise. But I couldn't help it. They thought I would harm Josh to protect my secret. The ludicrousness of their suspicions was so overwhelming that laughter was the only possible response I had.

They looked at me nervously. I could read their expressions. They were afraid I was becoming more unhinged. That they had triggered some sort of total breakdown.

It almost made me want to laugh more.

Almost.

'Josh didn't need to uncover any big secret as to my medical treatments.'

DC Collier drew back. 'He knew?' I could practically see her brain whirling, trying to fit this new piece of information into the puzzle in her mind.

'Sometimes.'

Their confusion grew deeper.

I smiled slightly. For all their power. All their research. Their questions. Their experience. They really had no idea.

'He knew what had happened at the time. He was always there for it. Involved.' I shrugged. 'Though he'd always conveniently *forget* later.'

'He caused your injuries?' I wasn't sure if DC Collier was asking me, or simply putting the pieces together aloud.

'Josh wasn't a threat to my secret. I was a threat to his.'

42

THEN

My phone vibrated quietly on the table, the sound drowned out by the fragmented conversations that surrounded me and the repetitive gurgle of the coffee machine that reached into every corner of the busy café.

Starbucks didn't have quite the same charm as our usual venues at the beach, but in its own way it was special too. I purposefully reached for my phone with my right hand, relishing the freedom of movement without the cast. It was sweet that Abhilash wanted to meet me to celebrate this moment. It might only be a cup of coffee in a café over the road from the hospital during his break, but it didn't matter. It was the sentiment behind it that was important.

On my way. Be with you soon.

I smiled at the message from Abhilash. I loved the way he did that. Messaged, even when he didn't need to, as though reassuring me that I hadn't been forgotten. That I *would never* be forgotten.

I relaxed back in my chair as I sent a smiley emoji in reply.

'Excuse me, is this seat free?'

I looked up from my phone to see a guy leaning on the chair opposite. 'Sorry, I'm waiting for someone.'

'No worries.' He started to back away but stopped. 'Do I know you?'

I studied his face. There was something a little familiar about him. I glanced at his blue scrubs. He was a doctor. A doctor at the hospital I had been treated at too many times. My stomach tightened. 'I don't think so.'

'Huh, sorry. I guess I have you mixed up with someone else.' He still looked puzzled, as though he wasn't convinced.

I shrugged. 'That's okay.'

I waited for him to walk away, but he lingered. He started to open his mouth to speak.

'Lauren?'

I practically leapt out of my chair at Abhilash's voice. I took a half step towards him and then froze. What was I doing? We didn't hug. Not yet.

His gaze drifted to the guy still standing by my table. 'Hey, Nick. Do you two know each other?'

'No,' I said too quickly.

Abhilash looked taken aback for a second before understanding registered on his face.

He'd guessed. I could tell. He knew that we'd met before. *How* we'd met before.

'I should get out of your way and let you two get on with your...' Nick paused. 'Date,' he added hesitantly.

'We're just friends,' Abhilash said.

'Ah.' Nick smiled. 'That makes more sense.' He lifted his hand in a half wave. 'It was great to meet you, Lauren.'

'You too.'

Abhilash slid into the seat opposite and glanced back over his shoulder, making sure Nick was out of earshot. 'He treated you before, right?'

I nodded, as I sat back down. 'Last year. Fractured ribs.'

'Right, I remember reading that in your file.'

An awkward silence descended between us.

Your file.

It was a reminder that I was a patient. Abhilash was my doctor.

'Maybe it wasn't a good idea to meet here,' I said, reaching for my bag.

'What? No, it's fine.' Abhilash leaned forward in his chair. 'Nick's the guy I rent the house with. He won't say anything.'

'Say anything?'

Abhilash cast a nervous glance around the café. 'Being seen with a patient could be...' He paused. 'Complicated.'

'You're worried someone else from the hospital will see us, aren't you?'

'I'm probably just being overcautious. I don't usually see many doctors here, aside from Nick. Actually, he was the one that introduced me to this café. It's good to get out of the hospital for a few minutes.'

'Ah, so this is where you bring all your ex-patients then.' I grinned at him mischievously, but I was only half joking.

Hurt flashed across Abhilash's face. 'You're the only patient I've ever taken anywhere. You're different. You're special.'

Guilt tore into my heart that I had made such an accusation. One that had caused him pain. He deserved better from me. And yet, at the same time, my regret was outweighed by something even more powerful.

Pride.

I was the only patient he'd socialised with. The only one he'd formed a friendship with. A bond.

I was special.

'And yet even this isn't really appropriate,' Abhilash continued, the anguish in his voice drawing me back to the present predicament.

'You treated me in the ED, it's not as though you're my GP.'

'You've had a safeguarding flag raised. If misconstrued, it might look like I was taking advantage of you and your...' Abhilash stopped.

'My mental health issues?'

'If you report Josh—'

'No.' I wouldn't do that. Not to Josh.

'He doesn't deserve your protection. Your loyalty.'

'You don't know the whole story. You don't know what he's done for me.'

'You're right. All I can think about is what he's done *to* you.'

I shuffled uncomfortably in my chair. Was Abhilash right? Was I wrong to keep Josh's secret?

Even though I knew what he did was wrong. Even though part of me hated him for it. I still loved him too.

There was a voice in my head that kept saying 'but'. *But* it was an accident. *But* it wasn't entirely his fault. *But* I antagonised him.

I was still trying to carry the blame for something he did. Just like always.

I kept thinking that if I changed enough, if I was good enough, he'd be okay. We'd be okay.

And yet, there was another part of me that was no longer certain I wanted to be with him at all.

A part of me that wanted something different. Someone different.

I met Abhilash's eyes. 'Just friends?'

43

NOW

'We need you to be very clear about what you are implying here, Lauren.'

I licked my lips. She was right. It wasn't enough to just imply it; I had to say it. 'Josh caused my injuries.'

'If that's true, if Josh hurt you, then why not come forward? Why not get help?' DC Collier asked.

I snorted. 'How many women whose partners beat them actually come forward?'

DC Collier let out a weary sigh. 'Not enough.'

'So, what makes you think I should be any different to them?'

'Because you are different,' her eyes met mine and she stared into my eyes as though trying to see into my soul. 'You've lived through abuse before. You overcame it. Why would you allow yourself to become trapped in it again?'

'Probably for the same reasons as all those other women stay, but also...' I licked my lips, searching for the strength to go on. To say the fear that had lived within me for so long. 'Because I am different.'

DC Collier frowned.

'What was your first assumption when you learned of my injuries? What was everyone's first assumption?'

'FII.'

I nodded. 'And now?'

She swallowed.

I chuckled ruefully. 'Still FII, right? Me accusing Josh doesn't change your assumptions. If anything, it probably makes you more convinced. You think I'm simply trying to deflect attention. Or maybe that I'm in denial and have convinced myself that my accusations are true. Either way...' I shrugged. I didn't need to finish my sentence. I'd made my point. Not that it was enough to change anything.

'Okay, so convince me. Tell me about the abuse. When did it start? *How* did it start?'

'Small,' I sniffed. 'It started so small that I didn't even see it coming.'

* * *

I drummed my fingers against the phone as I sat on the lumpy, second-hand sofa we'd bought to furnish our home. The TV flashed with images that made no sense to me. I'd put it on for a distraction and an attempt to drown out the voices in my head that told me something was wrong.

It wasn't helping.

How could I concentrate on anything right now?

He'd be all right.

He had to be.

I stared at the unanswered messages on my phone and swallowed.

What if he wasn't?

A heavy engine pulled up on the drive and I leapt from the sofa. I raced to the front door and swung it open, just as Josh stepped out of his car.

'You're so late!' My words gushed out on a wave of relief. He was here. He was home.

He stopped dead and stared at me. There was a hardness to his expression.

I shook that thought away. It was the harsh tone of the security light casting shadows on his face. That was all.

He resumed walking and marched towards me, his footsteps crunching across the gravel driveway. 'I didn't realise I had a curfew.'

'What? N-no, I didn't mean it like that.'

Josh barged past me, ignoring my outstretched arms that ached to hug him. To hold him. I needed tactile proof that he was real. That he was safe.

'I was just worried,' I told him. 'You usually call when you're running late.' I glanced at my watch. 'And you're later than ever tonight.'

'I was w-or-k-ing.' He dragged the word out as though I didn't understand its meaning.

'I know,' I soothed. 'You always work so hard.'

He glared at me again. 'For us,' he spat. 'For you.'

I wanted to nod. To assure him that I knew. That I appreciated it. That I loved him all the more for it. That care. That effort. That love.

But I couldn't move. His eyes seemed darker, more piercing as they glared at me.

I couldn't blame it on the lighting now. That hardness was real. It was deep.

No, I was overreacting. I scolded myself. I was always doing that. Overthinking. Over analysing. Looking for drama where none existed.

It was one of the lessons that Mum had taught me a little too well. And just like everything associated with her, it was hard to leave behind.

Josh had had a long day, that was all. He was tired. Hungry. Irritated. It was understandable.

'I'll re-heat your dinner for you,' I said, forcing a lightness into my tone that his presence seemed to kill the second the words left my lips.

'You could have waited for me.'

I stared after him as he stomped into the kitchen. He was right. I should have waited.

* * *

'Is there anyone who can corroborate your story? Someone who witnessed an altercation? An argument? Anything?'

I shook my head. 'Josh was too careful to slip up like that.'

'Is there at least anyone you confided in?'

I hesitated.

'Lauren?'

'What would that change? It would still be hearsay. They only know what I told them. That's not proof. That just drags them into this mess too.'

'I'm trying to help you here, Lauren.'

I arched an eyebrow. 'Just like before?'

'I was trying to help you then too.' She shook her head sadly. 'Even after...'

'You would have arrested me back then if you could have done. Same as now.'

'You don't make it easy to trust you.'

I nodded. 'I get that.'

'You and Josh had motive to want your mother dead. Just like you have motive to want Josh gone too.'

I tipped my head to the right. 'Accusing Josh of abuse is just another motive, isn't it? I mean, you don't believe me, but if it was true, or if I at least believed it was true, then it's another reason for me to want him gone.'

'Just like your mum,' DC Collier replied.

I closed my eyes. She had been gone for eleven years, but she was still with me. Still part of my life.

I would never escape her legacy.

No one would let me.

'We're done here,' I said abruptly as I opened my eyes and glared at DC Collier. I pushed my chair back and stood up, ignoring the grating sound that reverberated around the room as the chair legs scraped across the floor.

DC Collier leapt to her feet. 'Lauren, it's not a good idea to just walk out like this.'

'I'm here voluntarily, right? You said I could leave at any time,' I turned to PC Smith, seeking confirmation of his earlier words.

'Yes, but it's not advisable. Not if you want us to believe your story.'

'Story?' I snorted. 'That's the problem; it's not a story. It's my life! And I'm tired of you dissecting it, analysing it, and jumping to conclusions about it. About me.'

I marched towards the door.

'If you didn't harm Josh, then where is he?'

I froze with my hand on the door handle. 'What makes you think that I know?' I glanced back over my shoulder. 'Or even care?'

44

THEN

I traced my fingers along the edges of the tiny, pale blue flowers. 'I love them, thank you.'

'I told you I'd bring you a plant next time,' Abhilash winked at me across the table.

I shook my head in awe as I held the small terracotta pot which was overflowing with flowers. 'I can't believe you remembered that.'

'I always remember my promises.'

My smile grew bigger. 'I like that.' I tipped my head to the side. 'But why Forget Me Not's? I thought they were a weed.'

I glanced around the crowded restaurant, wondering what the other customers thought of my unusual gift. Guys usually bought their dates flowers, not plant pots full of weeds.

'Some people might say so,' Abhilash shrugged. 'But I think they are unappreciated. They're strong, resilient, and subtly beautiful.'

I turned back, my gaze fixed on him, suddenly no longer caring what anyone else thought.

Abhilash's eyes met mine and his cheeks flushed. 'Plus, I think their name is appropriate too.'

I slid the plant back into the silver gift bag and set it down on the table, playing for time before I could trust myself to speak without my voice cracking with emotion. 'Are you afraid that I might forget you?'

Abhilash took a deep breath. 'Lauren, there's something we should talk about.'

I braced myself, waiting for the words that I didn't want to hear. He was going to end it. Whatever this was. Whatever we were starting. He was going to end it before it had even begun. I couldn't let him do that.

'My family—'

I pressed my finger to his lips. 'Let's not talk about our families.'

Abhilash reached for my hand and lowered it from his lips. I waited for him to let go, to push my hand aside, but he held on to it. We were still connected. There was still hope.

'Our way, our customs, they're different to yours,' Abhilash said.

I arched an eyebrow. 'Do you really think that I don't know that families are different? They all have their ways. Their history.' I shrugged. 'But none of that matters right now.' I leaned forward, closing the gap that existed between us above the table. 'It's like what you said to me the first day we went for coffee together; that if you dwell on regrets about the past and worry about the future, you're missing out on the present. The now.'

Abhilash sat a little taller in his chair. 'You remember that?'

'I do,' I grinned at him. 'You were right. All we have is this moment. Here. Now. I want to focus on that. Not the past. Not the future. But the present. Our present.'

He nodded slowly. 'I do too, but—'

'No,' I said firmly. 'Nothing else matters.'

45

NOW

'You never asked us why you are here under caution,' DC Collier said.

I froze. She was right: I hadn't.

I wanted to know. And yet, at the same time, I didn't.

Ignorance was bliss.

Sometimes.

'It's not the typical procedure to interview the partner of a missing person under caution. Not unless there is a reason...'

I bit my lip. I wanted to ask what the reason was.

But I couldn't.

Don't ask questions.

I nodded slightly, acknowledging Mum's instruction. Even now, I still listened to her.

'Do you know why the jet-ski stalled?' DC Collier asked.

I turned back to look at her. 'What?'

'The jet-ski, do you know why it stalled?' Her question sounded more hesitant this time.

I shook my head. 'I don't know. I haven't really thought about it.'

'You haven't thought about the reason you ended up in hospital?'

'I thought it must have been because I did something wrong.' The words tumbled free from my lips before I'd had time to think about how they would sound.

Keep quiet.

Mum's reminder came too late. I'd said it now. My words were out there. Being analysed. Judged.

But they were true. It was how I always ended up in hospital. Wasn't it? Because I did something wrong. Again.

DC Collier held her hand out, signalling me back to my vacated chair. This conversation wasn't over, and we both knew it.

I hesitated for a second, debating whether to comply. I could still walk out of the door, leave them wondering. Guessing.

This time.

But I knew that wouldn't stop them. They wouldn't give up. Mum had learned that the hard way.

I sat down and met DC Collier's gaze. I wouldn't cower. Wouldn't look guilty.

Just tell them it hurts.

'The weather conditions were bad. I would never normally have gone out when the sea was so rough but I needed to get out of the house. I wasn't really thinking clearly. I thought going out on the jet-ski would help, but I wasn't in the right frame of mind to go out there. To go anywhere. Especially alone.' I shook my head. 'It was stupid. *I* was stupid.'

DC Collier and PC Smith were frozen in place, as though they thought the slightest movement might break my momentum. Might disrupt my confession.

'I was going so fast. Too fast.' I let out a deep breath. 'I know better than to be that reckless.'

They stared at me, waiting for me to continue. But there was nothing more to say.

'So, you're claiming the jet-ski stalled because,' PC Smith glanced at DC Collier, 'you were going too fast in rough sea?'

'Didn't it?' I looked from one to the other, searching their faces for confirmation. 'It must have been something I'd done, right? I mean, my car only stalls when I get the timing wrong on the clutch pedal, so...'

They stared at me silently. The gnawing in the pit of my stomach told me there was something more going on here. Something that I didn't know. Didn't understand.

'We had the jet-ski inspected after it was retrieved from the water,' DC Collier said slowly. 'There is evidence that the engine had been tampered with.'

'Tampered with?' I frowned. 'Wait, I don't understand. What are you saying?'

'The jet-ski didn't stall by accident. Someone wanted it to stall. They made sure it did. The ignition coil had been damaged, which would cause the engine to misfire or stall.'

'But...' my mind raced. 'Who would do that?'

'You.' PC Smith's voice was so blunt. So certain.

It felt like all the energy drained from my body. They thought I'd done this. Their accusations had been bad enough before. I knew they'd suspected me of harming Josh. But all they had were assumptions. No witnesses. No proof. No body.

'Let's say that you took Josh out on a sabotaged jet-ski in dangerous water at reckless speeds, knowing that it would stall,' PC Smith suggested.

They thought I was capable of something so premeditated. So callous. So... I shuffled uncomfortably. So desperate.

'That doesn't make any sense; why would I set myself up to have an accident like that? I could have been killed.'

'What better way to attempt to show your innocence? Harming yourself isn't new to you, is it?'

My breathing quickened. This couldn't be happening.

'It wouldn't be that hard to ensure that Josh was knocked off by a wave. Easier still if he was already unconscious before you set off. And without a life vest...'

PC Smith let his accusations hang in the air.

'I keep telling you, I was alone. Josh wasn't with me. He wasn't on the jet-ski. It was just me. I got knocked out. If that boat hadn't come by when it did... if they hadn't seen me...'

'An impressive way to deflect guilt. Playing the victim, unconscious in the water, almost drowning. And all you had to do was blame it all on the jet-ski for stalling.' He smiled. 'But you failed to consider that we would check it out.'

'I wouldn't even know how to sabotage an engine.'

PC Smith shrugged. 'The internet can make anyone an expert in anything.' He paused as his eyes narrowed. 'Especially someone who's an expert when it comes to the internet.'

My mouth gaped open. He was using my business against me. Just like Josh had done.

I slumped back in my chair as my body deflated. They had it all worked out. They had me all worked out.

And yet...

'Then why would I deny that Josh was there?'

PC Smith's brow crinkled and I knew that I was on to something. Something they couldn't explain. A loose thread in their whole neatly woven tale.

'If I was staging his death to make it look like an accident, then I would have told you he was with me, that we went out there together. I would have made us sound like the perfect couple that everyone around us thought we were. No problems. No domestic abuse. No breakup.'

'You only told us you'd broken up because we'd seen Josh's stuff in bags at your home,' PC Smith said smugly.

'True' I conceded. 'But I've told you Josh wasn't with me on the jet-ski from the beginning. I told you that at the hospital before you'd been in my home. Before you knew anything about us. About *me*.'

46

THEN

I waved at Abhilash as I stood on the shore, the waves threatening to wash over my trainers at any minute. I should step back. Retreat to drier sand. And yet, something inside me compelled me to stay, as though I needed to be as close to Abhilash as possible.

I held my phone up and took another photo as his kite lifted him over the crest of a wave. It was a shame I wouldn't be able to put these pictures on social media; they were so perfect, they would undoubtedly make an impact. I smiled. Then again, perhaps it was better that they were just for me.

Just for us.

Sometimes perfection wasn't meant to be shared.

'Lauren?'

I jumped at the sound of my name being called behind me. I spun around, taking a step backwards in the process.

'Doctor, er...' my mind went blank as I tried to recall his name. There had been so many. Too many.

I gasped as icy water slopped over my trainers and seeped into my socks.

'Sorry,' he said, reaching out his hand and pulling me higher up the beach, onto dry sand. 'I didn't mean to startle you.'

'No,' I shook my soggy foot. 'Not your fault, Doctor...' I scrunched my nose. Nope, still nothing.

'Just call me Nick.'

I nodded. 'Okay, Dr Nick.'

He laughed.

The sound surprised me. Other than Abhilash, I couldn't think of anyone else who I had made laugh. At least not for a long time. Certainly not Josh.

'Not quite what I meant, but it will do,' Nick said with a shrug.

My gaze drifted to his black wetsuit. 'You kite surf too?'

He nodded. 'Abhilash got me into it last year. He was always telling me how incredible it was. Eventually I decided to try it.' He leaned forwards and whispered conspiratorially. 'Mostly just to shut him up.'

My eyes narrowed 'And yet, you're still surfing a year later?'

He cringed. 'Turns out Abhilash was right.'

I laughed. 'He usually is.'

'So how come he hasn't talked you into trying it yet?'

I glanced at my wrist.

'Oh right, of course. You only just got your cast off.'

I shifted awkwardly on the sand. How did he know about my cast? When he'd seen me at Starbuck's, I'd already had it removed.

'Hey,' I glanced behind me at the sound of Abhilash's voice as he jogged out of the surf, fighting against the pull of his kite that soared above him.

Nick raced forwards to help. They lowered the kite to the beach and Abhilash released the clips from his waist.

'Are you done already?' I asked, glancing at my watch. 'I thought you'd be out there much longer.'

'I couldn't leave you on the beach on your own all morning,' Abhilash stared at Nick as he spoke. Was it my imagination or was there tension simmering between them?

'Right, well, I better finish getting set up,' Nick said. 'But it was really great to see you again, Lauren.' He gave a quick nod towards me, before turning away and heading up the beach to the kite that was resting on the sand.

'Did you two have a good conversation?'

I tipped my head to the right as I studied Abhilash, trying to decipher his tone. 'Yeah, he seems like a nice guy.'

Abhilash nodded. 'Yes, he is. But...' He cast a nervous glance in Nick's direction.

'Are you afraid that he will cause trouble for you? He's seen us together twice now. Do you think he'd report you for dating a patient?'

'No, we talked the other day. He knows the score. Besides, I'm not sure he's in a position to criticise.'

My brow furrowed. 'What do you mean?'

Abhilash stared at me, disbelief visible on his face. 'You know he likes you, right?'

'What?' I stared at him, my mouth wide open.

'He asked me about you after he saw us at Starbucks.'

'He did?' A spark of something lit inside me.

'Nick remembers treating you before. He said there was something about you. Something intriguing.'

'Right,' I nodded slowly. 'Doctors always find me intriguing. I'm sure my notes make compelling reading.'

Abhilash shook his head. 'Not medically intriguing. Just intriguing. You. Your personality. Your spark.'

'I have a spark?'

He laughed. 'Oh yes, you most definitely have a spark.'

'Huh,' I shifted my weight backwards, sinking my heels into the sand. 'Who knew?'

Abhilash reached for my hand and stepped closer to me. 'We all knew. We could all see it. You're the only one who didn't.'

I cast a glance up the beach at Nick. So, he liked me, did he? I smiled slightly. That could work out quite nicely.

'We'll be in touch if we have any more questions,' DC Collier said as she walked me out of the police station.

I could hear the frustration in her voice. They didn't have enough to arrest me, as much as they wanted to do so. A text from Josh to his brother, his car at the Harbourside car park by Baiter slipway, that was all they had to place him near the water with me. It wasn't enough. Not to be sure. Not to prove it.

All they had was a hunch.

Just like before.

'Your mother's case has tormented me for eleven years. I don't intend to let this do the same. I will uncover the answers this time, Lauren,' DC Collier said.

I nodded and watched her pivot and turn back the way she had come. Until Josh turned up, I had a feeling I would be seeing a lot more of her and PC Smith.

I took a shaky breath. Assuming Josh did turn up.

* * *

'What are you doing?'

My head jerked up and I stared at Mum standing in my doorway.

'I-I...' My brain failed to send signals to my mouth to allow me to form a sentence. I was too stunned. Too scared.

I followed her gaze to the half-packed suitcase lying open on my bed in front of me.

'I thought you were taking a shower.' My speech finally returned. It wasn't an explanation. Simply the reason I was packing now, at this moment, when I thought I would be unseen.

'The boiler isn't working. The water is stone cold.'

I nodded, knowing that our polite conversation skirting around the issue was only a temporary reprieve.

'You haven't answered my question.' Mum's voice was as icy the water she was avoiding.

The reprieve was over.

She wanted answers.

I sucked in a shaky breath, knowing that she wouldn't like the answers I had to give. 'I'm packing.'

'I see. Because?'

'I'm leaving.' My answers were short and clipped, and avoided telling her anything that she hadn't already figured out for herself.

She nodded stiffly. 'And where exactly are you going?'

I swallowed. 'I don't know.'

Her eyes narrowed as she glared at me. She thought I was lying. That I was keeping my planned destination from her.

'We haven't worked that part out yet.' It was Josh's plan. Incomplete and unlikely to succeed. But it didn't matter. He was trying. He was doing his best to keep his promise to protect me. Whatever it took.

'We?'

I cursed my slip. She didn't need to know that my plan involved anyone else.

'You and Josh, I assume?'

I didn't answer. I didn't need to. Who else would it be? There weren't many people in my life. Mum had made sure of that.

She tried to keep everyone out. Josh too. But he was persistent. He wouldn't give up. Wouldn't leave me.

He loved me.

I waited for her to yell. To scream at me that I couldn't leave. That I was betraying her. Abandoning her.

But she didn't.

'Do you think that's wise?' Her question was so gentle. So full of concern. Love. 'I know that you two think you are soul mates but,' she shook her head. 'You're so young. Too young to really know what love is.'

'Maybe,' I shrugged. She was probably right. Fifteen was too young to know things like that. 'But I know what love isn't.'

She swayed slightly and gripped the doorframe as though needing to steady herself. My words had hurt her.

I was glad.

They were meant to.

'Are you sure?' Her question threw me. It wasn't one I'd expected. 'Do you really think that you understand everything? Anything?'

'I...' I hesitated. The truth was that I wasn't sure. There were moments when everything seemed so clear. So bad. But those moments were driven by anger. Hatred for how she had treated me. What she had done to me. At least, what I thought she had done.

But there were other moments. Quieter. Less certain. When I remembered the other parts too. The good parts.

'Everyone makes mistakes, Lauren. No one is perfect. That's part of life. Part of being human. Being real. Do you think that you are above all that? That you are perfect? Blameless?'

Tears blurred my vision. I knew what she meant. My life had impacted hers. It had changed her. I had changed her.

We were who each other had made us.

'You need me to take care of you, Lauren. You can't expect someone else to sacrifice like I have. I'm your mother. I have to do it. But everyone else...' She shrugged. 'Do you really think Josh could cope with it all the way I have? To cope with you?'

'But I'm not sick. Not any more.'

'Not physically, no. At least not right now. But there is more to being well, to being normal, than just physical health.'

I shook my head. 'No, there's nothing else wrong with me. In fact, maybe there has never been anything wrong with me at all.'

'Not physically.'

'Stop saying that.'

'Why? Because you're afraid that it's true?'

I shook my head again. Faster. Persistent. I couldn't stop. She was wrong. She had to be wrong.

'What do you think will happen if you leave?'

If.

She said it as though my departure wasn't certain. But it was. It had to be. The alternative was to stay here. With her.

We wouldn't survive that.

I wouldn't survive.

I froze as clarity seeped into my thoughts.

Or she wouldn't.

48

THEN

'Hi,' I grinned at Abhilash as he met me on the promenade at the bottom of Fisherman's Walk. 'Thanks for meeting me early today.'

'No problem. Getting to see you sooner than expected is always a good thing,' Abhilash said with a wink.

I rolled my eyes.

'Seriously, I don't mind,' he said as he wrapped his arms around me and hugged me tightly.

Finally, we stepped back, but his fingers automatically linked with mine, maintaining the connection. 'You got big plans for this afternoon?'

'Sort of, I guess.'

Abhilash chuckled. 'You don't sound very sure.'

'It could be big,' I said as we stepped onto the sand and made our way towards the shore. 'Or it could be nothing. I don't really know yet. And I'm trying not to get my hopes up until I do.'

'Sounds intriguing.'

I stroked his arm. 'It's not that I don't want to tell you. It's just...' I scrunched my nose. 'It's kind of stupid, but I just don't want to jinx it by talking about it yet.'

'Then don't.'

I frowned as I studied him. 'You don't mind knowing I'm doing something, but not knowing what it is?'

'Of course not.'

'But don't you feel like I'm shutting you out and keeping secrets from you?'

Abhilash smiled. 'Not at all. Am I curious? Yes, absolutely. But that doesn't mean I have the right to know. You'll tell me when you're ready to share it with me. If you choose to do so.'

'And that's okay with you?' My eyes narrowed as I assessed his reaction. 'Really?'

Abhilash kissed my forehead. 'Really.'

I grinned. 'You're so different to—' I clamped my mouth shut.

'Josh?' Abhilash smiled. 'I'm glad to hear it.' He paused. 'But, speaking of Josh, what are we going to do about him, Lauren?'

My body tensed at the mention of his name. Thoughts of Josh weren't welcome here. This was our time. Abhilash's and mine.

'You and I are getting closer and closer all the time, but you're still with Josh and I'm—'

'I know,' I cut him off. I didn't need to hear all the issues that surrounded us. I knew them only too well.

But I still didn't know what to do about them.

Dealing with Josh was the priority. And yet, it seemed impossible.

'I know the last few months haven't been easy. I know that talking to me about Josh, acknowledging what he's done to you, has been a huge step.'

I nodded. He was right. It had been. It was a step I hadn't planned to take. Ever.

'I've often wondered what made you confide in me, instead of someone else. But I feel so honoured that you did. That you shared that part of your life, yourself, with me.'

I smiled. The truth was, I didn't know why I'd chosen him either. Perhaps it was simply that he'd been there at the right moment when I'd needed someone to talk to. A confidante when I had no one else to turn to. Back then he didn't know us. Didn't matter to us. Perhaps that's why I could talk to him. It didn't feel like such a betrayal of Josh to bad mouth him to a stranger that he would never meet.

When I walked out of the hospital it was almost as though my confession hadn't really happened. I'd left it behind me, along with Abhilash.

And yet, that decision had changed everything. Perhaps it was the act of telling him. Of putting it into words. Saying them out loud. Letting someone else hear them. They weren't just thoughts in my head. Tormenting me. They were free.

And with them, somehow, I felt like I was too.

A little less constricted. Restrained. Trapped.

I swallowed. They were strange words to think of. I wasn't trapped with Josh. I chose to be there. I *wanted* to be there.

I just wanted 'there' to be a little different, that was all.

'But it's not enough to recognise what Josh does. Defining it isn't enough. Understanding what's happening, knowing how bad it is, how harmful, that's all important. Essential even. But it's only the first step.'

'What's the second?' I already knew. Every fibre of my being already knew. And yet, I still needed to ask. Need to hear it from him.

'Deciding what we're going to do about it.'

I squeezed Abhilash's hand. I loved the way he phrased that. He wanted to help me. Talk through the options. Find a solution.

But the truth was, there was only one solution. 'I have to leave Josh.'

Abhilash nodded. 'But whenever you're ready to tell him you're leaving him, you know that I'll come with you, right? You don't have to do it alone.'

Was I ready? Would I ever be?

I needed to leave. I knew that now. I had for a while. Yet I kept putting it off. Not because I wanted to stay, but because leaving came with penalties.

'Leaving Josh means losing everything. Everyone.'

'Why not talk to his family, tell them the truth. Tell them what he's like. What he's done.'

'It would destroy them.' I rolled my eyes. 'Assuming that they even believe me.'

'If they don't believe you, then maybe they aren't the kind of people that you need in your life.'

I tipped my head to the side as I pondered his words. To Abhilash, things were so simple and clear cut. Friends trusted you. People you loved treated you well. I'd believed that once too. Until that theory had been tested.

Abhilash was naïve. Did he really think that they would believe me about the abuse? That they would shun Josh and choose me?

It was more likely they would just close ranks and protect one of their own. Flesh and blood were always going to come first.

'My friend, Emma, thinks you and I being friends is a sign of my insanity. She says I'm throwing away this perfect relationship with Josh.'

Abhilash shook his head. 'Your friends can't give you good advice because they don't know the real you. They only know the illusion you've created. The lies you've told them. The assumptions you led them to make. You did it so that you appeared to be like them. But you're not.'

My shoulders slumped. I wanted to dispute it, but I couldn't. He was right. And the worst part was that I was still doing it. Still hiding the truth. Protecting Josh. But perhaps in a way also protecting myself.

I was avoiding doing anything to resolve the situation. Avoiding the risk that it would all blow up in my face and I would be left with nothing. No boyfriend. No surrogate family. No friends.

I glanced at Abhilash. Well, maybe I wouldn't be left with absolutely nothing. I'd still have him.

'Assume for a moment that you told them, and they believed you. What do you think they would say?' Abhilash asked.

'That it's my fault.'

'Do you really believe they would think that about you? That somehow you deserve how he treats you?'

I shrugged. Why wouldn't they? I still did.

After all, Josh wouldn't just snap without reason. There had to be a trigger. A cause.

I was that cause.

I had been with Mum. And I was with Josh too.

Abhilash put his hand on my shoulder, drawing me to a halt. 'There is nothing that you could have done that would make you deserve a broken wrist, broken ribs, or anything else that you have suffered at his hands.' He stroked my cheek. 'Stop carrying the burden of guilt that isn't yours.'

I lowered my gaze and stared at the sand. It's what I always did. I carried someone else's baggage. Took the blame that wasn't mine. It was what I was accustomed to do. Trained to do.

But even if I could convince myself that I wasn't responsible for Josh's actions, I still couldn't place the blame fully on Josh.

The truth was I was complicit. I ignored what I didn't want to see. I allowed him to justify what couldn't be justified. I let it keep happening.

I'd stayed.

'If it was anyone else, anyone but Josh that had hurt you, what do you think his family would say then?'

'Probably the same thing that you said from the beginning. They would tell me to leave him.'

Wouldn't they?

Secretly I hoped so. It felt good to think that they would champion my stand. That they would rally around me. Protect me. Keep me safe.

But I also knew that it would never happen. Because it *was* Josh. They would never believe me. Not against him. It would challenge their perceptions of the world too much to think that someone like Josh could do something like that. I was the unstable one. The one with the history. Josh was the hero who had stood by me.

There was only one way this would play out. And it wouldn't be in my favour. No matter what I did I would lose them.

If I broke up with Josh, I would be cut off. An ex-girlfriend would simply be replaced.

If I told his family the truth, they wouldn't believe me.

Even if I managed to prove it to them somehow, it wouldn't do me any good. They would resent me for it. Not outwardly, perhaps. But subconsciously. I would always be the person who had shattered their family. Just as PC Collier had shattered mine.

I couldn't win.

Unless...

My mind raced as an idea started to form. Could it be that simple?

The downfall in every plan was that Josh would be the focus

of his family's attention. His new life without me would mean there wasn't a place for me any more.

But maybe there was one way to keep my place. Maybe not just retain it, but increase it.

I didn't need to disappear from Josh's life. He needed to disappear from mine.

From everyone's.

49

NOW

I glanced at the kerb where Emma had parked earlier when she dropped me off. There was another car there now. One I didn't recognise.

It wasn't a surprise. I'd told her not to wait. I had no idea how long I would be at the police station, I couldn't expect her to stay. Besides, I hadn't really wanted her to.

Part of me had been glad to step out of her car and walk away from her questions and accusations.

My relief had been short lived. Out of the frying pan and into the fire, as Mum used to say. The questions DC Collier and PC Smith asked were definitely worse. And they carried with them a far greater risk.

I actually missed Emma. We might not be close, but she was still a friend. Or the nearest thing I had to it. I needed that right now.

I slipped my hand into the top of my bag and fumbled for my phone. I sighed as it eluded me. Frustrated, I peered in as I rummaged to the bottom.

It wasn't there.

I glanced back at the police station behind me; had I left it inside? I frowned, trying to remember the last time I'd had it. I knew I had it with me when I left the house.

I sighed as I retraced my steps back into the station.

The officer at the front desk raised his eyebrows as he saw me. 'Back so soon?'

'I've lost my phone.'

'In here?'

I shook my head. 'I'm not sure. It must have fallen out of my bag somewhere.'

'Okay, jot down your name, address and details about the phone and if it turns up, I'll make sure we get it back to you.'

He pushed a notepad towards me and I scribbled down my address. 'Do you think you could call a taxi for me, please?' I asked hopefully. Without my phone I was stranded. And the police station was not somewhere I wanted to be for long.

'Sure,' he nodded. 'Are you heading home?' he asked as I gave him the notepad with my address.

'Yes please,' I replied but even as I spoke I felt nauseous at the thought of going back there. Of going home. Alone.

The officer picked up his phone and started to dial.

'Actually, I've changed my mind. Can I go to Bournemouth Hospital instead, please?'

* * *

I surveyed the quiet café opposite the hospital, debating where to sit as I tried not to spill my cappuccino in my trembling hands. I'd hoped it would be busy in here. I wanted noise and distraction. Not silence. It allowed too much time to think.

'Hi Lauren, back again?'

I pivoted to my right at the familiar voice. 'Dr Nick, hi.'

He grinned at me. 'Our paths seem to keep crossing recently.'

'They do, don't they?'

'Are you meeting your boyfriend?'

'B-boyfriend?' I stuttered over the word.

'Sorry, I thought Abhilash said that you were boyfriend and girlfriend now,' Nick said, casting me a puzzled look.

'He did?' I shifted uncomfortably. Wasn't that something that Abhilash should have mentioned to me first? 'Erm, I'm meeting him after his shift,' I added as I realised that Nick was still staring at me.

He glanced at his watch. 'You know that will be a while, right?'

I nodded. 'He told me when I stopped by the hospital to let him know I was here.' That was the downside to my plan. The empty hours between now and the end of Abhilash's shift. But the alternative was to go home to an empty house alone with nothing but memories for company.

I'd spent years learning how to live with the memories. How to shove them to one side and gloss over them, in a feeble attempt to pretend they weren't there. It was never entirely successful. They were always there. Lurking. Waiting. But they were manageable. Tolerable.

Until now.

Thanks to DC Collier, those memories had broken free from their restraints and it felt like my brain was under attack from the past.

'Join me?' Nick indicated the vacant chair opposite. 'We can keep each other company for the rest of my break.'

I hesitated as Abhilash's words raced through my head.

You know he likes you, right?

If Abhilash was right, then joining Nick for coffee in a practically deserted café didn't seem like the smartest plan.

Then again, perhaps I was wrong. Perhaps Nick was exactly who I needed.

'Thanks,' I said as I slid into the chair. I set my cappuccino down on the table between us and drummed my fingers against the side of the cup.

'Nick,' I hesitated. 'Could you do something for me?'

He tipped his head to the right as he studied me. 'Sounds serious,' he said with a mischievous grin. 'It's the first time you've called me Nick, instead of Dr Nick.'

'Oh,' I stifled a nervous laugh. 'It's not serious, it's just a bit, well, unusual, I guess.'

My understatement was almost as big as my lie. It *was* serious. Everything depended on what I was about to ask him to do. And for it to work, I needed to be able to trust him.

Could I trust him?

'Now I'm really intrigued,' Nick said, edging forwards in his chair.

'Could I send you something to keep for me?'

'What kind of something?'

I shrugged. 'Just something small.' At least it was small in terms of its size. But its implications were much bigger.

'You're not going to tell me what it is, are you?'

I shook my head. 'And you have to promise not to open it.'

Nick hesitated for a moment before nodding slowly. 'I can do that.'

'Thank you.' My shoulders relaxed at the tension I had been carrying in them lifted from me.

I sipped my cappuccino, conscious that now I'd asked my favour I didn't know what else to say. I wasn't in a particularly talkative mood.

'So, you and Abhilash, huh?' Nick said, leaning back.

I nodded. Not entirely sure if there was actually a question there.

'You seem pretty serious.'

I eyed an empty table in the corner which suddenly looked incredibly appealing.

'So, how come you didn't ask Abhilash to look after this mysterious item for you?'

I swallowed. I had my reasons. But they weren't ones I wanted to share.

'I know he stayed over at yours last night,' Nick raised his hands as I started to open my mouth to object. 'I know that's none of my business, and Abhilash has already warned me off, but—'

'Warned you off?'

Nick shrugged. 'It a guy thing, you know, just making sure that I know that you're taken. I don't blame him. I'd do the same if I was in his shoes.'

I slumped back in my chair. It didn't sound like Abhilash. Could he have been mistaken? Nick knew Abhilash had stayed at my house last night, which meant he thought Abhilash and I were getting more serious. Was it possible that in his jealousy he was making up accusations about Abhilash?

'The thing is, Abhilash is a friend but...' Nick glanced around the café, as though afraid of being overhead. 'I'm worried that you are getting in too deep.'

My instinct was to push my chair back and head over to that vacant little table away from Nick and whatever this was. *Abhilash is a friend, but...* was hardly reassuring. It made me question just how much of a friend Nick really was.

And yet, I stayed.

Perhaps because I already knew what it was like to be in too deep. I'd made that mistake before. I was still trying to clamber my way out of it. If I was making another mistake with Abhilash, then I needed to know now. While I could still do something about it.

'You make a great couple. And I don't want to rock the boat for either of you.'

I waited for Nick to continue, even though he was rapidly losing credibility. Rocking the boat was clearly exactly what he intended to do.

The only question was, what information did he hold that he thought was so powerful to be able to do it.

'But I have to admit that I was surprised when Abhilash told me you two were dating.'

I nodded slowly. 'Because of how we met.'

'Because of him.'

'Him?' I shook my head. I must have misunderstood. I was the reason for concern. For hesitation. Not Abhilash. I could understand Nick being surprised that Abhilash would date me. I could see him warning his friend to stay away from me. From my craziness. My complications.

But Abhilash being the source of concern didn't make sense. Unless... my body edged forwards in my chair as I leaned towards Nick, desperate for clarity. What was it that I didn't know?

'I see you two getting closer and closer, and it just worries me that you're going to get hurt.'

I swallowed, bracing myself for the big reveal. Whatever it was, I could handle it. After all, I'd been hurt before. So many times. So many ways. Nick was afraid for me, but he didn't know what I'd lived through. He didn't know that I could look after myself.

But knowing what I was up against in advance would be a new development. Usually, I was too slow to catch on. And even then, I lived in denial for as long as possible.

Not this time though.

I knew better now.

I would be proactive. Efficient. Different.

'He's not being fair to you,' he shook his head. 'I would never treat you like that.' Nick clenched his fist as though fighting with his frustration. 'I told him that. I told him that you deserved better.'

Better.

Was there better? Was Nick?

The questions circled in my brain.

Perhaps better was something fictional. Something that was always just a little bit out of reach.

At least, out of my reach.

'Abhilash is leaving soon,' Nick at least had the decency to look pained at delivering this news.

'You're wrong,' my words were punctuated with hostility. Perhaps it was unfair. Nick was trying to help. He didn't know that his claim was like acid burning into my flesh.

Abhilash wouldn't leave. He couldn't. Not after everything I'd done so we could be together.

Nick grimaced. 'He's going back to India.'

50

THEN

It's my mum,' Abhilash said, glancing at his phone as it played a repetitive tune.

'Take it,' I told him.

He hesitated for a second, his eyes silently seeking reassurance.

I smiled as I nodded. Of course he should take the call. It was his mum. Family was everything.

At least, the right family was.

My smile fell away as he scrambled up off the sand. He turned his back to me and walked a few steps away, as though seeking privacy. Not that he needed it. The sea breeze carried the occasional word back to me, but they were meaningless to me as he slipped back into his native language.

In time I would get him to teach me.

If we were together long enough.

I shook that thought away. Of course we would be together long enough. We had to be.

He needed me as much as I needed him. I could see the treacherous path that he was on. He didn't realise it. He was blind to it. Blind to the betrayal and manipulation of the people that surrounded him. The people that he trusted.

Just like I had been once.

I could be his guide. Help him navigate. Lead him to safety.

Lead us to safety.

Away from Josh. Away from everyone else who would separate us. Harm us.

I watched him pacing along the seashore. He seemed agitated. I tried to read his expression, wishing I could hear and understand at least one side of the conversation.

Why had he gone so far away? To be thoughtful and not disturb me with his call? Or was there another reason?

I recalled the photo of his family he'd shown me the other day. I could picture his mum on the other end of the phone. But her image was meaningless without context. What did she sound like? Not just her voice, but her tone. What was hidden beneath the words she spoke out loud?

Abhilash talked about her with pride and affection, just like he did the rest of his family. But the little I knew about them was enough. I could see what he couldn't. He was too close. Just like I had been.

I needed him to open my eyes to Josh, and Abhilash needed me to show him the truth about the people around him too. Alone we were vulnerable. Together we were stronger. He didn't realise it yet. Didn't see what they were like.

I wasn't really surprised. It was who he was. How he was. He saw the best in people.

Even when he shouldn't.

51

'Are you sure you're okay?' Abhilash asked as he pulled his car up to the kerb in front of my house.

I fixed a smile in place as I twisted in the passenger seat to face him. 'I'm fine. It's just been a long day.' I was holding back. Keeping things from him.

'I'm sorry I couldn't drive you home earlier.'

'No worries,' I shrugged. 'I knew it would be a while before your shift finished. Although you were later than I'd thought.'

Abhilash ran his hand through his short black hair. 'Yeah,' he puffed out his cheeks as he exhaled. 'I had some stuff to deal with.'

'Is everything okay?'

'Complications with a patient.'

'I'm sorry,' I stroked his cheek with my fingertips. 'I hope it all works out okay.'

'It'll all be fine,' he said in a more upbeat tone, but his frown remained.

'Your job is so tough. I don't know how you do it.'

'Some days I wonder the same thing.' He shook his head.

'Anyway, nothing more I can do about it today. I'm just sorry I kept you waiting so long. Although I still don't really understand why you didn't just get the taxi to drop you straight home instead of coming to the hospital.'

I glanced at the house through the window. 'I just wasn't ready to come back, I guess.' I reached for the door handle. The truth was I still wasn't ready to come home. But I also knew that I couldn't avoid it forever.

I pushed the door open and swung my legs out of the car. I frowned as I realised the engine was still running. 'Aren't you coming in?'

'I want to head home and take a shower. But I can come back after if you like?' Abhilash added as my face fell.

'Why not just take a shower here? It would save you going backwards and forwards.'

Abhilash's gaze drifted over my shoulder to the house. 'I don't know. I mean, it just feels a bit weird with Josh missing. You could come home with me.'

'To the house you rent with Nick?'

'Y-e-ah,' Abhilash's shoulders sagged. 'Not such a good plan, huh?'

I shook my head. 'Not really.' But not for the reason he thought.

I didn't want to see Nick. Not right now. And not with Abhilash. I didn't want Abhilash to learn of what he'd told me. Once that happened, Abhilash would want to discuss it. I wasn't ready for that.

I wanted to be an ostrich and bury my head in the sand. At least for today. I had too many other things to worry about after my police interview. If I avoided the subject, then I could convince myself that Abhilash's departure was an old plan. One from before he met me. Nick didn't know that things had changed. That I had changed them.

Hadn't I?

Abhilash turned the key. 'Then I guess I'm staying here.'

My lips curved upwards into a tight smile. It was a minor victory. He was staying. But for how long?

We walked up the driveway hand in hand. It felt good to be like this. Together. My smile relaxed as I slipped the key in the lock. Coming home with Abhilash was definitely better than coming home alone.

The door banged against something as I pushed it open. I poked my head around the door to see what it was and rolled my eyes. Nestled below the letter box was my phone.

I bent down and picked it up. 'I thought I'd lost it and it was here the whole time.'

Abhilash kissed my forehead as I stood up. 'You've had a difficult few days.'

'That's true,' I nodded. But my gaze remained locked on the phone in my hands. I was so sure that it had been in my bag when I left the house.

52

THEN

'I haven't heard from you all day.' There was a hint of accusation in Josh's voice as he stomped into our bedroom.

The irony of it grated against me. It was 10 p.m., I was already in my pyjamas, and he'd only just come home. Yet, he was complaining that he hadn't heard from me.

I shook my head, resisting the urge to point out that he could have called. That he could have told me he wouldn't be home for dinner.

I knew better than that.

I set my hair brush down on the dressing table and glanced at my phone propped up against the mirror. 'It's been a crazy day. I got contacted last week by a senior executive at a marketing consultancy. A big one.' My excitement bubbled to the surface, displacing my irritation. 'He'd been following my progress and wanted to meet with me to discuss my ideas.' I was rambling, I knew it, but I was so enthusiastic I couldn't contain my words. 'We met today.'

After I'd met Abhilash.

My omission felt like a lead weight pressing down on me. I hadn't been busy all day. Not with work.

Josh tugged his tie off and unbuttoned his shirt. 'Why would he want to meet you? He must have staff that handle that social media stuff.' His tone was flat and dismissive. He didn't understand. In all my babbling I'd failed to tell him the most important part.

I grinned. 'But that's just it. He wants me to be one of those members of staff. He wants to hire me.'

Josh's head snapped back and he glared at me. 'You had a job interview without talking to me.' His voice was full of contempt.

I felt my weight shift backwards as I withdrew from him. 'Sorry,' the apology left my lips before I'd even paused to question why I felt the need to apologise.

What had I done wrong? I'd had a meeting, that was all.

Perhaps I should have told Josh in advance. I could have mentioned it as soon as I'd received the invitation. But what for? To be talked out of it? To be told I was wasting my time?

I'd wanted to go. Even if I took the job it wouldn't intrude on any time Josh and I spent together. He was at work. I was stuck here. My business was a success, but it was isolated. Maybe working for a big company, going to an office each day, meeting other people in real life, would be good for me.

'I haven't accepted it yet.'

'Yet? You're not actually considering it, are you?'

I gazed at him blankly. This wasn't the reaction I had anticipated. I knew he didn't have much regard for my business. Didn't understand how effective I was at it. To him it was just me, sat at our kitchen table, messing around on the internet. But this was a job. A real job. I thought that would make a difference to him. I thought he'd be excited for me. Proud.

Right now he didn't seem to be either.

'Obviously it's a mistake. Why would they want you?'

'Oh.' It was the only word my brain could form as disillusionment settled over me. His question stung. The implication that I wasn't good enough for anyone to want was scathing and cruel. How could he not see that?

But then, for a long time, I hadn't seen it either. I hadn't wanted to.

Now it was the only thing I could see.

'Well?' Josh held his hands out in front of him, impatiently waiting for my explanation.

'I have a degree in marketing.'

'That was years ago. It's not like you ever actually did anything with it.'

'I run my own business.'

'I mean, you haven't done anything *real* with it. You've never had a proper job.'

'Because you didn't want me to.' I knew that they were the wrong words to say. The wrong tone. The wrong time.

I saw anger flash across Josh's face. In that split second my brain registered what was about to happen, but it was too late now to outrun the fall out.

53

NOW

'You should have called us.' Janice flung her arms around me the second I opened the front door. 'We would have come and picked you up from the hospital.'

I hesitated for a moment before hugging her back. I hadn't expected this kind of greeting. Not any more.

'We tried to visit you,' Keith added behind her. 'But the doctor wouldn't let us.'

I cast a glance at the stairs, conscious of the distant sound of the shower running and hoped the Carters wouldn't notice it. I wondered what doctor they had spoken to. If I'd been moved to the ward when they came to visit, hopefully they wouldn't recognise Abhilash. Then again, I was pretty sure discovering any guy taking a shower in the home I had shared with their son would not end well.

'He said it was family only,' Keith added.

Family only.

The words grated against me. Another reminder that I wasn't one of them. Not truly. Not fully.

I'd thought marrying Josh would change that. I'd officially be a member of the family. I'd share their name. I'd be their daughter.

Finally.

But Josh had destroyed that dream. He didn't want to marry me. He didn't want me to be one of them.

'The doctor wouldn't listen when we told him we are family,' Janice told me, stepping back to look at me. 'As good as, anyway.'

I tried to smile, but it felt more like a grimace as Janice's words got stuck on repeat in my brain.

As good as.

Except it wasn't. You were either family. Or you weren't.

And I wasn't.

'That's okay, I appreciate you trying,' I told them. It felt famil- iar. Soothing someone else when I was the one who was hurt.

'Paul and Sasha send their love,' she added.

The tension in my body eased a little. I might not be family. But they did still care. 'Tell them thanks from me.'

'They would have come with us, but someone needed to stay at home just in case...' Her voice trailed away, letting the silence speak volumes.

Josh.

It was always Josh.

'Sasha's been an angel,' Janice continued, as she slipped off her coat and handed it to me. 'She hasn't left our side since we heard Josh was missing. I don't know how we would have got through the last two days without her.'

My skin prickled.

All seems a bit fast to me.

Josh had been right. It was fast. Not just for the engagement but for everything. Sasha had barely been around five minutes and she was more a part of the family than I'd ever had been.

I'd been replaced.

I'd worked hard for my place, and she'd just swooped in and taken it from me.

A ring was all it had taken.

'We're all so relieved that you're all right. I just pray that Josh...' Her voice broke, and she dropped her head into her hands as she started to sob.

Guilt punched me in the gut. I was being selfish. Putting my feelings, my pain, ahead of theirs. I wrapped my arm around her shoulders and guided her down the hall. 'Come and sit down in the living room.'

The front door clicked closed behind me and I heard Keith's footsteps follow us along the hall floor tiles.

'What happened to our son, Lauren?' Janice asked desperately as she collapsed onto the sofa.

And there it was. The real reason they were here.

The switch had been so fast. So seamless. I hadn't seen it coming. Josh had the same trait. He could switch from concern to accusations just as easily as Janice had. And there was no mistaking that's what this was. An accusation.

She thought I knew something. Or perhaps even that I had done something. Something that prevented their son from being with them. That prevented their family from being whole.

Keith sat beside her and gripped her hand. They both stared up at me. Their eyes pleading for information. For answers. For hope.

'I don't know.' My reply was insufficient. But it was all I had.

'What did you do with his belongings?' Janice asked, glancing back over her shoulder at the empty hallway.

'I moved the bags into one of the spare rooms.' It was pointless to feign ignorance. We all knew what she was talking about. 'I wasn't sure when he would be round to collect them...'

'Is he *able* to collect them, then?'

'Of course, whenever he wants to.' I pretended I hadn't noticed the emphasis Janice placed on 'able'. She was testing me. Seeing if I believed Josh was still alive.

'Why are his clothes in bags, Lauren?' Janice's eyes narrowed. 'Bin bags at that. As though you are throwing out the rubbish.'

'No, it's not like that. I just didn't have anything else to put it all in.'

'Okay,' Janice said, but her expression told me she didn't think it was okay at all. 'But why would you need to put his stuff into bags at all?'

She was pushing me. Making me say it out loud.

'Because we broke up,' I forced my voice to stay strong. I'd known this moment would come. That Josh's parents would have questions. The police had got their belief that Josh was with me from Paul. It stood to reason that his parents would too.

'Why would you say such a thing?'

I took a deep breath and sank onto the armchair opposite. 'Because it's true. We broke up on Saturday. Josh is moving out.'

'No, that doesn't make sense. You couldn't have done. Why would the two of you go out jet-skiing together if you'd broken up?'

'We wouldn't. We didn't.'

They stared at me as though I was speaking another language. One they'd never heard before.

'I don't know where Josh is, but he wasn't with me on the jet-ski.'

'He texted Paul on Sunday morning. He told him you were both going jet-skiing together.'

'I know, the police told me, but it isn't true.'

'The police found his car in Harbourside car park,' Keith said.

'That doesn't mean—'

'Doesn't mean he was with you?' Keith cut through my words.

'Then what does it mean, Lauren? My son's car was found by Baiter slipway where he always went jet-skiing, on the day he always went, and he'd texted his brother to tell him that that was exactly what he was about to do. With you.'

With you.

The accusation resounded around the room. Their son was missing, and they thought I was responsible.

They weren't the only ones. Given the tone of the police interview, they clearly thought I was involved too. I couldn't blame them. The police didn't know me. Not even DC Collier. They only knew my past. But to the Carters, I was more than that.

Wasn't I?

'The police came to see us again this afternoon, they asked us something else about Josh that didn't make sense. They asked if he had a temper. Or if we'd ever witnessed any violence.' Keith's glare bore into me. 'Did that come from you too?'

I pushed myself up from the chair. 'Maybe we should talk about this another time.'

Keith leapt to his feet. 'Another time? Josh is missing. There isn't another time.'

'The problems Josh and I had are between us.' He hadn't treated me well, but I wouldn't turn his family against him.

'You're claiming he was violent with you?' Janice asked, standing up beside her husband.

I lowered my gaze to the floor.

'He's Josh. Our Josh. He wouldn't hurt anyone. Especially not you, Lauren. He loves you.'

I swallowed. Janice's words were so familiar. I knew them well. I'd told myself the same thing before. And not just about Josh...

'Josh disappears and now you're making all these crazy accusations.' Keith spat the words at me. 'If they were true, why didn't you say something sooner?'

'I couldn't.' I shook my head. 'I just couldn't do that to you. I know what it's like to hear that kind of truth about someone you love.' Everyone always said the truth would set you free. But they were wrong. The truth was a prison too.

'I know you've had a difficult life, Lauren.' Janice spoke softly. 'And as much as we have tried to be there for you, I realise that we will never fully know what living through that kind of trauma, that kind of betrayal, does to you. But you can't let that be an excuse to lash out and hurt the people who love you, who have only ever tried to help you.'

'I'm not lashing out. This isn't some kind of rebellion or breakdown.'

'Then tell us what really happened. Tell us where Josh is.'

I stared at her blankly.

'Just tell us what you did to him,' Keith yelled as he lunged towards me. 'What did you do to my son?'

I froze. I knew I should step back. Defend myself somehow. But I couldn't.

He reminded me too much of Josh.

There was a time when I'd admired Josh's passion. His fire. I thought it was a sign of how strong his emotions were. Of how strong his love for me was. But now I felt my stomach contract at the reminder.

Janice tugged at his arm, pulling Keith back. 'That isn't the way to reach her.'

'Well, your tiptoeing around her isn't getting us anywhere, is it?' Keith snapped but he allowed himself to be pulled away.

I stared at Janice. How had she done that? I could still sense Keith's anger simmering within him, but it was controlled. Janice's voice, her touch, was enough to guide him back to his own restraint.

That's what was missing from Josh. That balance. That containment.

Or perhaps it wasn't what Josh lacked. Perhaps it was me. I didn't possess Janice's skill. Her ability to defuse the situation. To instil calmness.

Occasionally I managed it. But it was different. It took compliance and apologies for things that I hadn't even done wrong.

* * *

'Come on, we're going to be late.' Josh clapped his hands in the doorway of our bedroom, as though a rhythmic beat would somehow make me go faster.

'I'm coming. I'm coming,' I assured him as I twisted my right arm behind my back and coaxed the zipper on my dress up. 'I wish you'd told me you wanted to go earlier than we'd planned.'

I froze as the clapping ceased.

'What?'

The only sound was the faint rumble of cars driving down the street past the house.

I cursed my stupidity. I knew better than that. 'N-nothing, I was just—'

'Just blaming me for your inability to be ready on time.'

'Sorry.' The apology fell from my lips so quickly; it had become instinctive. A look. A tone. And the sorry just emerged. 'I'm just flustered. It wasn't fair of me to take it out on you.'

Our eyes were locked across the bedroom.

Usually our room felt large and spacious. Its size had been one of the most appealing points when we bought the house. And yet somehow on days like this, even our large bedroom felt tiny and claustrophobic.

A few strides were all it would take Josh to cross the room and reach me.

'You should have been ready when I got home. I told you I was leaving work early today so we could get there on time. The party starts at 7 p.m.' His body was rigid, his jaw locked.

I nodded. 'You're right. I should have been. I must have lost track of time. I'm sorry.'

Josh's jaw relaxed slightly and I took a slow step forward.

No arguing back. No sudden movements. I knew the unspoken rules that guided our standoffs.

'I let you down.' I edged forwards. 'I'm sorry.'

I kept a silent count of my sorrys. Not too few. Not too many. They had to be used right.

'Yeah.' Josh rolled his shoulders. 'Next time just make sure you're ready.'

I nodded and smiled at him. Not a grin. Just a tiny smile. Moderated. Cautious.

We were so close now. I reached out my right hand slowly and stroked his arm. 'I'll do better, I promise.'

He covered my hand with his. 'I know you will, Lauren.'

He turned away, letting my hand fall. I watched him disappear down the stairs before I allowed myself to breathe out.

I cast a glance at my reflection in the mirror and tucked a stray strand of hair behind my ear. It had gone well. This time.

I was learning.

Slowly.

* * *

'Please, Lauren,' Janice pleaded as she clasped my hand in hers.

I studied her, wondering if she knew. If some part of her deep down, beneath the denial, could recognise the truth of my accusations.

'He's my son.'

Her words were like an icy wave crashing down on top of me, extinguishing the tiny sliver of hope. No matter what her subconscious might know, it was irrelevant; she would never accept it.

'I'm telling the truth. I don't know where he is.'

I waited for them to argue. To accuse me of lying. But they didn't. They didn't do anything. They just stared at me.

There was something different about their expressions now. Like a realisation dawning on them. Perhaps the sheer desperation in my voice had convinced them of my innocence. Perhaps they finally accepted that I would never harm anyone, least of all Josh.

Janice's hand fell from my mine and she took a step back.

'You really don't know, do you?'

I shook my head. Relief washing over me like the first rainfall after a drought.

They finally believed me.

They knew me.

'She's just like her mother.' Keith's words tore into me, depriving me of oxygen.

I understood their expressions then. It wasn't trust. It wasn't acceptance.

It was fear.

54

THEN

Josh's breathing became rhythmic and calm. He was asleep. He'd hit me, hurt me, and yet he slept like nothing was wrong.

It's what I'd wanted, for him to fall asleep, to leave me alone, and yet at the same time it seemed so unfathomable. How could he sleep?

It shouldn't surprise me. Not after all this time. But it still did.

Memories of the first time he'd hit me washed over me. Submerging me in the past. The pain.

My hand trembled as I pressed it to my eye. Pain seared through my face, penetrating deep into my head.

He'd hit me.

Josh had hit me.

I stared at him through one eye, desperate to make sense of what had just happened.

I had to be wrong.

He couldn't have hit me. Not Josh. He wouldn't.

I knew I should do something. React somehow. Yell at him. Tell him to leave. Or better yet, I should leave instead. I should run.

But I did nothing.

I reached for the wall to steady myself.

'Oh Lauren, I'm so sorry,' I heard the anguish in his voice as his arms wrapped themselves around my waist, just like he normally did.

Except there was nothing normal about this.

'I'm sorry,' he repeated.

I squirmed, trying to break free, but the pounding in my head made the room spin. I wasn't strong enough.

Again.

'You need to sit down,' he said, guiding me to the bed. I staggered and leant against him. Too stunned to do anything other than comply.

'Are you okay? Can I get you anything? Ice or...?' His words ran out of steam.

I shook my head, unable to speak.

He sat beside me and hugged me to him. 'I love you so much.' I winced as his shoulder pressed against my bruised face. 'I'm so sorry,' he whispered.

I nodded. I knew he was. I could feel it. His guilt. His sorrow.

That meant something.

Didn't it?

'It's late. We should get some sleep.' I didn't know why I'd said it. I knew I wouldn't sleep. Not now. How could I? My brain felt dazed from the force of the blow, but my mind was racing like a Scalextric race car driving in loops, stuck on a track.

He'd hit me.

Josh stood up and lifted me on to the bed, before lying down beside me. He was so attentive. So careful. Taking care of me as though I was sick.

But I wasn't sick.

I was hurt.

He snuggled against me and held me close as though he was afraid to let go. Afraid to lose me.

But all I wanted was for him to leave. I wanted space. I wanted to think. To cry.

I couldn't cry while he was here. It would make it worse. He'd keep apologising. Keep fussing. I didn't want that.

I just wanted to be alone.

He flicked off the light and I lay there staring into the darkness.

I should leave.

It's what you were supposed to do, wasn't it? If your partner hit you, you should run. It was common sense.

All I had to do was just stand up and walk to the door. Simple. Easy.

Yet, my body didn't move. I felt paralysed.

Maybe it was shock.

Maybe it was fear.

I shoved that thought away. No, it wasn't fear. I wasn't afraid of Josh.

Whatever it had been. Whatever had happened. It was done now. Finished.

Everything was calm now.

Josh was Josh again.

My Josh.

He hadn't meant to hurt me.

He was sorry.

But he had still done it.

My thoughts felt like they were colliding into one another. My brain couldn't process it. Everything had shattered in the space of a few moments.

To throw him out now would mean the end. It was a decision I didn't feel able to make. Not right now. I was too confused.

Yes, perhaps this was what shock felt like. Numb. Disconnected. Still here. Still present. And yet, at the same time, somehow not.

It was an accident.

Josh would never mean to hurt me.

The image of his fist flying towards my face replayed in my mind. I couldn't see out of my left eye now, but I could still see that. I could still feel the impact. Hear the crunch of his knuckles hitting bone.

I could see it and yet I still couldn't believe it.

Perhaps that was what silenced me. The impossibility of it. It couldn't have happened. Not really. Not by Josh.

He nuzzled against my neck, covering it in gentle urgent kisses. There was a sincerity to his touch. I could feel it. So tender. So caring.

I'd never known concern like that before.

I'd always believed he loved me. He'd always said he did. And yet, somehow this was more.

I could feel it with a certainty I'd never known before.

He loved me.

* * *

I knew differently now though. I knew better.

This wasn't love.

The tears came then. I couldn't stop them. Silent. Broken.

I stared at the ceiling, illuminated in the soft glow of the early September sunrise. My head hurt from crying so long. I thought it would have made me feel better. That my silent tears would wash away some of the pain.

But they never did.

It still lingered. If anything it felt worse now. My eyes stung and my head throbbed. But I had no more tears left. Just an ache that I couldn't ignore.

I didn't even attempt to wipe my tears away. I couldn't move. Couldn't make a sound. If I did, I might wake him.

I savoured the last few minutes of stillness before it was time for him to get up. I knew what would happen then. It was part of our routine. One that kept repeating. Its frequency increasing.

He'd be sorry. I'd comfort him and forgive him. And the cycle would reset.

Just like always.

I was treading water. Battling constantly against the current but barely even managing to keep my head above water. I wasn't getting anywhere. I was surviving.

Just about.

I'd spent years excusing his behaviour. Rationalising it. Absorbing the blame. Telling myself that it wouldn't have happened if I hadn't hurt his pride. It wasn't how he was. Not in normal circumstances.

I'd screwed it up.

Just like with Mum.

There's always a way out. A first step.

Abhilash's voice whispered through the darkness. My gaze drifted to the doorway, silhouetted in the faint morning light.

Josh was a light sleeper. If I shuffled out of bed, he'd be awake before I even reached the door. And yet I knew Abhilash would be disappointed in me if he could see me now. After everything that had happened last night, I was still here. I'd stayed.

Again.

I couldn't blame it on ignorance. Not this time. It wasn't like before. I knew what the danger was. I knew who it was. That should have been enough to make me run.

But I hadn't.

I no longer hoped that this time would be different. This time he'd change. For me. Nothing in our history gave any reason to think that. After all, he never had so far.

I was tired of doing the same thing, hoping for a different outcome. The only way to change things was to change my response.

And I had changed.

Josh just didn't know it yet.

55

NOW

I sat on the sand at the Fisherman's Walk, my attention fixed on the white cliffs of the Isle of Wight. From here the polar bear was clearly visible and yet I knew by simply walking along the beach I could change its shape. Distort it.

Appearances were always subjective.

A movement to my right caught my attention and I squinted up at Emma. She wasn't my usual Friday companion for a trip to the beach but given I hadn't heard from her since she drove me to the police station on Tuesday, I didn't think I could refuse when she'd called. Not if I stood any chance of keeping our friendship, however tentative it might be.

'Thanks for meeting me here,' she said as she flopped down onto the sand beside me.

'Sure.' I shrugged as though it wasn't a big deal. But after our last encounter, that's exactly what it was.

'I wasn't sure you'd come.'

I chuckled ruefully. 'To be honest, neither was I.'

We sat in silence watching a group of teenagers play football in front of us.

'That used to be us,' she said wistfully.

I didn't respond. Before Mum's death, I'd done exactly what I was doing now. Sat on the sand and watched everyone else having fun. It wasn't until after she'd gone that I was able to join them. But somehow even then it had never felt as though I quite fitted.

Perhaps I'd sat on the side-lines too long to ever truly belong.

'Why are we here, Emma? I doubt it's to reminisce.'

'I want to talk to you about Josh.'

I sighed. I knew this had been a bad idea.

'I spoke to Paul.'

'I'm guessing he told you everything I said to Josh's parents, right? The real reason for all my injuries.'

Emma's lips grew taut. 'He told me about your allegations.'

I stood up and dusted the sand from my clothes. 'They aren't allegations, Emma. They are facts. Facts no one opened their eyes enough to see. Not even you. Not even my supposed friend.'

I pivoted on my heel and headed towards the promenade.

'It's that doctor,' Emma said, trailing after me. 'He's got in your head. He's poisoning you against Josh. Against all of us.'

I stopped and turned to glare at her, anger burning behind my eyes. I wanted to yell at her. To scream the truth into her face. But what would be the point? She would never believe it.

I swung back round and marched up the chine towards the cliff top. It was futile to argue with her. But I wasn't going to stay and listen to her tear Abhilash down.

'You're throwing away an amazing relationship with a guy who adores you and all the history you have together. And for what? Some random stranger who patched you back together and is just looking for a quick fling. You always try and create perfection, even when there's nothing there.'

An amazing relationship.

It was the perfect image I'd created. The lie.

Emma couldn't understand why I was chasing the fantasy of a perfect relationship with Abhilash, when I already had a real one with Josh.

I couldn't blame her for thinking I was crazy to give it up. In her position I would probably think the same. How was she to know she was defending a lie? That neither were really perfect?

I'd never told her the truth before, so why would she believe me now?

It wasn't really fair of me to be mad at her. I'd created this illusion the moment I'd covered up the first bruise with extra make up. I could have told her then. I could have shown her. Asked for her advice. Her help.

But I also knew that it wouldn't have made any difference. We would just have had this conversation sooner, that was all.

The only difference now was Abhilash.

My pace slowed and I turned to face her again. 'I didn't leave Josh for Abhilash.'

She arched her eyebrow. She didn't believe me.

I shrugged. 'It's not for him, but it is because of him.'

'It's the same thing.'

'No.' I shook my head. 'It really isn't. Abhilash made me face the truth. If I hadn't met him, I wouldn't have found the courage to leave. I needed to. I wanted to. But the truth is I wouldn't. I couldn't.'

'But Josh loves you.'

'Sometimes love isn't enough,' I repeated Abhilash's words. He was right. I knew that now.

'You could go to counselling, work through things, deal with all this resentment.'

I ran my hands through my hair. 'I don't need counselling, Emma. I just need my friends to believe me.'

I caught Emma's arm and guided her to the bench a few metres away. Halfway up the chine wasn't the best place to reveal the dark details of my relationship with Josh, but I knew if I put it off any longer I would find a way to talk myself out of it.

It was time she knew the truth.

At least, some of it.

'Do you remember the broken wrist I had in the spring?'

Emma nodded.

'We were getting ready for work that morning. I was making Josh's breakfast, just like normal, but...' My voice cracked as the memories consumed me.

'What the—'

I swung round, turning my back on the toast that I had been buttering. Josh sat at the kitchen table, his phone in his hands, his face pale and shocked.

My stomach lurched.

'What's wrong?' I forced the words out; my throat felt tight and constricted.

'I was just about to transfer some money from the savings account to cover this month's mortgage, but...' His finger flicked against the phone screen, scrolling frantically.

I stepped forwards, gripping the worktop. 'But...?' My voice was barely audible. What had happened to our savings? We couldn't have lost them, could we? I heard about cases of identity theft so often, but that happened to other people, right? Not us. Please, not us.

His lips parted and closed, but no words escaped.

I rushed towards him and peered at the phone screen over his shoulder. My breath caught in my chest as my gaze locked onto the account balance.

I frowned. 'I don't understand. It's all there.'

Josh twisted in the chair to look at me. 'All there?' He spoke slowly, as though I was stupid. 'Lauren, that's not our money.'

I blinked.

'The bank must have made an error,' Josh continued. 'There's no way they will let us keep it.'

I laughed nervously. 'Of course they'll let us keep it. It's ours. It's in our account.'

'We don't have savings like this.' Josh shook his head as he went back to scrolling through the transactions. 'But I don't understand where it's come from. There are all these deposits, but they all have your name on them.'

'Josh.' I rested my hand on his shoulder, a broad grin spread across my face. 'When was the last time you looked in the savings account?'

'I don't know. Not for months. I mean, it's not like there's much in there to look at. At least there shouldn't be.'

'Yes, there should be.'

He looked up, his eyes meeting mine. Bewilderment shining through them.

'I told you I'd been transferring some money to savings from the business.'

'What business?'

'My business.'

'Your social media thing?' Josh waved his hand dismissively.

Thing.

I tried not to flinch at his condescension. That's all my business was to him. A thing. Trivial and unimportant.

Just like me.

'You couldn't earn amounts like these.' He shoved his phone in front of me, showing me the transactions. 'Not from that.'

His tone cut into me.

I'd stopped talking about my business months ago. I didn't share the details of my day with him. It was better that way. But I'd quietly transferred a portion of my earnings into our savings each month, waiting for him to acknowledge them.

And me.

But he'd never commented.

I knew better than to rush him. Josh needed to come round to new ideas in his own time. When he realised that it was a regular occurrence, when he saw that it was dependable, then in time he would recognise that my business was working. That I was capable.

He'd be proud of me then. I was sure of it.

I stood up straight, and grinned. Now was that time.

'But it does make that kind of money.'

I waited for that look of admiration, the one I hadn't seen on his face for so long. I missed it. I'd been a burden on him and his family for too long. Financially. Emotionally. But now....

My grin grew broader. 'The business is doing so well. It's grown faster than I'd ever anticipated. I can barely keep up with demand.'

He stared at me. I could see understanding start to clear his features, but he still looked stunned.

'I've kept some cash in the business account to reinvest but I've been transferring some into our savings each month.' I wrapped my arms around his shoulders and snuggled against his neck. 'We can finally go on holiday or buy furniture for the spare bedrooms like we've talked about. We're finally in a position to think about starting a family, Josh. Our family.'

Josh tensed against me. 'You're not satisfied with what I provide for us, is that it?'

I drew back. 'What? N-no, it's not like that.' I stammered. What had just happened? This wasn't how it was supposed to go. He was supposed to be proud of me, not resentful. 'I know how hard you work and I'm so grateful for that. But it shouldn't all be on you. I want to help too.'

I felt as though I was grovelling. Pleading for him to acknowledge my appreciation, and yet where was his? Shouldn't he be appreciative too? Hadn't I done something nice for us? For him? Confusion rained down on my life, like an April shower. Shouldn't this be a moment of celebration, not accusation?

He jerked free from my hug and stood up. 'I told you I don't need your help.'

'But—' I clamped my jaw closed.

'But what?'

Josh's first statement circled back through my brain. 'Why did you need to move money from the savings account?' Between his wages and the extra I'd already put in, there should have been plenty in the current account to cover our monthly bills.

He glared at me.

I stepped back. I'd seen that look before. I knew what it meant.

I'd said the wrong thing.

Again.

* * *

I wrapped my fingers around my right wrist. It had been free of the cast for almost three months, but I could still remember the feel of it. The weight. 'The irony of all this is that I only met Abhilash *because* of Josh.'

'Oh, Lauren.' Emma shook her head slowly. There was such pity in her eyes. 'You really believe that, don't you?'

She was judging me. She thought I was crazy. That I believed some fictionalised story that I told myself. But I knew better. I'd lived it.

'It's the truth,' I told her firmly. I stood up and straightened my spine. 'Josh isn't the guy you think he is. There's another side to him. I don't care if you don't believe me. I know it's the truth and that's all that matters.'

She licked her lips. 'There's something that I need to tell you.'

Her manner had changed. Shifted from assertive and self-assured to... I frowned, as I realised what her expression was. Nervous. She looked nervous.

'I didn't know. I swear I didn't know.'

I let out a breath and my body seemed to deflate as though the only thing that had been holding me together was the fear that no one would understand. No one would believe me.

But she did. Finally. Emma believed me.

'And I know that it was bad,' Emma continued. 'So unbelievably bad. I told him that.'

'You told him?' I frowned. 'You told Josh?'

She nodded.

I put my hand to my head as I tried to comprehend what she was telling me. She'd told Josh what he had done was bad, but until two seconds ago she hadn't even believed that he had hurt me. She couldn't possibly have told him.

Unless she had always known.

And lied for him.

'But I understand why he did it.'

Cold dread seeped into my bones as I staggered backwards. She was on his side. She knew what he'd done and yet she was condoning it. Excusing it.

Who else knew?

The Carters? The police? The doctors?

My fingers traced a shaky path along my cheek to my lips. I covered my mouth, supressing the cry that threatened to erupt from somewhere deep inside me.

Maybe Mum had been right all along. It was me. I drove people to this.

'He's willing to forgive you. He just wants you back.'

Emma blurred in and out of focus.

He wants you back.

The only way that Emma could know what Josh wanted was...

'He was desperate, Lauren. Desperate, scared, and stupid. But you at least need to hear him out. You owe him that.'

I felt numb. 'W-where is he?'

'Hi Lauren.'

The voice behind me, higher up the chine, welded me to the spot. It couldn't have been what I thought. *Who* I thought. But as I watched Emma's gaze shift from my face to something over my shoulder, the corner of her mouth lifted and I knew that voice was real. I hadn't imagined it.

He was back.

56

THEN

I stood in the kitchen doorway, waiting for him as his car pulled up on the drive. I knew that sound. The heaviness of the engine. The squeak of the brakes that he still hadn't got the garage to check. The thud of the car door slamming shut. One, two, three... I counted his footsteps up the gravel driveway. Four, five... I took a deep breath. This was it.

He was home.

The lock clunked as he turned his key and pushed the door open. His eyes met mine as I stood in the kitchen doorway at the other end of the hall. A flicker of surprise passed over his face before his features settled into a smile. It had been a long time since I'd greeted him as he came through the door and welcomed him home.

His smiled wavered when he realised that I wasn't smiling back.

My expression was neutral. Calm. But inside I felt everything. Every emotion that I had kept bottled up for too many years. The fear. The anger. It was almost overwhelming and yet at the same time it was reassuring. Because I finally knew what I needed to do.

'Are you having a clear out?' Josh asked as his gaze fell upon the row of black bin bags lined up along the side of hall. 'I didn't know we had so much rubbish.'

'Neither did I,' I replied without shifting from my position in the kitchen doorway. 'It took me a while to realise it.'

Josh stared at me. I could feel him trying to read my expression, my thoughts. I thought he had lost the ability to read the vibes between us years ago, but as I watched him, I realised he hadn't lost it; he'd just chosen to ignore it.

He couldn't ignore it now.

It was too prominent. Too obvious.

He bent forwards and opened the bag closest to him. 'Wait, this is...' He grabbed the next bag and yanked it open, before moving on to the next. 'This is my stuff. My clothes.'

He looked back at me, his confusion so tremendous that it was almost tangible. He straightened his back as he released the bags. 'You're still thinking about it, aren't you?'

It.

That's all the events of last night were to him. It. Unnamed. Irrelevant.

Like me.

Josh shut the front door behind him with more force than it required. 'When I left this morning, we agreed to forget about last night. We put all thoughts of it out of our heads, but it's back again now.'

I swallowed. He was right; that thought, that memory, was still with me. But it had never really left. It never did. I used to pretend to be okay because I wanted to make him feel better. That was what he needed.

But Abhilash was right. What about what *I* needed?

I glared at Josh. The man I had once loved so completely was a stranger to me now.

'Don't look at me like that,' he instructed, but the anger had gone out of his eyes now. 'It wasn't my fault.'

'No,' I said automatically. It never was. 'But that doesn't mean it's okay.'

'You're being dramatic, again.'

I gritted my teeth. I knew him well enough to know that I should stay quiet. Be soothing. Apologetic.

I shook my head. Not this time. 'I'm being honest.'

I waited for the fall out.

'It's how we are,' Josh said.

'It's how *you* are.'

'You've never had a problem with it before.'

'I've always had a problem with it.'

'If that was true then you would have left.'

He made it sound so simple. If I wasn't happy with the way he treated me, I could just leave. And yet, I'd stayed.

My belief in us, my hope that he'd change, my fear of my own inadequacies had all kept me here. And as a result, I'd effectively condoned his behaviour. After all, love was pain. For me, the two were intertwined. But there were no consequences. Not for him.

'We work the way we are. We fit.'

He made it sound as though I liked it. But there was no pleasure in being yelled at or hit. I didn't want that part of the relationship. I'd just wanted the rest. The good parts. The kind parts.

'No, we don't. Not any more. We haven't for a long time.'

Josh waved his hand at the bags. 'That's what all this is about, isn't it? You're throwing my stuff out because occasionally we don't see eye to eye about things.'

I didn't respond. It didn't really require a reply. It was obvious. And we both knew it. But the truth was that it was bigger than *occasionally.* It was about every dismissal, every punch, and every lie he'd told me when he promised that it would never happen again.

'Look, Lauren—'

Josh took a step towards me, but I held up my left hand. He stopped dead.

His action stunned me. Instant compliance. I'd never had that ability before. That presence. That control. Not over him.

It was invigorating. Powerful.

Except I knew that it wasn't simply holding up a hand in a stop signal that had caused his reaction.

I followed his gaze to my right hand. The hand that had remained out of his view until he had moved forward. My grip tightened around the worn tape wrapped around the handle.

'W-why do you have my old cricket bat?'

There was something satisfying about the stutter in Josh's voice. That hesitation. That uncertainty. It was so familiar to me. Except usually I was the one who felt it. Not him.

'I found it when I was clearing out your stuff.'

Josh nodded. 'Okay, but why are you still holding it?' I heard him swallow. 'Like that?' he added.

I shrugged, our gazes still locked on the cricket bat I held in my hand. I raised it as if ready to play baseball instead of cricket. I wrapped my left hand over my right, adding more support and strengthening my grip. I stepped forward away from the doorway to give the bat more room to swing.

'L-Lauren?' Josh took a tentative step backwards. 'Let just talk things through, okay? Just you and me, without the bat.'

'But I like the bat.' I sounded like a child even to my own ears. Insolent and stubborn.

'What are you planning on doing with it?'

My gaze shifted and I studied him. 'I haven't decided yet.'

'Okay.' He took a shaky breath. 'Maybe I should leave for a while. We can talk later. When you're calmer.'

'When I'm weaker, you mean?'

Josh shook his head. 'No, that's not—'

'When I'm defenceless and vulnerable. When I won't fight back.'

'Lauren, I...' Josh's words ran out.

'See, even you can't argue with that, can you? Because you know I'm right.'

'I didn't mean to hurt you.'

I nodded. 'No, I know. You never mean to.' I snorted. 'But you still do it anyway.'

Josh hung his head. At least he finally had the decency to look remorseful. Not that it mattered now. It was too little. Too late.

'I finally figured out why you do it.'

He looked up, curiosity piquing his interest. There was a hint of hope in his eyes. Almost as though he wanted me to understand, so that I could explain it to him.

'Because you can,' I replied. 'Because I never stop you. I never fight back.'

I shifted my arms, lifting the bat into a better position.

'Until now.'

57

NOW

I turned slowly, still praying that I was wrong. That it hadn't been Josh's voice behind me.

But I knew it was.

He smiled as our eyes met. 'It's good to see you, Lauren.'

'I...' I took a shaky breath.

'Let me guess, you didn't expect to see me again?' Josh chuckled. 'No, I don't suppose you did.'

I shook my head. The movement was so slight that it was probably barely perceivable to him. I had expected to see him again. At least at first.

In those first few hours after the police had visited me in the hospital and told me he was missing; I'd waited for this moment. His triumphant return. I'd been so certain that it was imminent.

Except days had passed and there had been no sign of him. It was only then that I'd started to wonder. To doubt...

What if he couldn't return? What if my actions prevented it?

Just like with Mum.

'I'll leave you two to talk,' Emma said.

I swung back round to face her. I glared at her, silently channelling the anger that I couldn't put into words. She'd betrayed me. She'd set me up. And yet, right now I needed her more than ever. The only thing stronger than my anger and hurt was my desperate desire to beg her not to leave me alone with him. I just needed to find the right words that would make her understand. That would make her stay.

'Call me later?' she added, and for a moment I felt hope resonate through me. If she wanted me to call her that meant she did care. She did...

My hope faded into a dark abyss as I realised her gaze wasn't fixed on me. She was talking to Josh. She wanted him to call her, not me.

Fury raged inside me like a fire that was out of control.

It was still him she believed.

I understand why he did it.

I realised what she'd meant now. She wasn't talking about Josh hitting me. She still didn't believe that. She meant she understood why he'd left. Why he'd run away.

From me.

My body swayed. My anger was still there. But I could feel it wavering. Displaced by the fear that had lived within me since Saturday.

It was only a matter of time before everyone knew. And once that happened, I would lose them all.

Even Abhilash.

I watched Emma walk back down the chine to the beach. My feet shuffled sideways to follow her, whilst caution told me not to turn my back on Josh.

'You know if you leave now, you'll only be postponing the inevitable. We need to talk.'

I studied him. I didn't want to talk to him. I'd already said everything I had to say.

'You can't avoid me for ever.'

He was probably right. But that didn't mean it wasn't tempting to try.

'We can sit on the cliff top and talk.' He signalled up to the top of the chine. 'There are plenty of witnesses there.' He smirked. 'For both of us.'

I swallowed.

We were part of an *us* again, bound together by each other's secrets. I told myself that mine weren't as bad as his. But the truth was, they had almost been worse.

I nodded my reluctant agreement. At least out here someone would hear me if I screamed. But then, the mere fact that I could be heard was the reason that I wouldn't need to be. I knew how this worked. How he worked.

I was safe in public. At least physically.

He turned and walked up the chine, his long legs striding up the slope with ease. I trailed behind, allowing the gap between us to grow with each step he took. This time, I didn't run to catch up.

I followed him to a vacant bench. He signalled for me to sit down. Before, I would have been touched by his display of chivalry. Now, it just felt false.

I strode past the bench and stood by the railing. I preferred to stay on my feet. Alert. Ready to run.

As he joined me, I realised the flaw in my plan. My gaze drifted down the overgrown cliffside to the promenade below. Would witnesses truly protect me? Or would they just be able to substantiate my claims about Josh when it was too late?

Josh stopped a few paces away from me. It wasn't far enough for me to feel safe. But it wasn't close enough to warrant starting to scream.

Not yet.

'It's been a long time since we came here,' Josh said, glancing at Café Riva over his shoulder. 'Do you remember the summers when we used to sit out here listening to the bands in the evening?'

I wanted to say no, I didn't remember. But I remembered everything about us. The good and the bad. It's why I'd stayed so long.

But reminiscing about the good times was no longer enough.

'The police think you drowned,' I said bluntly.

He shifted and his gaze dropped to the floor.

I recognised that expression. 'You already know that, though, don't you?' Even as a kid he always looked sheepish when he got caught doing something wrong.

'I heard.'

My body tensed. 'So why didn't you come back sooner?'

'It's what you wanted, wasn't it? Me gone. Permanently.'

I couldn't deny it. It was exactly what I'd wanted. His departure just hadn't gone quite to plan.

'Why let us all suffer fearing that you were dead?'

His chin lifted as his gaze shot back up to meet mine. 'You were upset?' There was a hopefulness to his tone.

'No, mostly all I felt was relief. But as the days passed, there was a tiny part of me that started to wonder if maybe...' I swallowed. 'After the way things ended between us, I wasn't sure what you might do.'

There was a possibility that I had tried so desperately to prevent myself from thinking about. Had the breakup driven him to do something drastic? Something final?

The police suspected me of being responsible for his death and I couldn't escape the possibility that I might have been.

Just not in the way that anyone thought.

The guilt of that burden was so familiar.

The corner of Josh's mouth twitched, and a queasiness settled in my stomach as realisation dawned on me. 'That's what you wanted. You wanted us to think you were dead. Why would you—'

The question died on my lips. There was only one reason.

'You wanted me to take the blame for your murder.'

'No, Lauren.' Josh stepped towards me.

I leapt back, colliding into the railing behind me.

He stopped and raised his hands in surrender. 'Sorry,' he murmured as he backed away. 'I didn't mean to scare you.'

I gritted my teeth. I hated the fact that he still had the power to do that. To make me afraid. To make me cower.

And worst of all, he knew it too.

I glared at him, anger outweighing my fear. 'The police are convinced that you and I were together on Sunday morning. There was something wrong with the jet-ski. They think I'd tampered with it to stage the accident.'

'Lauren, I can explain,' he edged forwards another step.

'No!'

Josh froze and I realised that the forcefulness of my voice had surprised us both.

I couldn't recall when I had ever shouted at him before. Even when we'd broken up, I hadn't raised my voice. I hadn't needed to.

Like Mum always said, *actions speak louder than words.*

58

THEN

'So, that's it? We're over? You're just going to throw me out of the house?'

I shook my head. 'I'm not just throwing you out of the house. I'm throwing you out of everything. Your friends' lives. Your family's. You're going to disappear from all of it.'

'That's ridiculous. You know that they will all stand by me. Without me, they won't want you.'

'Not if we broke up, no. That's why we're not going to tell them.' My grip tightened on the bat. 'You're simply going to disappear.'

'What?'

'No messages. No goodbyes. Just gone. Everyone will be so devastated. Me especially. But your family will help me through it. We will be united in our quest for answers and finally in our grief when we realise that wherever you are, you aren't coming back.'

Josh laughed. 'You really are your mother's daughter.'

'If I was like her, you wouldn't be leaving under your own free will.'

'I'm not leaving at all. This is absurd. That bat in your hands might keep me a few metres away from you, but it won't make me disappear. Not unless you're actually planning on using it.'

'I haven't decided yet.' My tone was flat and detached. I wasn't afraid to use it. Not now. But I also wasn't sure how much good it would do me.

I saw uncertainty flash across Josh's face. I'd shaken him. He thought I was predictable. Obedient. I'd never stood up to him before. Never fought back.

'You know I'm stronger than you. That bat won't protect you.'

'It doesn't need to. I have something far more powerful.'

'Right, sure you do.' He was mocking me.

'Check your email.'

Josh laughed. 'Right now?'

I nodded. 'I sent you a message as you arrived.'

He rolled his eyes but fished his phone from his pocket.

'Open the attachment.'

The amusement faded from Josh's expression. He stared at the phone screen. 'What is this?'

'It's us. It's you.' I lifted a shoulder in a half shrug. 'Don't you recognise yourself? That's who you've become.'

'This is...' Josh's gaze didn't lift from his phone.

'It's last night,' I confirmed what he already knew.

'You filmed me.' He sounded so indignant. So betrayed.

'You hit me!' I retorted. 'I think that's worse.' The bat in my hands gave me strength to answer back. But I knew it was an illusion. Josh could overpower me easily if he tried. I would only get one chance before he took control again. One swing.

It would need to be a good one.

Our voices fell silent as Josh jabbed at the screen. 'Give me your phone.'

'So you can delete the video?' I laughed. 'It won't do you any good. Do you really think I didn't make copies of the file?'

Josh's gaze darted around the hall.

'Or that I would be stupid enough to keep them on memory discs in the house?'

He glared at me. 'The cloud. You saved them to the cloud.'

'And other places.'

'Tell me your password.'

'You're not listening, Josh. You won't find every copy.'

'I can make you give them to me.'

I shifted my stance, bracing myself for him to charge at me. 'Probably. Which is why I don't have them any more. I can't give you what I don't have. No matter how much you beat me.' Josh's nostrils flared as he took a step towards me. 'And before you decide to test that theory, bear in mind that those copies I sent out carry instructions with them. If anything happens to me, that video will be distributed to your family, your friends, your boss. Every single person in your life will finally get to see you for who you really are.'

Josh hesitated. His gaze shifted from me to the bat and back again. I could practically feel the vibrations coming from him as his mind raced, debating his options.

I was playing a dangerous game. Betting that he would choose to keep his secret over his desire to vent his anger on me. It was a gamble that I could easily lose, especially as I hadn't sent copies to anyone. But the prize was too tempting not to take that bet.

I watched as his shoulders fell. He knew he was beaten.

I'd won.

He kicked the black bin bags as he turned back to the door.

'You can leave your keys; you won't be needing them again.'

Josh inhaled sharply, but he threw his keys onto the table beside the door. 'This isn't over, Lauren.'

I shook my head. 'No, I don't suppose it is.'

59

NOW

'Stay away from me.' My voice was level and firm; it didn't betray the tremor that I felt inside.

'I just want—'

'I don't care what you want.' I realised as I said it that it was true. For the first time since we had met, I didn't care what Josh wanted or what he needed.

I only cared about my own survival.

'You need to leave. Now.'

He shook his head. He didn't try to approach me but he didn't back away either. 'Not until you let me explain.'

I snorted. 'Oh, I think I've figured it out for myself now. You must have known everyone was worried about you. That they thought you were in the accident with me. I had so many messages on my phone, you must have done too. And yet, you didn't answer any of them. You just let me take the blame.'

'You told me to go.'

I nodded. 'I did. And this was your way of getting revenge.'

'No, that wasn't my intention.'

'But it is what happened.'

Like Emma said, perhaps I couldn't blame him for it. Trying to banish him from his own life had been a desperate move. I'd known he wouldn't just accept it.

'It wasn't supposed to.' Josh sounded so desperate. So honest. But I knew how well he played that part. Hurt. Misunderstood. Innocent.

He was always so believable.

But not this time.

'If that were true then you would have gone to see your family. You would have shown them you were alive.'

'I couldn't.'

'Why not?'

His shoulders slumped. 'If the police knew I was alive then they could have figured out that I was the one who sabotaged the engine.'

My breath escaped in a gush. 'Of course. I told them they had made a mistake, that whatever had happened to the engine must have been an accident. But it was you. You planned it.'

I'd thought Josh had just taken advantage of the situation. That my accident had been fortuitous for him. I'd known at some point he would return. He'd come to my rescue. Prove he was alive and that I hadn't killed him. I needed him back. He was the only person who could get me off the hook. But there would be a price for it. An exchange. My proof for his.

That's what this was. Here. Now. This is where he would set out his terms. Perhaps it was only fair. After all, I'd blackmailed him first.

I'd always anticipated that my success was likely to be short lived. But this, I hadn't expected.

His plan had been so clever. And yet, there was something that didn't make sense.

'How did you manage it? You couldn't have known that by messing with the engine I would get knocked unconscious.'

'I didn't. I just thought it would stall. That you would be stranded out at sea.'

I stared at him. It felt like I was seeing him for the first time. Who was this man? Where was the guy that I had once loved? That I had wanted to spend my life with? Josh had hurt me before. So many times. It was no longer a shock that he would want to harm me again. But this was different. This was premeditated.

He'd sabotaged the jet-ski in advance. He'd planned for me to get stuck out at sea alone.

And yet...

'It's a busy spot for water sports. You must have realised that someone would come to my aid.'

'I did.' Josh shrugged. 'I just thought it would be me.'

60

'You?' I stared at Josh, my mind racing. I must have misunderstood. 'I don't understand. You sabotaged the jet-ski so you could rescue me?'

'It sounds so stupid when you say it like that.'

'It is stupid. It's insane, Josh.' But then again, who was I to criticise insane plans?

'I'd arranged to meet an old friend from school who has a boat. I knew the route you preferred. I was going to make sure we were close enough to come to your aid straight away. I thought if I helped you, even just in a small way, you might see me the way you used to. The way you did after your mum...' His words trailed away as he lowered his gaze to the path.

I brushed his reference to Mum aside. She wasn't important. Not now. Not here. 'So what happened? How did you go from staging a rescue to framing me for murder?'

'M-mur...' He looked horrified at my wording. Unable to even repeat it. 'No, that's not what it was. I didn't.'

'It's what everyone suspects. The police. Your parents. Emma. No one's said the word. Not yet. But it was only a matter of time.'

He shook his head slowly. 'It wasn't supposed to turn out like that. The guy was late. By the time we got out there, you'd already been pulled from the water by another boat.'

'I was unconscious. If they hadn't pulled me out when they did, I could have drowned.' I glared at him.

'I know.' Josh turned away and paced the cliff top. 'You think I don't know that? I hate myself for that.'

'But not enough to come forward and tell everyone you were alive.'

'I didn't even realise that anyone would be looking for me at first. At least not to try and save me. Arrest me, maybe, but not save me.'

'Of course.' Clarity seeped into my shellshocked brain. 'You thought once the police discovered the jet-ski had been tampered with that they would realise that it was you.'

'After everything I've done to you, you didn't have any reason not to think the worst of me. I figured once you realised I'd endangered your life, you would show them the video.' He fumbled for his words. 'Once they'd seen that, and you told them that you'd kicked me out, I was afraid they would think this was some sort of retaliation. That I was trying to hurt you again.'

'You were.'

'No, I wasn't.' His voice was so desperate as his eyes silently pleaded at me to believe him. 'I hadn't anticipated the strong current, but even if I had, how could I know that you would get knocked off like that?'

I didn't answer. I couldn't answer. Perhaps he was telling the truth. Perhaps he hadn't thought about the possibilities. The danger.

But it was irrelevant.

He should never have placed me in that situation to begin with.

'I figured the best thing was to lie low for a little while, just to give me time to work out what to do. I wanted to see how much the police had on me.'

'They didn't have anything. Other than the fact you were missing. And everyone believed you were with me.'

'That was unintended.'

'You'd told Paul we were going out together.'

'He messaged to ask if we were going out on the jet-ski, or if I could meet him for coffee. It was just a casual question. If I told him we weren't going then we would have wanted to know what I was doing. I couldn't tell him my plan. And I didn't want to tell him we broke up. I couldn't. I was going to fix it. I was going to win you back before anyone ever had to know that.'

'Fix it? Is that what you call staying quiet while the police started interrogating me and accusing me of killing you?'

'I didn't know. At least not at first. I saw a newspaper article about my disappearance the next day. There was a photo of me and a plea for witnesses. I realised then that things had got out of hand, and I was about to come back, but I stopped.'

'That was Monday, Josh. It's Friday now.'

'I was afraid that you would have told everyone what had been going on. That you'd told my family. With the police involved, I knew I couldn't expect you to stay silent. And I couldn't face them, not if they knew. I couldn't bear to see their disappointment. Their contempt.'

'So you just hid?' I was stunned by his cowardice. In all the years that I had lived in fear of him, I had never realised one important detail. He was more of a coward than I was.

I felt like Dorothy, drawing back the curtain to find the wizard who was so powerful and commanding was just an illusion. One that I had believed so fully, so completely, that I'd almost let it destroy me.

'I asked my friend to do some digging and find out what you'd said. He didn't like it. He wanted me to come forward. He'd been with me on the boat. He was afraid someone might have seen us. That he might be implicated. But I persuaded him to talk to Emma. I knew that if you'd told anyone, she would know.'

He was right, of course. Emma knew everything now. Not that she believed it. Not that anyone did.

Except Abhilash.

'I realised then how much trouble you were in.' He took a deep breath and straightened his shoulders. 'So that's why I'm here.' He sounded almost proud. There was an air of expectation about him, as though I should be proud of him too. Not just proud: grateful. He was coming to my rescue. Again.

But his logic was flawed. He couldn't be the hero when he was also the villain.

A random thought sprang to the forefront of my mind. 'Tim?'

Josh blinked. 'What?'

'Your friend with the boat, it's Tim Harris, isn't it? I remember him now. I remember you being jealous when he bought the boat.'

'I wasn't jealous.'

I shook my head. 'Really not the point right now, Josh.'

'Right, no.' He rolled his eyes. 'Yeah, it was Tim. You're not going to say anything to the police, though, are you? It wasn't his fault.'

I snorted. 'You're worried about him? Some guy that you've barely spoken to since school. But you were going to let me take the fall for your murder? When you aren't even dead?'

'No, that's why I'm here. As soon as I knew you were in trouble—'

'Don't lie to me, Josh.'

'I'm not, I came back strai—'

'Straight away?' I shook my head. 'Emma told me on Tuesday that she'd spoken to Tim. That was three days ago, Josh.'

The colour drained from Josh's face.

I crossed my arms, waiting for him to deny it.

'Okay, so maybe not exactly straight away.'

'So, you knew I hadn't turned you in, and yet you still stayed away.'

Josh hung his head, hiding his face from me. Unable to look me in the eye. It was his usual pattern. First anger. Then guilt. It was our routine. He had a way of making me feel sorry for him. Feel responsible for causing his actions. I always ended up consoling him. Making him feel better.

But not this time. I wouldn't make him feel better about this.

Josh lifted his head, but instead of remorse I saw fear in his eyes. 'Do you blame me? After what you did?'

61

NOW

'I thought you were going to kill me that night, Lauren. You had a look in your eyes like...' He shook his head. 'I don't even know how to describe it. Angry. Crazed. It was terrifying. *You* were terrifying.'

It wasn't my proudest moment. Discovering the anger that simmered within me, knowing it could engulf me like that.

And yet, at the same time, I knew there was only one reason that it was there. One reason that it had ignited at all.

Him.

'I have issues, Lauren. I can admit that now. But so do you. I think all that stuff with your mum, it messed us up. I didn't realise it until now. These few days away, taking a step back, looking back in on our lives from the outside, it woke me up. It changed me.'

I scoffed. 'You expect me to believe that you're a reformed man now? That you won't hit me again the next time you have a bad day?'

'Truthfully, I wish I could say yes. But I'm not stupid. I know I have a problem. A big problem. One that's not that easy to fix just by a few days apart. But that time changed my perspective. And that's a start. A first step.'

A first step.

His words echoed in my head, but it wasn't his voice I heard now. It was Abhilash's.

'I know I have a long way to go to earn back your trust. To make you feel safe with me again. But if you'll give me a chance, I won't let you down ever again.'

I stared at him. He wanted me to take him back, after everything we had been through. Everything he had done. He still wanted my forgiveness.

He was wrong. He hadn't changed at all.

'I'll go and see the police, show them I'm alive. Explain that I'd just needed some time on my own after our breakup. You'll be free from any suspicion.'

'And the sabotage?'

Josh shrugged. 'With me alive and well, they won't have any reason to pursue that.'

'In other words, you want me to keep quiet and not reveal that you were the one who tampered with the engine.'

'What good would it do, Lauren? Besides, I think that makes us even. After all, I don't plan on telling anyone that you tried to kill me with a cricket bat.'

'I wasn't trying to kill you,' I objected.

'Neither was I.'

We stared at each other. We were in a standoff. I couldn't prove he had tried to kill me, and neither could he. I wasn't even sure that either of us actually had tried to kill each other. Not really. We'd both just been reckless and stupid.

The indignant self-righteous part of me wanted to point out that he'd started it. All I'd done was retaliate and defend myself. But I also knew that I'd had other options. Less violent ones.

I'd chosen to keep our secret. To isolate myself from the people who could have helped. I'd had my reasons. Good ones. Or at least I thought they were. But that didn't mean I'd made the right decisions.

'Fine.' That one word felt like I was conceding defeat. He was going to get away with everything he had put me through, not just this week, but the months and years before that as well. But what other choice did I have?

'And you'll delete all the copies of the video?'

I'd known it would only be a matter of time before he asked. Perhaps I couldn't blame him. If I was in his shoes I would use all the bargaining power I had to get that evidence destroyed.

But then, I would never have been in his shoes.

I shook my head. 'The video is my assurance that you will stay away from me. I'm not letting that go. But I know I can't expect you to disappear again. Not now. Your family have been through too much. The video will stay our secret, as long as nothing ever happens to me.'

It sounded a fair deal to me. He could have his life back and I could be assured of my safety. But from the look of disapproval on his face I could see he didn't think so.

'But—'

'It's non-negotiable, Josh. You've been seen now. People know you're alive. You don't have as much bargaining power here as you think. You want me to stay quiet about the sabotage, then I keep the video. Otherwise, both get revealed.'

Josh nodded slowly. 'I could have come to you on the quiet, you know. I could have made sure no one else knew I was alive.'

'Why didn't you?'

'Because I don't want us to be like that. I wanted to prove to you that I've changed. That you can trust me.'

'You don't need to worry about regaining my trust, Josh. We're done. I'll ask Emma to collect your stuff from the house.' It was the only consolation. It was over. We were both alive. Both free. And I would never have to see him again.

I'd lose his family too. They'd slip from my life now. Emma too, probably. But maybe it was for the best. The last week had shown everyone's fallibility.

Maybe they aren't the kind of people that you need in your life.

Abhilash's words repeated in my memory. He'd been right about them. About me.

'We can try again, Lauren.'

I shook my head. We were past that point. Maybe this time was different and he had changed, but I wasn't going to risk testing that theory. Not again.

'Is it because of that doctor Emma told me about?'

That doctor.

That's all Abhilash was to him. To Emma. An inconvenience that didn't even deserve the use of his name. Their disdain for him irritated me. He deserved better. I was no longer tormented by guilt over our friendship. Our relationship. I didn't owe Josh that. I didn't owe him anything.

I only owed myself the truth.

'No. it's because of you. I'm done. We're done.'

His chest lifted and fell as he took deep breaths. I braced myself for what was to come.

'Okay.'

I blinked. I hadn't expected him to cave in so easily. In fact, I hadn't expected him to cave in at all.

'You don't need to look at me like that. I'm accepting defeat. We don't work unless both of us want it to. I know that. If you're sure this is what you want—'

'I am,' I said without hesitation.

Josh nodded. 'Then we're done.'

I waited for the impact of the meaning of his words to hit me. It was over. This time it was official. I wasn't just throwing him out in an angry rage. We'd talked. We'd agreed.

Yet instead of feeling relieved, all I felt was numb.

'Right, so, erm, you'll go to the police station today?'

Josh nodded.

I wondered if I could trust him to do it alone. It was tempting to escort him there, parade him in front of DC Collier myself. But the problem with that was it involved spending time alone with him in my car. Emma had already left. It was just me and Josh now.

And I knew what happened when we were alone.

But what if he simply disappeared again?

I glanced around us. There were witnesses here, but none would remember us after we left. Emma had seen him. She knew he was alive. But could I trust her to confirm that if Josh asked her to lie for him?

She knew what he'd done and she'd still defended him. She was an unreliable friend. At least to me.

I needed proof. Something I controlled.

I pulled my phone from my pocket and flicked it to the camera app. I lifted it up, aligning us in the frame.

'You want a memento of our breakup?' Josh asked, bewildered.

The memory of his first kiss flashed through my mind. We'd taken a selfie that day too. The difference was I wouldn't be keeping this one. Not once the police had closed the missing person's case.

'Just some insurance.'

'You don't need it, but I understand why you feel like you do.'

'Bye Josh,' I said, slipping the phone back in my pocket as I stepped away. I wouldn't look back. The past was behind me now. He was behind me.

'Lauren, just one thing...'

I froze. I should have known that this was too easy. That he wouldn't let me just walk away.

'That doctor of yours, he's bad news.'

62

I laughed as I turned back to face Josh. 'Seriously? That's coming from the guy who just tried framing me for his own murder?'

'Maybe that means I know what I'm talking about.'

'What, so it takes a villain to spot one?' I rolled my eyes. He was unbelievable. 'If this is some feeble attempt to win me back—'

'It's not,' Josh interrupted. 'Don't get me wrong, I would love to win you back. But this is just me looking out for you.'

My eyes narrowed as I studied him. 'R-i-ght.' I dragged the word out. He was lying. Again.

'He's using you.'

'And how could you possibly know that?'

'I've been keeping an eye on things.'

'You mean you've been spying on me? On us?'

'I was looking out for you.'

I scoffed and started to walk away.

'You don't know this guy, Lauren,' Josh said, racing past and stepping in front of me. 'You don't know what he's capable of.'

I glared at him. He thought blocking my path would make me afraid. But he didn't intimidate me any more.

'You mean like I didn't know you? I didn't know what I was getting into by being involved with you. What that would lead to. How much pain that would cause me.'

Josh was wrong. I did know Abhilash. I knew he would never treat me the way Josh had.

Josh hung his head. 'I know I hurt you.'

His agreement threw me. I had expected denial. Resentment. Redirection. Anything but agreement.

'That's why I did this. I owe you this.'

'Ah.' Suddenly it all made sense. 'You owe me. So that's what this is. Retaliation. Vengeance. I left you, so you want to destroy my new relationship. A relationship that makes me happy. Safe. You can't hurt me with your fists any more, so you thought you'd find another way.'

'No!' Josh grasped my hand, but I snatched it free. 'Sorry,' he said, instantly stepping back as though he'd been burnt. 'I shouldn't have done that. I'm just so desperate to make you understand. This isn't for me. This isn't anything to do with me.'

'Exactly,' I spat at him. 'So, leave us alone. *Both* of us.'

'He's using you, Lauren.'

I rolled my eyes and veered round him. I was done engaging with him. He would never listen to me. He would never back down.

But I realised as I walked away that it no longer mattered. Josh was irrelevant to me now. He was my past. Abhilash was my present. We were building a life together. One that Josh wasn't part of. One I wouldn't let him take from me.

'You're not the first patient he's dated.'

63

NOW

I stopped dead. Indignation causing me to swing round and glare at Josh. 'Of course I am,' I snapped back. But I knew the fact that I'd stopped made my declaration less convincing.

Doubt niggled somewhere beneath the surface. What if I wasn't the first? What did it mean?

'Being a doctor is just a way to meet women for him. Vulnerable women. He uses his position to get them to trust him. They think he's a friend. A confidante. It starts out platonic, but then...'

I should have left. I didn't need to listen to this. Not from him. He couldn't know anything about Abhilash. And even if he did, I couldn't believe he would tell me the truth. He just wanted to break us up. To break me.

I took another step.

'I know you have no reason to trust me. No reason to believe what I'm saying. But if you won't listen to me, then at least listen to her.'

'Her?' I turned back. I cursed myself for my curiosity. I was doing exactly what Josh wanted. I was falling into his trap. Listening to his story. But I couldn't stop myself.

I couldn't risk being played again. I needed to know who I was dealing with this time. Josh had fooled me for years because I let him. I wouldn't do the same with Abhilash. If what we had was a lie then I would deal with that. As long as I knew.

Josh nodded his head towards a bench further along the clifftop. A young woman sat at an angle, twisting back, watching us instead of the sea.

'Who is she?' I asked, even though an uneasy feeling in my stomach told me I already knew.

I see you two getting closer and closer, and it just worries me that you're going to get hurt.

Nick had warned me that Abhilash wasn't good for me. I'd brushed his comments away. I hadn't wanted to hear them. To face them. But I hadn't forgotten them. I couldn't.

'Her name's Helen. She's the patient that has come forward about what Dr Menon did. She made a complaint against him on Tuesday.'

'Tuesday?'

Josh nodded.

Complications with a patient.

That's what Abhilash had said when he drove me home on Tuesday. He'd been late leaving work because he'd had a bad day.

I stared transfixed at her across the cliff top.

Was she the complication?

Pieces started to fit together in my mind. But the picture they were creating was all wrong. It had to be wrong.

'And how do you know her?'

Josh winced. 'I've been hanging around the hospital. I may have incentivised a few people to talk to me.'

'You threatened them?'

'No, I paid them.'

I groaned.

'They wouldn't give me a name, but they did tell me she had made an allegation and was coming back in to make a formal complaint to management on Tuesday. So I waited to talk to her as she left.'

'You stalked her too?' I shook my head. 'Are there no depths you won't stoop to?'

Josh shook his head. 'Not when it comes to protecting you.'

'You realise how preposterous that sounds coming from you, right?'

'Like I said, I owe you.' He glanced back at the woman on the bench. 'Just talk to her, Lauren. Hear what she has to say. What you do with that information is up to you.'

I wrung my hands together. To speak to her felt disloyal to Abhilash. As though I doubted him. That I thought the accusations that Josh was making against him were possible.

And yet could I really afford to allow blind trust to dictate my life again?

I nodded.

Josh smiled. 'Come on, I'll introduce you.'

I raised my hand to stop him. 'I'll talk to her alone.' If I was going to do this, I was doing it my way. Without him.

Helen stood up as I walked across the dried grass towards her.

'Hi,' she said quietly. She looked as uneasy as I felt.

I swallowed. 'Josh says...' I paused. 'He says you know Abhilash.'

Helen nodded. 'Unfortunately.'

The pain in her voice made my breath catch in my chest. What if Josh was right about her? What if her accusations were true? They didn't just have the potential to destroy Abhilash's career. They could destroy us too.

Abhilash was the one who had made me face the truth about

Josh, but what truth was he hiding about himself? If I couldn't trust him, did that undo everything he had taught me?

I glanced back at Josh as he leaned against the railing where I had left him. If I'd been wrong about Abhilash, could I have been wrong about him too?

'He treated me in ED,' Helen said, without prompting, and I shifted my attention back to her. 'I was going through some personal stuff at the time.' She ran her fingers across a scar on her wrist. 'Bad stuff.'

I bit my lip, searching for the right thing to say.

'Anyway.' She shrugged. 'Abhilash was so supportive. It was like he could feel my pain. As though he understood it. Understood me. You know?'

I didn't respond. But I knew.

'We started meeting after that. Just as friends. At least at first.' She took a deep breath. 'He seemed to know what I needed. He never crowded me. Never made me feel pressured. He was such a comfort. A support.'

I could feel my heartbeat reverberating through my body. Our stories were so similar. She was describing Abhilash so well.

My Abhilash.

Except what if he wasn't?

What if he'd been hers first?

He said I was the only patient he'd ever dated. It was the only time he'd ever taken that risk. The only time he'd ever been tempted to. But the way she described their relationship...

I swallowed.

Had he lied to me?

'Our relationship evolved quickly,' Helen continued. 'It seemed natural. It seemed right. It wasn't until later that I realised I'd been played.'

'How do you mean?'

'Once he got what he wanted from me, once I'd slept with him, he dropped me. Cut me off completely. It was as though I'd never meant anything to him. Never even existed.'

'That must have been difficult.' If what she was saying was true, if they really had dated, then what did that prove? The relationship she was describing had unnerving similarities to ours, but that didn't mean that Abhilash had done anything wrong. Did it? Misguided perhaps. Getting involved with past patients. But had he abused his position? Was it enough to get him struck off? Had he taken advantage of us? I couldn't speak for her, but for myself I didn't feel like he had.

I'd made the first move. I'd sent him the Facebook friend request. I'd followed him to the beach. If anything, it was me that had stalked him.

'I realise now that if I hadn't kept running into him, we would never have got together.'

'Running into him?'

'Yeah.' She scrunched her nose. 'He kept turning up in places that I always went to. I thought it was fate bringing us together.' She tipped her head to the side. 'Now I realise it was just creepy.'

A chill washed over me. It had been me stalking him that brought us together, hadn't it?

Memories of the day we met on the beach flashed through my head. I always went to Café Riva on Fridays for lunch. I posted about it on social media each week. Was it coincidence that Abhilash had happened to be not only at the beach, but at the spot just below the café, at exactly that moment?

The timing of his acceptance of my friend request had always seemed odd. He accepted straight after we'd talked. Almost as though he'd already known the request was there. If he did, then that could mean he'd already checked out my profile. Already learned my routine.

My breathing quickened. I was looking for him on that beach, but had he been looking for me too? Waiting for me?

I shook my head. No, this was crazy. I had to be rational. Even if he had set up the circumstances for our first meeting, I had gone willingly. In fact, he'd done no more than I had. Used social media to manoeuvre an encounter. That didn't make him creepy.

At least, no worse than me.

I could feel Helen watching me. Studying my reaction.

'Why are you telling me all this?'

'If I can save you from going through what I did...' She smiled ruefully. 'I was in a bad place when Abhilash and I met. I was worse when he dumped me. He knew I was vulnerable. He knew I'd become attached to him. Reliant on him. I think he liked that. Needed it, even. And then he just disappeared from my life. No warning. No explanation. Nothing. It just about destroyed me. Just like he must have known it would. No one should experience that.'

I stared at her, mesmerised. Her words flowed freely. She spoke so openly. So calmly. I was impressed by that. She didn't need encouragement or support from me. She just needed to talk.

She needed me to hear.

If it was me, I wasn't sure that I could have been that strong. I was only listening to her and I could feel my body trembling.

Was I reliant on him? The unsettled feeling in my stomach told me I was. There was no question that I had been vulnerable, desperate for a friend, a connection, something. Had Abhilash seen that? Had he used that against me?

If I believed that then everything we had would be thrown into question too.

'The worst part is he'd promised no matter what happened between us, he wouldn't hurt me, that he might not be able to take me lifelong with him, but he would never abandon me.'

It was as though the air was suddenly sucked from my lungs. I couldn't breathe. Those were the words he'd said to me too. The exact words. So specific. So memorable.

I thought his promise had meant something. It had been special. It had been just for me.

But it wasn't.

Hurt battled with anger inside me.

It was just a line. One he'd used before.

64

NOW

I stumbled away from the clifftop. Away from Helen. From Josh.

My whole world had turned upside down in a few short moments.

Josh was alive. And yet, instead of feeling relieved that the police would have to leave me alone now, I felt more betrayed than ever. He'd caused the accident. I could have drowned because of him. He'd sparked a police investigation, with me as the prime suspect. He'd turned everyone I loved against me.

Was he telling the truth? Had it all spiralled out of his control? Was the police investigation an accident, or had he used my past against me? Had he realised that everything that had happened with Mum would place me under suspicion? Or was that just a coincidence?

But regardless of his intentions, he'd done it all out of fear of losing me.

Did that make his actions more understandable? He'd still been wrong, but perhaps simply misguided rather than unforgivable?

I knew what Abhilash would say. He'd tell me to stop making excuses for Josh. To stop letting him manipulate me.

But was he really someone who I should be listening to? Hadn't he done the same thing, just in different ways?

I might not be able to take you lifelong with me, but I'll never run away from you. I'll never abandon you.

Abhilash's words repeated in my head. They had meant so much to me. But they weren't just for me. They were meaningless.

I thought we were kindred spirits. Connected. When I was just being used.

Again.

Mum, Josh, and now Abhilash. They were all as bad as one another. Different lies. Different betrayals. But the same result.

There was only one difference remaining now.

Mum and Josh had been dealt with. They couldn't hurt me any more. But Abhilash...

My pace quickened as I fumbled in my bag for my car keys. I needed to see him.

* * *

Tears blurred my vision as Abhilash opened his front door to me.

'Lauren, hi, I didn't exp—'

'How did we meet on the beach that first day?' I interrupted his surprised greeting and barged past him into his hallway.

'What?'

'I thought I'd stalked you, but now that I think about it, it kind of seemed as though you'd been searching for me too.'

Abhilash's eyebrows lifted as his eyes widened. 'You stalked me?'

'I'd already sent you the friend request. You could have seen from my Facebook posts that I always went to Café Riva for lunch on Fridays. Was your choice of location and timing for kite surfing coincidental or planned?'

'It, er...' Abhilash hesitated.

A strange, strangled noise escaped my lips. It was planned.

'I should have known. I mean, the flowers should have been a clue. Why would you give me flowers the first time we met for coffee? And roses at that?'

'You didn't like the flowers?' Abhilash sounded bewildered.

'You knew I had a boyfriend. Not one you approved of, but you still knew I was in a relationship. Surely guys don't do that, give flowers to someone else's girlfriend, not unless they were making a move. Do they?'

And yet, somehow it hadn't felt like that. It hadn't felt inappropriate. It hadn't felt like anything more than a thoughtful gesture. It's what people did: give flowers to friends who were sick or injured. And the fact they were roses wasn't important. He'd just given me what happened to grow in his garden. It was economical. Practical.

I nibbled my nail. The problem was that it was also thoughtful.

Picking up a bunch of flowers when buying your groceries at Tesco was easy. Going out and picking them from your own garden took purpose and effort.

'Lauren, I don't understand what's going on here.'

'Josh came to see me.'

'Josh?' Abhilash blinked. 'He's back?' He stepped towards me, his brow furrowed with concern. 'Did he hurt you?'

I shook my head. He hadn't hurt me. Not physically, at least. 'He just wanted to talk.'

Abhilash drew back, stunned. 'You're talking to him? After everything he's put you through?'

'He wanted to talk about you.'

'About me?' Abhilash's eyes narrowed. 'You and I are none of his business. He's out of your life now, Lauren. That's what you said.'

I nodded. 'He is. I'll never be able to trust him after what he did to me. But...' I swallowed.

'You're not sure if you can trust me now either.' Abhilash finished for me. It wasn't a question. He knew what I was thinking. What I was afraid of. My doubts were too big to keep hidden. Too important. 'Because of the flowers?'

'Because of Helen.'

He stopped as realisation seeped into his expression. 'How do you know her name?'

'You said you were late leaving the hospital on Tuesday because of complications with a patient. She's the patient, isn't she?'

Abhilash nodded, but he looked confused. 'She's made allegations against me. But there's nothing to them. They're all false. She's just desperate.'

'She doesn't seem desperate. In fact, she just seems hurt.'

'You've met her? Lauren, you can't pursue this yourself. The hospital has procedures that have to be followed.'

'It's not as though I went looking for her,' I replied curtly. 'I'm not stupid.'

'No, of course you're not. I didn't mean to imply that you were. But wait, if you didn't go looking for her, how did you meet her?'

'Josh introduced us.'

'I don't understand. How does Josh know anything about her?'

'He's been asking questions about you at the hospital. Bribing people for information.'

Abhilash's eyes widened. 'Seriously?' He shook his head in

disbelief. 'But even so, no one would tell him about Helen. It's confidential. We take that kind of thing very seriously.'

I shrugged helplessly. Josh's involvement still felt odd. His motives couldn't be trusted and yet here I was confronting Abhilash with evidence supplied from Josh.

Something felt off.

The question was, though, which one of them could I believe?

'She's lying, Lauren. You have to believe that. She came into the ED a few weeks ago claiming she needed painkillers. But there was no reason for them. She showed all the classic signs of addiction. I refused to give her a prescription and tried to get her the help she needed, but she stormed out. Then suddenly, three days ago, I got hauled into the office and told she's accusing me of having some sort of relationship with her. There's going to be an investigation. But there's nothing to investigate. It's crazy. I didn't do anything. You have to believe me, Lauren.'

I'd always believed Josh. I'd trusted him completely, no matter what. In the early days it never occurred to me to doubt him. And even when I finally did, I felt guilty for it. Because doubting him was to doubt us.

I'd paid the penalty of that blind trust. I couldn't make the same mistakes again with Abhilash. I wouldn't. 'I know it's all going to blow over. I flagged the incident at the time in case she tried to con another doctor into giving her medication.'

'You did?' Doubt started to gnaw at me.

'She's obviously just trying to get back at me, but...'

'But what?'

'I don't know, I guess I just can't figure out why now? I mean, she came into the hospital weeks ago. And then suddenly she makes these accusations now, weeks later. It just feels odd.'

Odd.

The word resounded in my head. He'd echoed my own thought.

'Lauren, are you okay? You've gone really pale.'

'But you told her the same thing that you told me: "I might not be able to take you lifelong with me, but I'll never run away from you. I'll never abandon you".'

Abhilash looked as though I'd slapped him. 'I've never said that to anyone else. I wrote that to you. Just you.' He pulled his phone out and thrust it towards me. 'You can check my messages, my calls, my contacts. I've never spoken to her since she came into ED.'

'Your messages,' I repeated slowly. 'You wrote that in a message to me, didn't you?'

'Yeah, so?'

I pulled my phone from my bag and stared at it. 'I lost my phone.'

'Lauren, you're holding it.' I could hear the concern etched in Abhilash's voice.

'Not now. Tuesday.'

'Right, but you hadn't really lost it. You'd just left it at home.'

'On the floor by the front door.'

'So you must have dropped it as you were leaving.'

'I know I had it in my bag when I stepped outside. I'm sure I did.'

'Then how could it have got back inside?'

'It was beneath the letter box.'

'So,' Abhilash shrugged, 'maybe you have a good neighbour who spotted it on your driveway and posted it back inside for you?'

'A good neighbour?' My gaze lifted from my phone and my eyes met his. 'Or maybe a bad friend.'

65

NOW

A noise behind Abhilash caught my attention. He turned at the sound and we watched as Nick opened the front door and froze in the doorway as his gaze shifted from me to Abhilash, his left eye swollen and bruised.

'Nick!' I exclaimed in horror at the sight of his injuries.

He didn't respond, but it was as though calling his name spurred him into action and he brushed past Abhilash as he headed for the stairs.

'Are you okay?' I asked, as I rushed towards him, but he side-stepped out of my path.

'Fine,' he grunted. 'I'm going to my room.'

I watched him retreat up the stairs, gripping the solid mahogany banister as he limped up each step.

'What's going on?'

'What do you mean?'

'I saw the way he looked at you, Abhilash. He was scared. Of you.' Perhaps I should have been more subtle. Making an outright accusation was unlike me. But then, perhaps that was the point. I was tired of being subtle and careful. Of living in ignorance and denial.

All I wanted now was the truth.

'He's not scared of me, he's just—' Abhilash stopped abruptly and his eyes widened as he realised the implications of what I was saying. 'Wait, you think I attacked him?'

'You told him I was your girlfriend. You warned me to stay away from him. What else are you capable of? What else did you do?'

'I told him to stay away from you. I admit that. But that's all. Just words. No threats. No violence.'

I waved my hand up the stairs where Nick had departed. 'I saw him. I saw the bruises.'

'I'm not him, Lauren. I'm not Josh.'

I jutted my jaw out definitely. 'Aren't you?'

'Aikido.'

'What?'

'Nick does Aikido. He had a tournament last night.'

'Oh.' I stared at him. What had I done?

'There's no way I could beat him up, even if I wanted to.' Abhilash pulled his phone from his pocket. 'Look, he sent me photos on WhatsApp.' He pulled up a photo of Nick holding a trophy. 'That's how he got his bruises.'

I didn't speak. I couldn't.

'I can call him down; you can ask him yourself.'

I shook my head. 'No, I believe you.' I did. I should always have done. I owed him that much. After all, he'd always believed me.

I turned and stared up the empty staircase. 'But,' I frowned, 'the way you two looked at each other...'

'He's not scared of me, Lauren. He's avoiding me.'

'Why?'

'Because of this.' Abhilash stepped towards me before turning to the stairs and bending down to pick up an envelope that was perched against the wall on the bottom step. He held it out towards me. 'It arrived this morning. Does it look familiar?'

My jaw dropped. I was right, I had come between their friendship. Just not in the way I'd thought.

'It's your handwriting, Lauren. On a letter addressed to my housemate.'

'I can explain.'

'Great, I was hoping that you would, because Nick refused to. He said I should talk to you.'

'You didn't open it?'

'It's not addressed to me.'

Fresh tears formed in my eyes. But they were different this time. They weren't tears of anger or despair. They were of love and adoration.

How could I have doubted Abhilash? If it had been Josh who had found a letter I'd sent to another guy, he would have torn it open within seconds. But here it was. Still sealed. Its contents and purpose a mystery to Abhilash.

'I asked Nick to do a favour for me,' I confessed.

'What kind of favour?'

'Just to keep it. Not to open it. Not unless something happened to me.'

'Happened to you? What did you think was going to happen to you?'

I didn't answer.

'Josh. You think he's still a threat to you, don't you?'

'It's more that I'm a threat to him.'

'How?'

I nodded at the envelope still in Abhilash's hands. 'Because of that.'

'What is it?'

'Proof of his abuse.' Abhilash's eyes widened. 'Two days before he disappeared, I videoed him on my phone. When he went out the next day I made copies. I saved it to my cloud, but I knew that it was only a matter of time before Josh hacked my password or persuaded me to give it him, so I made a couple of hard copies too. I saved them to memory sticks and hid them. I bluffed and told Josh that I'd given copies to other people to keep, but I didn't have anyone to give them to. When I saw Nick at Starbucks the other day, I asked him to help. I told him I wanted to send him something to keep safe for me.'

'Why didn't you just give it to me?'

'At first because I was ashamed. I didn't want you to know that I was blackmailing Josh. That I'd made him disappear or I would take the video to the police.'

'And then?'

'When the police interviewed me and their suspicions that I'd harmed Josh became apparent, I knew it was only a matter of time before he'd come back. He'd know my position was weakened and I expected him to come after the video. I had to get at least one of the copies out of the house. Emma had told Josh about you. But he didn't know about Nick. I told him to keep it somewhere safe, out of the house, just in case Josh came here looking for it.'

'Let me guess, Emma would be the bad friend that you think stole your phone.'

I nodded.

Abhilash tapped the envelope against the palm of his hand.

'Oh, Abhilash,' I said as I walked towards him. I stopped just in front of him and gazed up at him desperately. 'I'm sorry.'

Abhilash shook his head slowly. 'I'm not him, Lauren.'

'No.'

I swung round at the sound of the familiar voice in the kitchen behind us.

'You're most definitely not me.'

'Josh.' His name was barely a whisper on my lips as my gaze locked on the knife in his hand.

66

Abhilash lurched forwards, his arm outstretched as he reached for me. He pulled me behind him, positioning himself between Josh and me.

'You really should keep your back door locked,' Josh said as he grinned at us.

'What do you want, Josh?' I demanded over Abhilash's shoulder.

Josh jerked his head towards the envelope still in Abhilash's left hand. 'That.'

Abhilash raised his hand slightly as his head dropped and he stared at the envelope. 'You know what this is?'

'I was standing outside. I heard Lauren explaining it to you.' Josh chuckled. 'It seems I have impeccable timing. I figured I'd have to hunt for it. Nice of you to make it so easy for me.'

'I have other copies,' I told Josh defiantly.

'You mean you *had* other copies. I found the one you'd hidden in the house.'

'You got in the house?'

'You took my key, but my parents still had one.'

'They've seen you? They know you're alive?' I knew it shouldn't be the priority right now, but knowing that his parents were no longer suffering, fearing their son had died, was a relief.

'Not yet, I wanted this resolved first. Emma borrowed it for me.'

Emma, of course.

'Still deceiving everyone who you supposedly care about, then?' Abhilash spat the words at Josh with contempt.

Josh's jaw tensed. It was the only acknowledgement he made of Abhilash's accusation. 'I've also deleted the original on your phone and the copy on the cloud.'

I yanked my phone from my bag and scrolled through the video clips. 'How?' I groaned as I realised he was right. The file had gone.

'You really should be more careful where you leave your phone.'

Rage boiled in the pit of my stomach. 'Emma.'

Josh smirked. 'She's such a good friend. You know she didn't even ask why I wanted her to borrow your phone. She just got it for me.'

I nodded slowly. I'd always known her loyalty was to Josh. I should have thought about how easily it would be for him to manipulate that.

'I knew your password, so the rest was easy. Even managed to use the opportunity to track your phone.'

'That's how you found us.'

'I knew you would have given him a copy. It's not like you have any other friends to entrust it to. But I couldn't find his address. I tried following him, but I'm not very good at it. And when I did succeed, he kept staying at *my* house. But I knew you would lead me to him eventually. Especially with a little motivation.' Josh paused as though waiting for recognition of his cleverness. He shrugged as he realised his audience wasn't impressed. 'Now I'll take that copy too.' Josh held his hand out.

Abhilash glanced at me, and I nodded slightly. It wasn't worth risking our lives to try and keep it. I knew how dangerous Josh was, even without a knife.

'I told you I wasn't going to use it,' I said as Abhilash tossed the envelope at Josh's feet. 'I was just keeping it for protection, in case...' I waved my hand at him. 'In case of something like this.'

Josh chuckled as he scooped the envelope from the floor. 'I guess that plan rather backfired on you, didn't it?'

He stood up and surveyed us.

'You can leave now,' Abhilash said firmly.

'I could.' Josh shrugged. 'But I don't really want to.'

'At least put the knife down, please,' I begged.

'You don't like it, huh?' Josh turned the knife in his hand. 'Now you know how it felt when you threatened me with a bat.'

Abhilash pivoted to stare at me. 'You had a bat?'

'Ah, so she didn't tell you about that?' Josh looked gleeful.

I glared at him. I knew what he was doing. He'd already tried to turn me against Abhilash with his lies, now he wanted to jeopardise our relationship by exposing my secrets. My flaws.

'It doesn't seem as though you two know each other very well at all.'

Panic tightened my chest as I turned to Abhilash. 'I'm sorry. I know I should have told you. Our breakup wasn't as amicable as I said, I—'

Abhilash's fingers entwined with mine. 'We know enough.'

I gazed at him. I'd kept secrets from him. I'd accused him of terrible things. And yet he was still standing by me.

'So, this is who you left me for.' Josh appraised Abhilash with disdain.

'He's just a friend.'

'A friend!' Josh snorted. 'Don't lie to me, Lauren. You know better than that.'

He was right, of course. I knew the penalty when Josh suspected me of lying. This time was different, though. This time his accusation was actually true.

Now was the moment when I should apologise, just like I'd always done before. Be meek. Grovel for forgiveness. Soothe his ego. His pride.

But even the twinge of guilt I felt for my lie wasn't enough to override one unescapable truth. I wasn't sorry.

Every stolen moment I'd had with Abhilash was wrong. I'd been in a relationship. I had a boyfriend.

And yet, I didn't care.

I wasn't with Josh out of love. I was with him out of need. Out of fear. And so was he. Abhilash was right: Josh's treatment of me stemmed from his own fears that he wasn't good enough. That he couldn't live up to the expectations he'd placed upon himself. We'd both been trying so hard to be perfect that we'd failed beyond measure.

I didn't owe him any apologies. Not any more. I'd apologised enough to last a lifetime. My betrayal was nothing compared to his. He'd failed me. Failed us.

And I was done accepting that.

'Just go, Josh. You have what you came for.'

He shook his head. 'Not everything I came for. I came for you.'

My body went cold. I gripped Abhilash's arm as I braced myself, waiting for my punishment. Whatever Josh dished out, I would take it. I gritted my teeth and jutted out my jaw. It was the last time he would ever hurt me.

Josh lowered the knife to his side. 'I want you back.'

67

NOW

I felt Abhilash's muscles tense at Josh's words, but he stayed silent. This wasn't his battle.

It was mine.

I scoffed. 'You can't seriously think that I would come back to you now, can you?'

'I meant what I said on the clifftop; I can change.'

'You say that while you're holding a knife. I see changes, Josh. But not good ones.'

'You can't just leave me.' He stared at me, voicing the words that I'd said to myself thousands of times in the last few years.

'Why not?'

'Because...' The certainty in his voice wavered. 'You just can't.'

I pursed my lips together.

'I need you and you need me,' he pleaded.

It was the foundation of our whole relationship. Our mutual need for each other. As though somehow we were incomplete if we weren't together. But was it true?

I sighed softly. Perhaps for him it was true. But for me...

'I love you.' It was an afterthought he tagged on after a pause that had lasted too long.

Abhilash cast a sideways glance at me, as if waiting to see my reaction to Josh's declaration.

I shrugged. 'If that was enough, it would have been your first reason. The only reason.'

Abhilash let out a breath and I realised that he'd been afraid. Not of Josh. But of me. Of my resolve.

I didn't want Josh to need me. I didn't want him to depend on me to the point he felt he couldn't cope without my presence. I'd just wanted him to love me. Unconditionally.

It was all I'd ever wanted.

It was the way I'd loved him.

Perhaps that was part of the problem. I'd loved him without fail. Even when I shouldn't. It was why I'd stayed so long. Or at least part of the reason.

He wasn't the only one who was too needy. Too dependent. My life revolved around his. My independence had been his first casualty. Not that either of us had realised it at the time.

I had surrendered it willingly. *He* was more important

'It's because of him, isn't it? He's brainwashed you. Turned you against me.'

'This has nothing to do with him.' But even as I said it, I knew it was a lie. My outlook had changed since I'd met Abhilash. He'd opened my eyes to the reality that I'd been refusing to see alone. It wasn't ignorance, or naivety that had kept me in the dark. It was fear.

I'd chosen to stay with Josh because he was better than the alternative.

He was better than being alone.

'We'll figure things out, Lauren. We'll get better.'

We.

I was done being part of the problem. He viewed me as being as guilty as him. I was the reason for his anger. His violence. I'd not only accepted his blame. I'd blamed myself as well. I provoked him. Triggered him. It didn't take much. Just my presence. My existence.

It never occurred to me that it wasn't reasonable.

But if I was the reason for his anger then I should remove myself from the situation. Without me he would be calmer. Happier. And if he wasn't, at least I would no longer be in his line of fire.

'Marry me.'

'What?'

'Marry me,' Josh repeated. 'It's what you want. What you've always wanted. So, let's do it. Let's get married.'

My heart raced. They were the words that I'd longed to hear for years. Josh had finally said them. I'd always imagined that this moment would be filled with love and excitement. And yet, all I felt now was confusion.

'But...' I hesitated as I cast a quick glance at Abhilash before my gaze returned to Josh. 'You didn't want to.'

'I do now.'

He was offering me everything I wanted. Marriage. Acceptance. A name. *Family.* All of it.

And yet, it still wasn't enough. I knew that now. It never had been. It never would be.

His proposal wasn't a life-changing moment of joy. It just made me feel empty and sad.

'What are you waiting for, Lauren? For him?' Josh asked, jerking his head towards Abhilash. 'He'll never give you what you want. He'll never marry you. He can't.' Josh paused as he gazed pityingly into my eyes. 'He's going to marry someone else.'

I stared at him. Straight backed, head held high. He looked so triumphant. He thought he'd won.

Thought he'd crushed the final bit of rebellion that lived within me. That he'd eradicated the one thing that stood between us.

Abhilash.

'I know,' I replied and watched his expression fall.

68

THEN (MAY)

'Ah, Dr Menon is treating you.' The radiographer smiled as she positioned my wrist under the x-ray machine. 'He's lovely, isn't he?'

I nodded. 'Yeah, he really seems to care about his patients.'

'He does. Well, we all do of course, but...' she paused and her focus drifted to somewhere beyond me. 'He's so empathetic. Almost as though he knows what you're feeling.' She chuckled. 'And maybe even what you're thinking.'

I stared at her. It was exactly how he'd made me feel. Seen. Understood.

'Hmm,' I murmured, perhaps that was why I had felt able to talk to him. I'd told him a secret that I'd never told anyone before. Something I barely even admitted to myself. I couldn't understand why I'd done that. Why now? Why him? But listening to the nurse, perhaps it wasn't all that surprising. There was something about Dr Menon, an ability to empathise. To connect. Something that drew out the things that normally people were too afraid to say out loud.

That I was too afraid to say out loud.

He knew my secret now. Part of me regretted it. Feared what he would do with that knowledge. And yet, at the same time, another part of me, a bigger part, felt relieved. I wasn't in it alone. Not any more. Someone else knew. He might not understand. Might not know all the details. But he knew enough.

The radiographer gave herself a little shake as though physically pulling herself away from thoughts of Dr Menon. 'We're certainly going to miss him around here.'

My head jerked up. 'He's leaving?' I heard the note of panic in my voice. It was too much. He was nothing to me. Just a kind doctor, another in a long list. His departure shouldn't mean anything to me. He shouldn't mean anything to me.

'Yes, sadly. He's returning to India at the end of his training.'

'India. But that's so far.' I thought she'd say another hospital, another city, maybe even another county. But another country...

She nodded. 'It is.'

Sadness seemed to seep into every pore. I felt it as strongly as if she had told me a lifelong friend was leaving, not someone I had only just met.

It wasn't as though I planned to see him again. Not that I could rule out the possibility, given he worked in the ED. But knowing he was here. That someone knew the truth. Shared my secret. My pain. My dilemma. It helped. At least a little. If I really needed to, I could come back. I could find him. I could talk to him again. I wasn't alone now.

Once he left the hospital, though, that connection would be lost. Our paths would diverge. He would continue with his life and I would continue with mine.

There was something sad about that.

The one person who knew the truth would be gone.

I cleared my throat, attempting to keep the overwhelming

sense of desperation from my voice. 'How long until he finishes his training?'

'Oh, a few months, I guess.'

'Months,' I repeated. That was all the time we had.

I watched her shoulders rise and fall as she shrugged. His departure didn't matter to her. Not really. Her life wouldn't be impacted by the absence of his presence.

But then, mine shouldn't be either.

* * *

I sat in the cubicle facing Dr Menon again as he examined the x-rays on the screen.

'I hear you're leaving.'

His body flinched. It was the tiniest movement, but I caught it. Perhaps because I was in tune to such things. Reading body language, mannerisms, moods. It was a skill I'd refined living with Josh. I could adapt my own behaviours in response. It made things easier. Safer. And yet, perhaps, it also made them a lie.

'Sorry, I shouldn't have said anything.'

'No.' Dr Menon shook his head. 'It's fine. I was just surprised that you would know that.'

'The radiographer told me.' I cringed as I realised how that sounded. 'It wasn't as though we were gossiping about you or anything. She just saw your name on my notes and said how lovely you were and how much everyone was going to miss you.'

'Lovely?' His accent emphasised the word even more than he'd intended, and his cheeks flushed.

'Yeah.' I lowered my gaze, examining my white trainers.

'I'm going back home,' he said, and I nodded, already privy to that information.

'Why?'

He blinked.

'Sorry,' I shifted, suddenly uncomfortably hot. 'That's none of my business.'

'Not really, no,' he confirmed, but his tone was soft. He didn't seem offended by my intrusion. He tipped his head to the side. 'So, why did you ask?'

'I-I don't really know.' I wasn't being entirely honest.

He studied me for a moment. 'Yes, you do.'

I swallowed. The radiographer was right: he could read what you were thinking. 'Okay, I guess that I'm a bit disappointed that you're going. I know I shouldn't be. I know it shouldn't matter at all to me. We've only just met, and I don't know you. But...'

'I know your secret.'

My mouth fell open. 'How do you do that?'

He shook his head. 'Do what?'

'Read me so well. It's like you know what I'm thinking without me even needing to say it.'

He laughed. 'I'm not psychic, if that's what you're implying. I just pay attention to people. Their expressions. Their words. The ones they say and the ones they don't. At least not verbally.'

I nodded. We really were like kindred spirits.

'And I guess that if I was in your shoes, discovering that the person you have confided in is leaving, it might make me feel a little bit...' He paused, searching for the right word. 'Abandoned.'

I let out a breath. 'You're good.'

'And if I felt like someone was abandoning me, it's only natural that I would want to know why,' Dr Menon finished.

'Maybe you should have become a psychologist.'

Dr Menon shrugged. 'I did think about it for a while. But I like what I do.'

'You just don't want to do it here.' I tried to laugh, but it wasn't funny. It was sad.

'My family is all back home, I want to go back and be close to them, and also—' He clamped his mouth closed.

'And also?'

'It's nothing.'

I shook my head. 'I might not possess your level of skill, but I can tell that's not true.'

'Okay, I'm going home to get married.'

'Wow, that's definitely not nothing.' Jealousy slammed into me as though I'd collided with a wall. It was a sensation I was accustomed to. I felt it every time someone mentioned marriage, or showed me their engagement ring, because they had achieved the one thing that I wanted most. Somehow it felt as though they were stealing my dream from me. They'd got what I'd worked so hard for. It wasn't fair.

'Congratulations.' I forced my jealousy down and did what I always did. I smiled.

'Thanks,' Dr Menon said, looking a little awkward.

'I hope she appreciates your psychic abilities.'

He swallowed.

There was something about his reaction that felt off. 'She does appreciate them, doesn't she?' I knew it was none of my business. But I couldn't bear the thought that he might be marrying someone who didn't fully appreciate him.

'Actually, I haven't met her yet.'

I frowned. 'You're marrying someone you haven't met?'

'No, that's not what I meant.' He shook his head. 'It's really more of a plan to go home and get married, rather than being engaged or anything yet.'

'Oh.' I nodded slowly. I understood it now. He really was like me. He wanted that life too. To be married. To have a home. A family. It was part of his plan, just like it was part of mine. I sucked in a deep breath. 'I hope your plan works out better than mine is.'

He arched an eyebrow.

'My plan, my hope, is that Josh and I will get married.' I shrugged. 'Eventually.'

'Josh? The guy who broke your wrist?'

'Love isn't always perfect.'

'No, not perfect, but still...' He took a deep breath and shook his head, as though remembering his role. 'Well, we're in luck,' he said, his tone becoming more serious. 'Your wrist doesn't need manipulation so you can go to the plaster room for a cast and you'll be all set.'

'Set?' I repeated with a grin.

He groaned. 'That was unintentional.'

'Hmm, of course it was,' I teased as I stood up. 'Well, erm, thanks for...' I nodded at my wrist. 'And for listening.'

'You're welcome.'

I walked to the door but paused. 'I hope you find someone great.'

'Thanks, I'm sure they will.'

'They?'

He shifted his weight. 'Where I'm from, it's customary for your family to be involved in finding your bride for you.'

An arranged marriage. That's what he meant. A cold dread seeped into my bones. He was letting other people decide his future. His life.

It wasn't his fault.

He didn't know that the people you love couldn't always be trusted.

But I did.

That's why he needed me. Why he'd always needed me.

To save him.

'You k-know?' Josh stuttered in his surprise.

I smiled sadly. 'I've always known.'

'No, that's not possible. If you'd known, why would you be with him?'

'I didn't plan to be.' I'd chased after Abhilash in search of a friend. Someone who knew my secret. Who saw me for more than just my past. And at the same time, someone who needed my help.

'I hadn't intended to fall in love with him. I'd always known how foolish that was. There was never any illusion. Never any pretence. Abhilash has always been honest.'

Abhilash squeezed my hand in his. 'There has always been a countdown running in the background for us.'

'That doesn't make sense. Why would you choose him over me when he wouldn't marry you either? At least I was with you. I would always have been with you.' Josh's voice was desperate and confused. 'He's leaving. He wants someone else.'

'There isn't anyone else,' I corrected him. 'Not yet. It will be an arranged marriage. Abhilash's family will find someone for him.'

'That makes it worse, Lauren. You do see that, don't you? He doesn't even know the girl he's going to marry and yet he still wants her.' I could hear the scorn in Josh's tone. His contempt. His pity. 'He'd rather marry a stranger than be with you. Doesn't that tell you something? Doesn't that tell you everything?'

'It's not like that,' Abhilash said, casting a fearful glance at me. He was afraid that I would believe Josh.

But I knew better now. I always should have done.

'He is using you, don't you see that?' Josh urged.

I shook my head. I'd let Josh fill my head with his accusations once already. I'd done it out of fear, because I was so scared to lose the one good thing I had in my life. But that fear had jeopardised the very thing I was so desperate to keep. 'I don't care what you think. You don't know anything about him. About us.'

'Us?' Josh scoffed. 'You're not an "us". You're meaningless.'

Despite my declaration, his words stung.

I'd spent too long feeling meaningless. But not Abhilash. Never to Abhilash. Only to Josh.

'How can you leave me for him?'

I shook my head. 'Why does everyone assume I left you for him? Like I told Emma, I may have left you because of him. But it was never for him.' It was true. If I hadn't met Abhilash, I might never have found the courage to leave Josh. I wanted to. I needed to. But my fear of being alone always stopped me.

I left for the possibility. Not of Abhilash. But of someone.

'You don't—' Josh froze, his part-formed sentence forgotten as the faint sound of sirens caught his attention.

I glanced at Abhilash, but he looked as puzzled as I felt. The sound grew louder. Closer. Was it coming here?

'What did you do?' Josh growled.

'Nothing,' I assured him.

Abhilash squeezed my hand for a second, before easing his grip. He repeated the pattern again. And again.

I glanced at him, puzzled. It felt like he was trying to tell me something. But what?

Blue lights flashed through the glass panels of the front door.

'One of you called the police.' Josh spat the words at us as he raised the knife.

Abhilash edged backwards, and I mirrored his movements, even though I knew it was pointless. We were edging past the stairs towards the front door, but Josh wouldn't simply let us leave.

'Stop there,' Josh commanded, his voice booming through the hall as he charged towards us.

'Now,' Abhilash yelled as he swung round in front of me, shielding me from Josh with his body as he flung us towards the door.

'Argh,' I heard Josh yell as a thud vibrated the wall. I peered over Abhilash's shoulder, desperate to see what was happening.

'Nick?' I stared in bewilderment as Nick and Josh struggled for the knife.

Abhilash released me and raced towards them. I gasped, instinctively reaching for his arm to pull him back and keep him safe, but he slipped through my fingers.

The knife tumbled from Josh's hands as Abhilash grabbed his wrist and slammed it against the wall, while Nick kept Josh restrained.

'The door, Lauren,' Abhilash yelled, without turning his head.

I stumbled backwards, fumbled for the door latch and swung the door open. I found myself face to face with two police officers. Their gaze shifted over my shoulder before they surged forwards, pushing me to safety as they joined the fray.

The knife spun along the hall tiles as someone kicked it away.

Abhilash staggered backwards as the police cuffed Josh's hands behind his back.

I stood in the doorway, barely able to breathe.

'Lauren?'

Abhilash's voice filtered through the chaos, and I raced into his open arms.

70

NOW

I glanced back and forth between Abhilash and Nick. 'How did you...?'

'I felt bad about the way I greeted you when I got home, so I was coming down to apologise and I heard him.' Nick jerked his head towards Josh as he was guided into a police car. 'I heard you talking about a knife and I knew you were in trouble, so I called the police.'

'But you jumped him.' I raised my eyebrows as I turned to Abhilash. 'And you knew he was going to do that, didn't you? That's what you were trying to tell me when you were squeezing my hand.'

Abhilash grinned. 'I heard the floorboard creak. I know that sound. There's a loose board on the stairs. I realised that Nick was there. I figured if we could get out of the way and lead Josh to the bottom of the stairs, Nick would intervene.'

I shook my head in awe. 'You guys are amazing.'

Abhilash clapped Nick on the back. 'It was all Nick.' His expression turned serious. 'Thank you,' he said earnestly.

Nick smiled. 'That's what mates are for.'

'Lauren?' My stomach stirred at the familiar voice. I sucked in a deep breath and turned to face DC Collier. 'I think we need to talk, don't you?'

* * *

'You realise you could have made things easier for yourself if you'd just given me the video of Josh when we interviewed you?' DC Collier said as she walked with me out of the police station.

I snorted. 'You already suspected that I'd killed him, proving his abuse wasn't going to redeem me. It would just have strengthened my motive to want him gone.'

'Well, with the video evidence, and given today's events, Josh has confessed to everything, including sabotaging the jet-ski. Your friend, Emma, has also admitted to helping him gain access to your house and phone.'

Friend.

It felt a strange way to describe her given all she had done.

'I'm surprised she turned on Josh.'

'Once she learned of the charges against him, and that we had proof, she was very contrite.'

'And Helen, the patient who made a complaint against Abhilash, how did she get mixed up with Josh?'

'Apparently, he'd bribed a few people for information on Abhilash, that's how he heard there was a rumour about his planned engagement. Helen happened to be at the hospital at the time. She's admitted she was trying to get medication again. She was making a scene, blaming Abhilash for turning the other doctors against her, and Josh witnessed it.'

'He got her to make the complaint?'

DC Collier nodded. 'She said he gave her a script for what to say to you when you met. Josh has admitted he got the details from your phone messages with Abhilash.'

'Wow.' I shook my head. 'I really didn't know him at all, did I?'

'The important thing is that it's over now, Lauren.'

I took a deep breath, filling my lungs to capacity before exhaling slowly. It was soothing. Like letting go of all the negative energy. Letting go of the past.

'It feels good to have everything out in the open at last.'

'Everything?' DC Collier raised an eyebrow as she studied me cautiously. My innocence had been proved with regards to Josh, but she still had doubts about Mum's death.

'Everything,' I replied firmly.

'Ready to go?' Abhilash asked as he approached, his car keys jingling in his hand.

'Oh yes, please take me away from here.' I cast a glance back over my shoulder. 'I never want to see this place again.' My gaze shifted to DC Collier. And I certainly didn't want to see her again.

'Take care of yourself, Lauren,' she said as she turned away.

I nodded. 'I will.' I realised as I said it that this time I would.

'You won't take him back, will you?' Abhilash asked as we walked to his car.

'Josh?' I stared at him, stunned. 'I just got him arrested. I don't even think he would want me back.'

'That wasn't an answer.'

He was right. It wasn't.

'You found shelter with Josh, and you never tried to see the outside world. When the world was going faster, you never caught up with it. But now you've realised what the world is and have started to run to reach it. Don't go back to the shelter again. Run faster and keep up with the world. Your future will be so happy, exciting, and bright.'

Abhilash's words were so optimistic and comforting. But there was one flaw. 'You don't know that. Not for certain.'

'I believe it. That's enough.'

Was it? Perhaps if I believed it for myself, it would be. But I couldn't keep relying on his belief to give me strength and direction. Not when he wasn't even going to be here.

But one thing I did know for certain. 'No, I'll never take Josh back.'

71

'Nick was incredible today,' I said as Abhilash and I walked hand in hand along the beach towards Boscombe Pier. Neither of us had felt like going home yet.

'He was.' Abhilash's agreement seemed to hang in the air. I could tell there was more he wanted to say. 'You two seem to get on well.' There was a stiffness to his tone.

'Is my friendship with Nick causing you problems?'

'Physically no, but mentally...' His shoulders sagged. 'I know I don't have the right to have that problem.'

I cast a sideways glance at him. He was still jealous, I realised with surprise. It meant he cared enough to be jealous. But at the same time, it wasn't his place. He was planning to leave.

'He's not right for you,' Abhilash said quietly.

'And you are?'

'Lauren...' Abhilash said my name so softly. So sadly. 'I'm sorry.'

'I know.' I took a deep breath. 'But you don't have to worry. There's nothing between Nick and I.'

I wasn't interested in Nick. I never had been. Not really. I'd been flattered. Intrigued. Perhaps I'd even hoped that there could be something there. No, I shook my head. I was lying to myself again. The truth was that I *wanted* there to be something there.

Perhaps I'd been unfair to him. Smiling at him. Talking to him. Turning to him for help. Giving him hope that maybe he stood a chance. But then maybe I'd needed to believe in that possibility too. Perhaps even more than he did.

But as much as I wanted it, there was no spark. No connection. He was a nice guy. Friendly. Kind. Attractive. The kind of guy any girl would want. There was only one thing wrong with him. Something big. Something completely out of his control.

He wasn't Abhilash.

And yet Nick could give me the one thing that Abhilash would never be able to.

A future.

'Sorry,' Abhilash said, hanging his head.

I tried to shrug. 'It's okay.' But it wasn't. He reminded me of Josh. 'It's kind of sweet that you care enough to be possessive. But I know what that can turn into. I know how it feels to be on this end of it.'

'I keep telling you, I'm not him.'

I shook my head. 'No, you're not. I know that.'

I couldn't fault him for one tiny reminder of Josh. After all, I had my own similarities to Josh myself.

'About the bat.' I licked my lips. 'I know it was stupid. I should never have threatened Josh like that. I should have just reported him to the police and got them to help me. I can't believe that I actually thought I could blackmail him out of my life. I was just...' I shook head.

'Desperate?'

I nodded. 'Yeah, but that doesn't make it right.'

'No, it escalated an already volatile situation. But you thought it was your only way out.'

'Exactly.' I snuggled against his shoulder as we walked, relieved that he understood.

'I just wish that you'd realised you weren't alone. I'm here for you.'

'For now.'

Abhilash closed his eyes. My words had hurt him. But the fact remained that they were true.

'When your mum called you at the beach last week, it was to tell you they'd found someone for you, wasn't it?' I finally found the strength to ask the question that had gnawed at me relentlessly.

Abhilash lowered his gaze to the sand. 'I was going to tell you. I was just waiting for the right time. And then you had your accident and the police started questioning you...'

I nodded. 'I get it. You were trying to protect me.' I fixed a weak smile on my lips. I couldn't be mad at him for that. For caring. For protecting me. And yet, at the same time, I couldn't help but be disappointed that he'd kept it from me.

'It's too soon,' I said, shaking my head. I thought we'd have more time together. I thought I'd have more time to change his mind. 'Make an excuse. Delay your departure. Tell them you need to stay here longer. Buy us more time together. I need you.'

Abhilash shook his head. 'You don't need me, and,' he swallowed hard, 'I already said yes.'

'Oh.' The meaning of his words was as sharp as the knife that Josh had threatened us with.

He'd made his decision to marry her without me even knowing that she existed. I pulled away from him, desperately trying to hold myself together and not fall apart in the middle of the beach.

'We decided it was a good fit,' he added hesitantly.

We decided.

I closed my eyes. I understood now. He hadn't talked to me before agreeing to the match because I wasn't part of that decision. He was taking the next step to building a life with someone. A life that I wasn't part of.

I understood how Abhilash felt about Nick. That jealousy at the thought of me with someone else. I felt it too about him. Until now I'd just been jealous of an idea. A mythical girl who didn't exist in his life yet. But now she did. She was real.

'Josh was right about one thing: you're marrying a stranger.'

'I know you have reservations about arranged marriage. I wanted to explain it to you before but whenever I tried to broach the subject, you didn't want to talk about it.'

'No, I didn't.' Not then. And not now either. But I knew that his acceptance of the match meant it was a topic that could no longer be ignored.

'I just wish you could see—' I clamped my mouth shut. It wasn't my place to criticise his loyalty to his family.

'No,' Abhilash said. 'You don't need to do that. Not with me.'

'Do what?'

'Shut down. You bite your tongue and keep quiet. But you don't need to. Don't think. Don't worry about what I'll feel. How I'll respond. Just say what's on your mind. You can be yourself with me.'

'Are you sure you can handle my unrestrained, unfiltered thoughts?'

'You don't need to be worried with me, Lauren. We might not always agree. We might not even like each other's opinion at times. But you will always be safe with me.'

I nodded. It had been a long time since I'd trusted anyone

completely. But I realised for the first time in years that I trusted someone now. I trusted him.

'Okay, I think you're making a mistake. A huge one. One that you will end up regretting for the rest of your life. You wanted me to see the people around me for who they were, flaws and all. But you won't do the same. You're letting your family, your traditions, bully you into something you don't want.'

'But I do want it, Lauren.'

I shook my head. 'No, that's what they've made you think. They've manipulated you. Years of being told how it should be. Guilted into abiding by their ways. Their rules. They found you someone without you even being there. You weren't even part of the process.'

'I was.'

'What?'

'They aren't forcing me to marry anyone. I asked them for their help. I asked them to find me someone.'

'B-because you know that's what's expected of you.'

'No, because that's what I want.'

We stared at each other in silence as his words sank in. I'd convinced myself that his family was pressuring him. That they were the ones coming between us. I hated them for that. And I pitied him because he couldn't see it.

Perhaps it was easier to blame them. Because it prevented me from having to face the truth that was no longer avoidable.

He'd chosen this path.

'It's not how you think. I get a say in who I marry. We'll talk and decide if there's a connection. We're not required to marry. It's not forced. We decide.'

We.

The word cut into me again. There was a time when it had meant him and I.

'There are specialised websites that my family used to find potential matches based on education, occupation, family background, and heritage. They vetted the matches and then sent me the profile of the girl they felt was most suitable.'

The process sounded like it was essentially a narrow pool of online dating, with very specific criteria and a lot of family involvement. It didn't necessarily make it bad. It just made it different from what I was used to.

But for Abhilash, this was normality. It was the way he'd always expected things to be.

It wasn't as though he was being forced to marry. He chose to. He chose to honour the traditions that he believed in. That were part of his culture. His life. Himself.

I couldn't deny there were some advantages to an arranged marriage. A safeguard to ensure that you'd find someone. That you wouldn't end up alone. And perhaps, more importantly, that the person you ended up with had been vetted first.

Maybe if I'd had a family and they had vetted Josh, they could have warned me about how unsuitable he was. Of course, whether I would have listened, or just viewed them as intrusive, was another matter.

But there was still a flaw. 'It's all happening so fast,' I said, clutching his hand. 'Too fast. How can you know if you're choosing the right person, or if you'll just end up settling?'

'I just know,' he said with certainty. 'This is right for me.'

My grip loosened as I realised the arranged marriage wasn't the problem. I was.

I was the spanner in the works. Without my interference Abhilash would have returned home and got married without even a second thought. He'd said it himself: the girl his family had found was a good match. They even got on well. They would be happy together. He didn't have any doubts about her. The only hitch was me.

'I hadn't expected to fall in love,' Abhilash said quietly as he stopped and turned to face me.

I shook my head. 'Me neither.'

And yet we had. That one unplanned emotion jeopardised everything.

'Only a couple of my friends at the hospital know my family are planning an arranged marriage. Nick is one of them. That's why he disapproved of you and I getting together. He thought I was being unfair to you. He's probably right. I am.'

Everyone around us had their own opinions about our relationship. His friend thought he was making the most of his freedom before he married someone more worthy. Whereas mine thought I'd stalked a poor unsuspecting doctor because I was so desperate for attention. Just like my mother.

The reality was that neither were true. But we were the only two people that knew that.

We'd seen something in each other that made us think we each needed a friend. Falling in love had been an unexpected by-product.

I didn't regret it. But that didn't make it hurt any less.

He closed his eyes as a single tear tumbled down his cheek, and I knew that his heart was breaking too.

But the difference was, he was the one who was breaking it.

It didn't make sense.

'Why walk away from something so good? Something that makes us both so happy? So loved?'

'Sometimes love isn't enough.'

I flinched at the words he had said to me the first day we met. Back then he had referred to Josh's love for me. It wasn't enough. *He* wasn't enough.

But we were different. Abhilash wasn't like Josh. He never would be. Never could be.

Abhilash lowered his head, unable to hold my gaze.

His movement, so slight, yet so significant, told me more than any words could.

He would never choose me.

Abhilash pulled me to him, and I wrapped my arms around his waist, clinging on tightly. *This.* This is what I needed. What I wanted. His arms. His love. Him.

It struck me then that Abhilash didn't need to stay for us to remain together. There was another option.

I shifted in his arms so I could look at him. 'I could...'

Abhilash's eyebrows lifted in an unspoken question as the suggestion of going with him withered on my lips. I realised now that it wasn't the answer. Abandoning my own life for someone else's wouldn't work. It hadn't with Josh. It wouldn't with Abhilash either.

We'd be together. And yet, Abhilash was right: somehow that wasn't enough.

I shook my head. What more was there to say? I realised now there were no words I could say that would convince him to stay. I had to let him go.

We reached the pier and walked in silence as we made our way past the kids playing mini golf. We stopped at the end and leaned against the railing side by side.

'I think I'm going to sell the house,' I announced to the sea in front of us. 'It's time for a fresh start. Somewhere new.' Following Abhilash to India wasn't the answer. But maybe staying in Bournemouth wasn't either. It was time to let go of the past.

'And the job offer?'

I scrunched my nose. 'Running my own business is risky; it could fail. The job offers more security. More certainty.' I sucked in a deep breath. 'But maybe it's time I stopped being afraid of failure. My business has been successful so far and I'll fight to keep building on that.'

'I know you will,' Abhilash said with such certainty that it made my heart ache.

'I'm going to miss you,' I said, as my voice cracked.

'Me too, so much.'

'I want you to have a good and happy life,' I told him with tears in my eyes. 'So, I really do hope you have a happy marriage. But I can't promise I won't still be jealous.'

'I understand. I know I'll feel jealous when you meet a new guy. And I know it will happen in the near future. I want that for you. I want you to get the best. Far better than me.'

I wasn't sure there was anyone better than him. But maybe there was someone better for me.

OCTOBER

'Could I go to the platform to see my boyfriend off, please?' I asked the guard at the train station. My eyes pleaded with him. It would only give me a few more minutes with Abhilash, but every single second counted. They were the last ones we would ever get together.

The guard nodded and opened the barrier to let me through. Abhilash scanned the QR code on the app on his phone and followed me. We walked hand in hand up the stairs and across to the opposite platform, as he carried his suitcase in his other hand. For the first time since I'd known him, I couldn't think of anything to say.

'That Maroon 5 song, 'Daylight', keeps running through my head,' Abhilash said, breaking the silence.

'Mine too,' I agreed. It was a track I had heard so many times before, but when Abhilash played it for us while he'd held me in his arms last night, those words felt like they were written just for us. Just for that moment.

'I could come with you to the airport,' I said, repeating the suggestion that I had made countless times already.

Abhilash shook his head. 'It's better to say goodbye here.'

I nodded, but I wasn't sure anywhere would be good for goodbye.

I bowed my head as silent tears trickled down my face, just as they had done so many times over the years. But this time they were different. They weren't tears of fear. Of failure. They were tears of love.

'Will you remember me after I've left?'

My head jolted up and I stared at him in surprise. I was usually the insecure one in this relationship.

'Of course,' I replied. 'Look how much I've changed because of you.'

He shook his head. 'It's not because of me. It's because of you. You wanted to change. You made it happen.'

'I wouldn't have done it without you.'

'I believe you would have done. It just might have taken you a little bit longer.'

'Or I might have left it too late.'

He pulled me to him, hugging me tightly.

'Will you meet me if I come back to visit?'

'You'll be married then.' My voice was flat. What was the point in him returning? It wouldn't be the same. It couldn't be.

'But we can still be friends.' He gazed at me with pleading eyes. 'Can't we?'

'Of course.' I nodded automatically.

'So, we can still meet.'

'O-okay,' I agreed hesitantly. It was the last lie I would ever tell him.

I knew I couldn't meet him. At least not for a while. Perhaps a long while. Maybe in time, seeing him again wouldn't break my heart. But for now, I knew it would. I loved him too much to just be his friend.

I might have accepted his decision. I might even have agreed with his reasoning. But that didn't make it hurt any less. We weren't ending things because we didn't work or didn't love each other now. It was pre-emptive.

There was a logic to it. In the long run, it would probably be the right decision.

Probably.

But for now all I could see was that he was ending something that was only just getting started. Something with potential. With love.

It was hard to get past that.

'Do you have a photo of her?'

Her.

That's who she had become. We never used her name. Abhilash had never said it. And I'd never asked.

She was a distorted image in my imagination whenever I thought of the two of them together. I liked it that way. Hazy. Almost as though she didn't exist.

Almost.

'Yes,' Abhilash replied hesitantly. 'Do you want to see her?'

I swallowed. The sensible thing would be to say no. To leave her as a mystery. Half formed. Half real.

I nodded, as my curiosity got the better of me. Who was this woman who was stealing the man I loved away from me? What did she have that I didn't?

He pulled up a photo on his phone and positioned the screen so I could see it.

'Her name is Pooja.'

Pooja.

I stared at her. Examining her features. Her stance. Her clothes. Judging her from one tiny moment captured in an image on a phone. 'She's pretty,' I said, fighting the urge to find fault with her.

It wouldn't be fair of me to take my frustrations out on her. None of this was her fault. She didn't know she was taking the most amazing guy away from me. In fact, she probably didn't even know I existed at all.

And yet, despite that, my empathy was limited. She might not know what she'd done, or how much she had taken from me. But the fact remained, she'd still taken him. Still agreed to marry him. She'd still deprived me of a future with Abhilash. Whatever admirable qualities she may have, my ability and inclination to see them was clouded by my jealousy.

His gaze lingered on her photo a moment longer before he locked his phone and slid it back into his pocket. It wasn't much. And yet, at the same time it was everything.

In that split second, I finally knew the unescapable truth. He liked her. A lot.

Until that point, part of me hadn't really believed he'd go through with it. I was still clinging to the fantasy. But the reality was he'd already made his choice. In fact, for him there never had been any choice involved. He felt it with such certainty, that staying with me had never really been an option.

It's what he'd always known he would do. Where he would be. How he would live. I'd made him question it for a moment. But it wasn't enough. The temptation of a life with me wasn't enough to distract him from the plan he had already made. The life he had always envisioned.

I was the only one who hadn't accepted it. Even now.

The knowledge that he loved me was bittersweet. We'd never know for sure if that love would have been strong enough to have lasted. If we'd had more time together before his family had found him a match, perhaps he would have found leaving harder.

I knew it was a long shot. He might never have chosen a future with me. But I liked to think he would. I needed to think he would.

'I wanted to invite you to the wedding.'

My head jolted up as I stared at him, speechless.

'But I figured it might be too hard for you,' he continued, oblivious to my reaction. 'Plus, I'm not really sure how I would explain your presence.'

I laughed in spite of myself.

Abhilash's eyes widened as he watched me nervously.

I probably seemed unhinged to him, but I either laughed or I would cry. 'I don't think there would be any explanation for your girlfriend to be at your wedding to someone else.'

'Yeah.' the corner of Abhilash's mouth twitched. 'When you put it like that, probably not.'

My laughter faded. As much as I tried not to think about it, I couldn't escape the fact that some other girl was going to marry the guy I loved. And she had no idea how lucky she was.

'We will still keep in touch, though, won't we?'

'Yes.' this time my answer wasn't a lie. I might not be strong enough to see him again, but I wasn't ready to lose him completely.

He beamed at me. 'We'll always be close, Lauren. No matter what.'

'I hope so.'

He nodded and pulled me close to him. But even as he wrapped his arms around me, I knew that we were just fooling ourselves.

I hoped he would always stay in my life, that we'd always be friends, but it wouldn't be the same. I didn't even want it to be. If I couldn't have him completely then I needed to let him go. I couldn't wait for him to come back, praying that one day he would realise his mistake and regret what he'd left behind. I couldn't restrict myself to a half life, never letting anyone else in to take his place. I deserved better. I deserved more.

We would keep in touch. At least initially. But it would dwindle. It would change. It could no longer be as intimate or connected. We would have to take a step back. *I* would have to take a step back.

I was done giving anyone power over me. Not even Abhilash.

'Don't hate me,' Abhilash said, as passengers filed on to the waiting train before us.

I stared at him in surprise. 'How could I ever hate you?' He was breaking both of our hearts, but it was only because he believed it was the right thing to do. How could I hate him for following what he believed? Though it would be easier to walk away if I did.

Abhilash glanced at the clock on the station wall and I knew from his heavy sigh that it was time for him to go.

He stroked my cheek. 'I love you,' he whispered before he kissed me for the last time.

'I love you too,' I said, as tears streamed down my face. I knew that no matter what happened, I always would.

I watched him silently as he picked up his suitcase and boarded the train. It felt like something inside me was breaking. I wasn't sure that pain would ever ease. He turned back to face me and blew me a kiss as the doors closed between us. He pressed his hand to the glass. I stepped forward as I lifted my hand, reaching out for his.

'Stand back behind the yellow line,' the guard commanded.

My hand fell to my side as my feet complied, while my gaze remained locked on Abhilash.

I'd wanted someone who recognised what Mum had done was wrong. Who would tell me that it wasn't fair. That I didn't deserve it. That I was strong to have lived through it. To have survived. But that I didn't have to do it all alone any more. They would be there. They would protect me. Care for me. Love me.

I'd wanted someone to tell me I mattered. How I felt, what I wanted, what I needed, all of it mattered.

I'd thought Josh was that person.

He wasn't.

Abhilash was different. He said all the right things. Did the right things. How I felt mattered finally.

But even he was temporary.

I watched as the train stuttered forwards before gaining momentum.

With Abhilash I had found everything I had ever wanted, but it still wasn't enough.

My tears continued to flow as the train shrank into the distance.

You don't need me.

Abhilash's words repeated in my head. Despite the ache in my heart that felt like it would never be whole again, I finally understood what he meant now.

I wanted him. I loved him. But my survival wasn't dependant on him. What I needed was acceptance by the one person that mattered most of all.

Myself.

I took a shaky breath. 'It's okay,' I whispered to the empty platform. 'I'm going to be fine.'

And I knew that it was true. I would be fine. I would be better than fine.

I accepted my past. My pain. I knew where the blame belonged and was finally free from the doubt I had always carried, that somehow it had all been my fault.

It wasn't.

I wasn't broken. I wasn't unlovable.

I felt like I was in the ending scenes of a movie, watching his train fade into the distance while I stood crying on the platform, my world crumbling.

But I knew this wasn't really an ending.

It was a beginning.

Abhilash had shown me the way.

ACKNOWLEDGMENTS

To my wonderful boyfriend, Ahl: your patience and encouragement continue to amaze me. I'm so glad I get to share this journey with you.

Thank you to my parents for your continued support and encouragement.

Special thanks to Abhi for the inspiration for this book. Our story was, thankfully, very different, but the ending was the same. Maroon 5's 'Daylight' will always have a special place in my heart.

Thank you to Carlos for your insight and words of wisdom, which have always stayed with me.

To my incredible editor, Emily Ruston: your excitement for this book has meant the world to me. Special thanks to you, and the whole Boldwood Books team, for helping this story to shine. And thank you to my talented proof-reader, Rose Fox, who I've been lucky enough to work with on all of my books.

Thank you to Yvonne for your endless patience answering all my medical-related questions and Stuart Gibbon for your continued expertise on all the police matters and for giving me the inspiration for DC Collier.

Huge thanks as always to my writing mentor, Jonathan Eyers, for your encouragement and helpful feedback, and my fantastic writing buddies: Ellie Henshaw for your insight on early chapters of this novel and Kath McGurl whose brainstorming beach walks helped solve the ending for *The Other Girlfriend*.

Thank you to Alison May, Sheryl Browne, Noelle Holton, and

everyone in the Romantic Novelists' Association for your continued encouragement and support.

And finally, thanks again to all the wonderful readers who have supported my books with your purchases, reviews, social media posts and lovely messages. Thanks to you I get to keep living my dream.

MORE FROM ALEX STONE

We hope you enjoyed reading *The Good Patient*. If you did, please leave a review.

If you'd like to gift a copy, this book is also available as an ebook, hardback, large print, digital audio download and audiobook CD.

Sign up to Alex Stone's mailing list for news, competitions and updates on future books.

https://bit.ly/AlexStoneNewsletter

Explore more gripping psychological thrillers from Alex Stone...

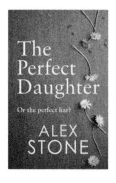 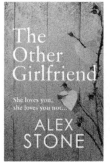 

ABOUT THE AUTHOR

Alex Stone, originally an accountant from the West Midlands, is now a psychological suspense writer based in Dorset. This beautiful and dramatic coastline is the inspiration and setting for her novels. She was awarded the Katie Fforde Bursary in 2019.

Follow Alex on social media:

 twitter.com/AlexStoneAuthor

 instagram.com/AlexStoneAuthor

 facebook.com/AlexStoneWriter

Boldw⚭d

Boldwood Books is an award-winning fiction publishing company seeking out the best stories from around the world.

Find out more at www.boldwoodbooks.com

Join our reader community for brilliant books, competitions and offers!

Follow us
@BoldwoodBooks
@BookandTonic

Sign up to our weekly deals newsletter

https://bit.ly/BoldwoodBNewsletter

THE

Murder

LIST

**THE MURDER LIST IS A NEWSLETTER
DEDICATED TO SPINE-CHILLING FICTION
AND GRIPPING PAGE-TURNERS!**

**SIGN UP TO MAKE SURE YOU'RE ON OUR
HIT LIST FOR EXCLUSIVE DEALS, AUTHOR
CONTENT, AND COMPETITIONS.**

SIGN UP TO OUR
NEWSLETTER

BIT.LY/THEMURDERLISTNEWS

Printed in Great Britain
by Amazon